Hard and Fast

ITALIAN STALLIONS, BOOK 2

MARI CARR

Hard and Fast

Penny is tired of being seen as the gamer, the crazy cat lady, the mom-jeans-wearing, YouTube-bingeing, quirky IT girl. She's barreling toward 29 and ready to make some changes...in her appearance and her nonexistent love life. But she's smart enough to know she needs help—*and* who she needs it from. Her billionaire playboy boss, Gage Russo.

Bachelor Gage's life is typically full of excitement, on the work front and in the bedroom. He's never lacking for female company and he rarely sleeps alone. Regardless, lately, he can't shake feeling bored. That is, until Penny challenges him to a friendly wager... one he promptly loses. Her prize? Lessons in seduction —from him.

Lines get blurred as Gage pushes harder...moves faster...teaching Penny things she's only ever fantasized about. But the playboy with all the smooth moves makes one big mistake when he fails to tell his sexy student that the lessons are no longer fake, and what he wants from her is very, very real.

Chapter One

Penny dragged herself into her small apartment and dropped down on the couch wearily. Of course, she didn't get to stay there for longer than a few seconds before she was besieged by a chorus of meows. Her cats—all four of them—were hungry.

She pushed herself up and trudged to the kitchen, nearly tripping over Harry, who was attempting to herd her toward the cabinet with the cat food.

"Dammit, Harry," she chided. "I'm not that late. Besides, look at you. You could afford to miss a few meals, buddy." Harry, a large Maine Coon, was way too fond of dinnertime, breakfast time, snack time, and the cat most likely to finish off whatever the other three had left behind.

She reached into the cabinet to pull out a can of cat food. Then she dipped out four portions into the personalized cat bowls under the kitchen window. Being a single woman with a good-paying job and zero social life meant she had too much money to blow on frivolous shit like the cute cat bowls. Of course, that wasn't her fault. Facebook had her number, constantly tempting her with ads for cat stuff, hilarious gamer shirts, and techie gadgets.

She rinsed off the spoon but left it in the sink then considered the box of Fruit Loops sitting on top of her fridge. She'd already had dinner, a bowl of macaroni and cheese—the orange stuff—at Jess's new apartment. Maybe she could call the Fruit Loops dessert.

"Nah," she said to no one. "I'm not hungry." She directed that comment to the cats so she wouldn't feel like an idiot talking to no one. Forrest briefly lifted his head from the bowl to give her one of his typical vacant-eyed expressions. Poor cat. The lights were on, but nobody was home.

At least he acknowledged she was speaking.

"I'd only eat it because I'm bored."

Forrest seemed to accept that reason and returned to his bowl, bumping heads with Harry, who had already scarfed his down and was now looking for more.

"Harry!" she chastised. "For shame."

Harry had none, but he was familiar enough with this routine to know he had to wait for the other cats to finish before he claimed the leftovers. He walked over to her, rubbing around her ankles, as if that would soften her up. She sat at the kitchen table then reached down absent-mindedly to pet him.

It had been quite an afternoon. She'd left work early at her new friend Jess's request. Jess had moved out of the apartment she'd been sharing with Penny's brother, Rhys, and his roommate, Tony, into a place of her own. She'd asked Penny to pick up her young son, Jasper, from elementary school, and she'd been more than happy to blow off early because Jasper was quickly becoming one of her favorite people on the planet. The kid was smart, sweet, and super adorable.

She'd been looking forward to helping Jess decorate her new place, but she had a feeling that wasn't going to be necessary now.

Penny had just finished her macaroni and cheese when Rhys and Tony showed up, with Tony's aunt Berta in tow. Aunt Berta had announced she was taking Jasper for the night because Rhys and Tony wanted to talk to Jess—alone.

Penny had left with Aunt Berta, who'd confided in a low voice, so Jasper didn't overhear, that the two men were in love with Jess and they were hoping to talk her into moving back in with them. For good.

"I think I'm going to be an aunt," she confided to Harry, who'd rolled over on his back, mooching for stomach rubs.

She silently hoped Tony and Rhys would win their bid for Jess's heart. Not that she believed they'd have to try too hard. Jess was obviously in love with them—both of them—and they felt the same. It was perfect and wonderful...and damn if it didn't make Penny feel even more alone.

Before she could sit too long with that heavy feeling, her phone pinged and she read the text.

dead by daylight

If she was a normal person, maybe a text like that would scare the shit out of her. As it was, she bounced up from her chair and headed down the hall to her office.

Waking up her PC, she fired a text back to her colleague and gaming buddy, Toby.

logging in

As she waited for the game, *Dead by Daylight*, to load, she slipped off her shoes, cleaned her glasses, then ran back to the kitchen for a sugar-free Red Bull. Toby was a huge fan of the game's premise, where famous movie serial killers chased them around, trying to kill them in spectacularly gory fashion. They had to outrun and escape Pinhead, Michael Myers, Leatherface, or Freddy Krueger to win. She and Rich, the other member of their gaming group, humored him every now and then by playing.

By the time she returned, Toby had added her to the game and set up a Discord channel. She frowned at the avatars.

"Where's Rich?" she asked. "And who the hell is Daddy_Morebutt$$?"

Toby chuckled. "Rich had to work late, so I invited Gage."

"Gage who?" Penny asked.

"It's me, Beaumont."

Penny recognized the voice in an instant, but even if she hadn't, she would have known who it was. Only one person in the world called her Beaumont.

She tried to figure out if she'd somehow fallen into a parallel universe, a place where it might be plausible for her to be playing video games with Gage Russo, her too-hot-for-words playboy billionaire boss.

"Uh," she said, super lamely. Because talking wasn't something she did so well whenever her sexy boss was around.

"Wow. I think I heard something there, Beaumont. Did you just try to talk or are you choking?" Gage teased. The man typically said hello whenever he stopped by IT to talk to Toby or Rich, grinning when all she managed was a flimsy wave. He never tried to engage her in anything more because in the world of gods like Gage Russo, her mere mortal status rendered her virtually invisible.

Goddammit. She was going to read Toby the riot act tomorrow. Their gaming group was her safe space. A place where she could kick back and be herself. Toby knew she became a mute idiot whenever Gage was around, so how could he invite the boss and not ask her first?

Not that it was particularly shocking he had. Toby suffered from a serious case of hero worship where Gage was concerned, always trying too hard to relate and laughing too loud at Gage's jokes.

She cleared her throat and tried again. "Uh. Hi."

Okay. That was a little bit better.

"Thought I'd check out life inside the nerd circle," Gage said.

Penny rolled her eyes, wishing she could be annoyed by the nickname. Unfortunately, Toby—taking a page from Fat Amy and *Pitch Perfect*—had given their department that stupid moniker, deciding if they called themselves nerds first, it somehow made them cool.

Sadly, she suspected Samuel L. Jackson barking orders at them drill-sergeant style about how to dress and behave wouldn't even manage to make their Island of Misfit Toys cool.

"I figured you'd have a date," Toby said to Gage—because God knew he wouldn't think that about *her*. "Lucky that I asked on a night you were available."

Gage chuckled—why did he have to have such a sexy laugh?— and said, "Scored at lunch, so it freed up my evening."

Toby laughed as if that was the funniest thing he'd ever heard in his life. Then asked Gage about his "lunch date." Apparently, Gage was currently dating some former *Sports Illustrated* swim-suit model, which sent Toby into orbit, firing off a million questions. To his credit, Gage answered them all, seemingly unannoyed by Toby's endless fawning.

"You still there, Beaumont?"

Shit. Penny realized she'd forgotten to speak for a while. Not that she'd had a damn thing to add.

Regardless, she spent way too much time alone with only her thoughts. Curse of living by herself for so long. She really needed to work on her conversational skills. Or consider getting a room-mate who wasn't feline.

"Yeah. We playing?"

Woohoo! She silently cheered for herself. Three whole words. Not one stammer.

"Yeah, man. Let's do this thing," Toby said excitedly. "Wait until you see the graphics on this game, Gage."

As always, once the game play began, Penny lost herself in the digital world, one where she fit in, where she felt comfortable. After a few minutes, she forgot all about Gage Russo, becoming the character she was playing, concentrating on nothing more than outrunning the serial killer.

"Dammit, Toby," Penny yelled. "Get your shit together. Because I'm telling you right now, I'm not spending the whole night saving your ass from Michael Myers."

She wasn't sure, but she thought she heard Gage laugh.

Toby scoffed. "I'm trying. Jesus. I spilled soda on my keyboard and the keys are sticking."

"You use that excuse all the time, but I know for a fact you never put drinks anywhere near your computer. Watch out!" she yelled.

"What a game," Gage muttered as he cut Toby down from where the killer had strung him up before Penny could reach him.

"Good save," she said.

"Behind you, Beaumont," Gage warned.

"I see him." She deftly escaped, though she took a couple hits before she was able to beat the villain back.

Gage whistled. "Shit, you're good at this."

She wasn't sure why, but something inside her warmed up at his praise. She didn't consider herself the type of person who needed other people's admiration, but it felt nice to be seen. Or not just seen but recognized as having an actual talent for...well, *Dead before Daylight* was a stupid talent, but at least it was something.

For the next two hours, the three of them ran through the digital woods, working together like a well-oiled machine as they defeated Michael Myers. Gage was a surprisingly good gamer, and like her, when in the heat of the moment, he cussed like a sailor.

When the game was over, she realized that for the entire night, she'd managed to talk to Gage with the same confidence and familiarity she shared with Toby and Rich. She'd broken through her tongue-tied insanity—and it felt great.

"Fuck," Gage said. "That was intense. I see why you like it, Toby."

Toby, clearly thrilled, said, "Right? I told you."

"Next time we play, one of us should take on the role of the killer. That's when shit gets real." Penny paused when she realized what she'd just said.

There was no way Gage was coming back for an encore of game night.

This was a fluke.

"I'm in…if I get to be Pinhead," Gage responded.

Penny groaned, delighted by the thought that he wanted to join them again. "I hate Pinhead. That guy creeps me the fuck out."

He deepened his voice. "No tears, please. It's a waste of good suffering."

"Jesus." She shuddered, hating how good his impersonation was. "Guess I'm sleeping curled in a fetal position under the covers all night."

"Gotta admit, I didn't realize you could talk so much, let alone cuss, Willow99," Gage teased before taking a jab at her screen name. "Buffy much?"

If Penny had one failing—okay, she had more than that, but in this instance—it was that she could never resist the urge to knock someone down a peg or two if they got too cocky. Her father called her his clever little smart-ass. And at least half the time, he meant that as a compliment.

"I was fifteen when I picked that name. Besides, Willow is awesome. And before you throw that stone, maybe *you* should have taken a few extra minutes to come up with a better screen name, Daddy_MoreButt$$."

"I do like the sound of you calling me daddy, Beaumont," Gage joked.

Aaaand she'd just made a cardinal mistake, forgetting that Gage was a consummate smart-ass himself. While she never engaged in conversation with the man, opting instead to keep her head down and do her job lest she make a jackass of herself, she watched him way too intently whenever he joked around and traded barbs with the other guys in IT.

She had long acknowledged that Gage wasn't the typical boss. He never played the power card with her or the others in the departments he oversaw. He also didn't seem to take things too seriously. She figured that was because his brother, Matt, was the CEO of Russo Enterprises, and nobody fucked around on Matt's watch. Because of that, Gage tended to play the "good cop" role, jovial and easygoing.

Penny didn't really have an opinion about Conor, the third Russo brother, because he was rarely in the office, opting instead to work out of one of the nightclubs he owned.

It wasn't unusual for Gage to stop by the IT department once a day, either to discuss business or, more often than not, just shoot the shit. When she considered it now, she wondered if Gage was serious about wanting to be included in the nerd circle.

Because she played video games, D&D, and possessed zero feminine wiles, she'd earned her all-access pass to the boys' locker room years ago, so she had been privy to Toby, Rich, and Gage's brand of sophomoric guy talk around the office pretty much since the beginning of her employment six years earlier.

She figured she was the most sexually knowledgeable virgin on the planet, thanks to too many years of listening to the guys she hung out with...and the dirty books she read...and the porn she watched...and the occasional WooHoo SIMS hookup, which was painfully PG.

"For your information," Gage said, as if her long silence wasn't weird, "I came up with that screen name when I was sixteen. My high school performed the musical *Annie* that year and I was hooking up with a couple of the orphans...and Annie. Thought it was pretty fucking clever."

"It's hilarious," Toby said, far too earnestly.

"The dollar signs are a nice touch," she said sarcastically.

"So you seriously want to play again, Gage?" Toby interjected, probably worried they'd start ragging on his stupid screen name, Freaky12, which was by far the least clever one of their group.

"Yeah. I would."

"Awesome!" Toby exclaimed, the first to cry uncle, pointing out that they all had work the next day. He said good night and exited the voice chat, leaving Penny alone with Gage.

Jesus H. She should have let Michael Myers kill Toby. The

witless wonder had just left her alone in the lion's den...with the lion.

The easiness of the past couple of hours started to fade despite her best efforts to stay cool. "So, um..."

Gage saved her from herself, interrupting before she could stammer out anything completely inane. "If I don't see you at the office tomorrow, I'll see you tomorrow night. Toby invited me to your weekly Dungeons & Dragons game."

"And you're coming?" She didn't mean to sound so shocked but, well...she was shocked.

"I love D&D."

"Oh. Okay."

"You all right with that, Beaumont?"

"Yeah."

"Good," he said. "I like you talking to me. Didn't realize you were so funny. Keep it up."

"Um. Okay. I will. Night, Gage."

"No, no, no. That's Daddy to you."

She snorted, forgetting to be intimidated or shy once and for all where Gage Russo was involved.

"Asshole," she called him.

Before he could reply, she exited the chat, catching only a split second of his loud laugh, and she grinned.

What a night.

Chapter Two

"**A**nd then, me and Billy won the prizes for being the fastest runners in the whole first grade!"

Penny nodded, enthralled as Jasper regaled her with the highlights from his school's field day. Apparently, the school system had bussed the entire elementary school to the local high school's football field and held competitions for each of the grades.

Penny suspected there were a shit ton of teachers facedown on their couches tonight, as Jasper detailed the countless events and games and—sweet Jesus—she was exhausted just hearing about it.

"He got a ribbon that says First Place. Aunt Berta has it hanging on the refrigerator." Her brother, Rhys, who was seated on the other side of Jasper, put his hand on the boy's head, beaming so proudly, you would think Jasper had just won the Olympic gold.

She'd been delighted when her brother had invited her to join his new family for dinner tonight. She was getting damn tired of eating alone. In addition to her, Jasper, and Rhys at the table, Tony, Jess, and Aunt Berta were also there. Penny was amazed by how quickly her confirmed-bachelor brother had upended his life, eschewing his assertion that he would forever be married to his work, and opting instead for this wonderful instant family.

He and Tony had been roommates for years, but that fact hadn't prepared Penny when they'd both fallen head over heels for Jess. While she knew committed threesomes weren't exactly the norm, there was no denying the three people sitting across the table from her were making it work. Tony had his arm draped loosely around the back of Jess's chair, and Jess, a single mom who'd been homeless when she'd crash-landed in their lives, absolutely glowed with happiness.

Rhys called her this afternoon and said they all wanted to try a new Italian place that had opened in Center City, and he wanted to see if she'd like to join them. Considering there was nothing but cereal in her house, she'd been only too happy to accept the invitation.

Penny had started her job search in Philadelphia after college because she'd wanted to live close to her brother, and their parents, who had also moved here from Connecticut right after she graduated from high school. Her family meant the world to her, so she knew she wanted to settle down near them.

"Sounds like you had an amazing day, Jasper. I'll have to stop by sometime and see the ribbon."

Jasper beamed then asked Rhys, "Can I have some more bread, Daddy?"

Every time Jasper called Rhys and Tony "Daddy," Penny's eyes misted with happy tears, so grateful that these incredible people all found each other.

Rhys reached into the breadbasket, spreading a bit of butter on the roll before handing it to Jasper. "Last one," he warned. "Or you won't eat that big plate of spaghetti you just ordered."

Jasper took the bread. "I can eat it all," he said with great confidence. "On account of my leg."

Penny frowned as she glanced down at Jasper's leg in confusion. "Leg?"

Tony laughed. "Aunt Berta swears Jasper has a hollow leg. The rascal is eating us out of house and home."

Aunt Berta grinned. "He's a growing boy. I suspect he'll be bigger than you and Rhys by the time he's done."

Jasper was clearly thrilled at the idea of growing taller than his two fathers.

Penny dipped her bread in the seasoned olive oil. "I appreciate you guys letting me tag along. I've heard good things about this place from Toby at work. He's already eaten here three times and the place hasn't been open a month."

"We haven't seen enough of you lately," Rhys said. "I was missing you, kiddo."

Penny grinned at her brother's nickname for her. Their parents had waited ten years between kids, but that age difference hadn't had a negative impact on their sibling relationship at all. She'd always been very close to her big brother, who'd never been too busy for, or too bothered by, the little girl constantly hanging around him when he was a teenager.

"Yeah. I need to get better about being more social, but by the time the workday ends, usually all I can think about is going home, stripping off the bra, and collapsing on my couch."

They all laughed.

"I think we have to face it. Work is crazy for all of us. It's hard to find a time when we're all free." Jess had been a waitress when she met Rhys and Tony, but since officially "moving in" with them—not just as a roommate—three months earlier, she'd cut back on her hours at the diner and taken on quite a lot of the office work for Moretti Restorations, the business Tony owned with his three brothers.

Tony nodded. "I can't complain because business is good, but we're feeling the loss of Joey, now that he's off filming that TV show of his. If you ever repeat this to him, I'll deny it, but he was a hell of a worker and it's been hard finding someone to replace him."

Tony's brother Joey had landed a gig hosting his own TV

show, *ManPower*, a few months earlier. Penny couldn't wait for the first episode to air. The Morettis were already planning a massive viewing party and she'd been invited. The Morettis, Italian to the core, knew how to party.

Aunt Berta leaned toward Tony, as if speaking confidentially. "There's no way I'm telling him you said that. That boy is a walking, talking contradiction. Works harder than anyone I've ever seen when it comes to building things, but my heavens, he's the laziest creature on the planet at home. Dirty dishes in the sink, laundry piled up everywhere. I stopped by his place one day to drop off a casserole I made him, and I counted no less that ten pizza boxes piled up by the door."

"You don't have to tell me," Tony grumbled. "I lived with the idiot for three years. Best day of my life was when Rhys and I decided to move in together."

The waiter came by the table to deliver their food and refill their wine glasses. "This smells delicious," Penny said.

For a moment, she thought Tony was groaning in agreement. Until she realized it was his Russo growl. She followed the direction of his now dark gaze, expecting to see Matt Russo, Tony's sworn arch enemy—for reasons Penny had only just recently learned from Jess. It had something to do with an old high school rivalry and, of course, a girl.

However, tonight's Russo in the crosshairs was Gage...who had his arm wrapped around a scantily dressed, heavily made-up redhead. Penny pushed her glasses up and squinted.

Wait. She was pretty sure that was Marjorie from accounting. Penny rolled her eyes. Gage was apparently starting to fish in the company pond. He'd mentioned some date with Connie from HR—for pity's sake—just last week. Penny would have thought at least an HR woman would know better than to mess around with the boss, but apparently not.

Gage saw her staring and waved.

"Damn Russos," Tony muttered. "Can't turn around twice without running into one."

"Down boy," Jess joked.

Penny turned her attention back to Tony and felt the need to defend her boss. "Gage, while a shameless playboy, is actually a pretty nice guy."

Crazy as it sounded, she'd actually come to view Gage as a friend lately. Which was just what she needed. Another fucking guy friend.

Since crashing their *Dead by Daylight* game three months earlier, Gage had become a somewhat regular fixture in the nerd circle. Not that any of them considered him a full-fledged member.

Gage Russo would never qualify as a true nerd, but he seemed to genuinely enjoy their company, loved D&D as much as she did—which was saying something—and had proven himself her biggest competition when it came to gaming.

So really, if he hadn't been a gorgeous, super-cool billionaire with stunning women fluttering around him like butterflies, he would have easily been inducted into the nerd circle, no questions asked.

Recently Gage had grown a beard—a ridiculously sexy beard—and now Toby and Rich were trying to do the same. She didn't have it in her to tell Toby his beard probably classified more as peach fuzz and he should probably just pack it in and shave.

Not that he'd listen to her. Toby and Rich were too busy hanging on Gage's every word—something that was completely annoying—while Penny's role in their ragtag gang was to simply keep the man humble.

Although, she had to begrudgingly admit Gage had been good for the guys. Toby and Rich had become more confident of late as they followed Gage's advice regarding women. Both of them, normally extremely shy and awkward around the opposite sex, had gone out on several dates, and it sounded like Rich was on his way to landing himself an honest-to-God girlfriend, something that had eluded every member of the nerd circle since the three of them had started working together six years earlier.

Regardless of her reassurance about Gage's good-guy status, Tony mumbled something indecipherable under his breath. Probably because it included some bad words regarding the Russos that he didn't want Jasper to hear.

Jess winked at Penny across the table, shaking her head. Like Penny, Jess had worked for Russo Enterprises, though for a short time, and she shared Penny's opinion that whatever the Russo guys had been like back in school, they weren't pure evil, like the Morettis continued to insist.

"So what are we doing for your birthday next month?" Jess asked Penny, adeptly finding a way to change the subject.

Penny groaned. "Nothing. I'm not celebrating this one."

"Why not?" Tony asked.

"It's not a milestone I'm particularly excited about."

Rhys frowned. "This isn't a milestone birthday. You're going to be twenty-nine, right? Not thirty."

"Twenty-nine is a milestone," Penny insisted. "Last year in the twenties. Then...I'm going to be ancient. Like you."

Rhys reached over Jasper's head to playfully pull her hair. "Et tu, Brute? It's not enough I have to deal with Tony calling me old man all the time."

"We're having a party," Jess interjected, refusing to be swayed.

"Bah humbug," Penny grumbled.

"We'll go out for a girls' happy hour with Keeley, Gianna, and Liza to come up with a menu and guest list," Jess continued.

For the first time in her life, Penny actually had a few girlfriends to hang out with. They were women she'd seen occasionally over the years at Moretti parties or get-togethers but had never really talked to because, hey—wallflower. Jess had been the one to help her break the barrier, moving her out of the acquaintance column to the girlfriends one with Keeley Gallo, Gianna Duncan, and Liza Moretti. So far, they'd gone to one happy hour and had met up for lunch. Penny hadn't contributed much to the conversation at either event, but she'd been thrilled to her toes to be invited and included.

In high school and college, she hadn't managed to find common ground with many girls, her interests landing her more male companionship. She'd never been the type to go to parties or bars, preferring to hang out in some pal's dingy basement playing *Warzone* all night.

She had zero interest in hair or makeup—though lately she'd been thinking she might like to try something different with her looks—and she viewed shopping as the equivalent to getting a pap smear.

Then her mind drifted back to *dingy*. Hmm. That would be a good Wordle word.

"Penny," Jess said, trying to draw her attention back to the conversation at hand.

"Sorry. Um. Can we just do the happy hour and forget the rest?" she muttered, not even bothering to feign enthusiasm about the party.

"Come on. A birthday party will be fun. You can invite that hot guy across the hall," Jess added.

"Hot guy?" Rhys asked.

"I have a new neighbor," Penny said, recalling the way her jaw had dropped the first time she'd seen him on his move-in day. The clean-cut man reminded her of a younger Brad Pitt, with his dirty-blond hair, dazzling blue eyes, and deep, sexy dimples she could get lost inside for days. Something she'd shared with Jess a few weeks ago. "But I'm not inviting him. I haven't even introduced myself to the guy."

Every time Penny ran into the new neighbor in the hallway outside their apartments or on the elevator, her brain cells evaporated, and she wound up just staring at him and grinning like a goofball. The guy probably thought she was touched in the head because the last couple of times he'd seen her, he'd avoided making actual eye contact.

"We'll make you a cake," Jasper chimed in. "And there will be presents and games and everybody will sing to you. And pizza!" he added, clearly all in on the birthday party plan.

Penny grinned. Jasper basically owned the keys to her soul, so the chances of her bailing on the party idea were nil at this point. "Sounds awesome."

Jasper wiggled with what she thought was glee until he said, "I need to go to the bathroom."

Aunt Berta and Rhys both started to rise, but Penny beat them to the punch, waving them back down. "I'll take him." She was anxious to escape all talk of birthday parties. She'd go through with it, but she wasn't looking forward to it.

Jasper hopped up and grabbed her hand, leading her through the restaurant. She glanced over at Gage's table. He was sitting very close to Marjorie, his arm draped around her shoulders as he leaned close to whisper something into her ear. Marjorie laughed, turning her face to his as he nuzzled her cheek.

The whole thing looked...nice, and Penny felt the same pang of loneliness that kept sneaking in and sucker punching her lately. They entered a small alcove where the bathrooms were.

"I can go in by myself," Jasper said, pointing to the men's room door. It was a single stall, so she opened the door, did a quick scan, then nodded.

"I'll be just out here."

Jasper walked into the bathroom and locked the door. Penny leaned against the wall and sighed.

"Tired, Beaumont?"

She looked up, surprised to discover Gage had followed her.

She shrugged. Her sigh had nothing to do with exhaustion, but she wasn't going to admit that to him. "Hot date?"

"Always," he said with a shameless grin.

"You better pace yourself," she joked. "You don't want to run out of single women at work to date too quickly."

Gage leaned his shoulder on the small wall she was currently holding up. "Yeah. Matt's gonna be pissed when he finds out I've been dating women from work, but it's not like I'm purposely seeking them out. The truth is, Marjorie asked me out tonight."

"And the word no isn't in your vocabulary?"

He frowned, as if puzzled. "Say the word again. I'm not sure I've ever heard that one. No, you said?"

She snorted. "You're an ass, and I should let you hang, but I'm worried about you."

"Me?"

She shrugged casually. "I'm worried you're going to mess with the wrong woman at work, someone vindictive who might decide to label your advances harassment if you break her heart."

Gage scowled. "I don't come on to women at the office, Beaumont. Don't touch them or say inappropriate things. You know that. The women I've dated from there have approached *me*."

"Fine, but still...be careful. Okay?"

"I will." Then he looked her over, taking in her outfit. "New shirt?"

She glanced down, shocked that he would notice something like that. She had stopped by Goodwill on the way home, wanting to find something decent to wear tonight. Her wardrobe was in bad need of a freshening up, most of her stuff worn out or faded. She'd grabbed this striped patch shirt because she loved the vivid colors. She was aware it was probably a bit in-your-face loud, but it was easy to partner with her best pair of jeans. She hated trying to put outfits together, figuring out if shit matched.

"Yeah. Well, *old* new. I found it at Goodwill. Can you believe someone got rid of this? Still had the original tags on it."

"I like it."

Penny studied his face, searching for the slightest indication of insincerity. Either Gage had one hell of a poker face, or he really meant what he said.

"Guess Moretti's annoyed by my presence." Gage looked a little too pleased by that idea.

"Not sure he noticed you were here," she lied, feeling the need to defend Tony, since he was practically family now.

"Mmmhmm," Gage hummed as he reached out to tug on her braid. "Liars go to hell."

"So do shameless playboys, so I guess I'll see you there."

He chuckled. "Followed you here to ask if D&D is at Rich's apartment again or if we're moving it back to Toby's. Knew it would piss Moretti off if I approached your table, which was tempting, believe me. But it looks like you and Jess are having a good time, so I opted to keep the peace."

"Very mature of you. D&D is at Rich's place again. Toby's is still a wreck." Toby had gone home last week to soggy carpet due to an overflowing bathtub in the apartment above his. He'd been crashing at Rich's place while the landlord made the repairs.

"Great. Then I guess—"

The bathroom door opened. "Penny. I can't get my pants buttoned," Jasper said.

"No worries. I got you." She knelt before him, quickly slipping the button into place. "Did you wash your hands?"

He shook his head. "No. I was frustrated."

"Aw. I bet." She grinned at his very adult word as she pointed into the bathroom, toward the sink. "With soap, please."

"Okay." Jasper returned to the bathroom, the door closing behind him.

"Smart kid," Gage observed.

"So smart," she said. "I'm crazy about him."

"You'd be a cool mom, Beaumont, with your mad *Mario Kart* skills. Ever consider it?"

She'd done way more than merely consider it. Penny dreamed of the day she'd start a family of her own.

No. Dreamed was too weak a word. She longed for it, *yearned* for it.

Of course, before that happened, she had to find a guy, lose her virginity, convince said guy to marry her...

She was twenty-eight years and eleven months old, and managing just step one of that process felt impossible. Find a guy?

Yeah right.

"Someday, maybe," she said, fighting hard to keep the sadness from her tone.

Jasper reemerged, holding his hands up for her inspection. "All clean."

"Excellent job, Jasper." Then she jerked her head toward Gage. "Say goodbye to my boss, Gage."

"Bye, Gage."

Gage smiled at Jasper. "Good night, Jasper."

The three of them reentered the main room of the restaurant, Gage returning to his date, while she and Jasper trudged back to their own table.

"How do you feel about some dessert?" Rhys asked them when they reclaimed their seats.

"Yes, please," Jasper said loudly.

Penny nodded. "Sounds good."

They all placed their dessert orders when the waiter stopped by, then Penny let the others at the table do the majority of the conversing for the rest of the evening.

Her gaze kept flitting back to Gage and Marjorie, observing the way the other woman flirted, flipping her long hair over her shoulder, batting her thick eyelashes, laughing and leaning close.

Every move Marjorie made seemed so natural, so...feminine. And it was obvious Gage was attracted to her, his attention focused solely on his beautiful date.

Penny had started observing Gage more closely of late, her lifetime membership to the locker room still holding strong. He often regaled the nerd circle with stories—okay, he bragged—about his sexual conquests, so she knew there weren't too many nights Gage went to bed alone. Though he'd also pointed out he did *not* do sleepovers.

Toby and Rich had started a list of "Gage Excuses," keeping track of all the clever, sometimes creative reasons Gage had given his dates for leaving right after doing the deed. Something Penny told them was juvenile and stupid. Not that they listened. Instead, they insisted they were just compiling the data for their own future dates.

Which always made her snort. As if Toby or Rich would ever

need an excuse—or use one. If a woman ever let one of those guys in her bed, she'd have to hire a moving company to get their asses out the next morning.

However, the more she heard—and witnessed for herself—the more she realized that Gage understood what made women tick.

He was an expert when it came to her sex, while she—despite being a damn female her entire life—felt like queen of the cluelessness.

She mentally compared her outfit to Marjorie's, her too-loud, too-buttoned-up shirt and jeans versus Marjorie's black minidress that left nothing to the imagination. Then she glanced across the table at Jess. Even her friend had taken special pains tonight, wearing a simple but elegant white blouse that hinted at the cleavage below—something she'd noticed both Tony and Rhys appreciating—and crisp black slacks.

Jess, like Marjorie, wore her hair down and loose, both women managing those soft waves that looked effortless, but no doubt required a hair dryer and curling iron and would involve her needing to put her Switch down.

As if that would happen.

Her cute little town on *Animal Crossing* needed tending. Those bugs and fish weren't going to catch themselves.

And while Jess's makeup wasn't as overdone as Marjorie's, it enhanced her beauty. Penny ran her hand over her chin, aware that if the zit residing there got much bigger, it was going to need its own zip code.

She took in the way Rhys was holding Jess's hand, the way he squeezed it familiarly, the way he gripped it like he couldn't sit next to her without touching her. The way Tony toyed with her hair.

Then she looked back at Marjorie, at the way Gage kissed her cheek before they rose to leave. The way he helped her put on her jacket. The way he wrapped his arm loosely around her waist.

She wanted what Jess and Marjorie had. Wanted it with every fiber of her being.

Silently, she made a vow, right then and there, that she would do anything, change anything, to get what she wanted. And she gave herself a deadline.

Because she wasn't going into the thirties as a single woman *or* a virgin. Which gave her one year and one month to get her shit together.

But she needed a tutor, an expert, someone who knew not only what made women attractive to men but someone with bedroom skills as well, someone who could teach her not only how to flirt but how to *seduce*.

She took one last look toward the door as Gage and Marjorie left.

Penny knew exactly who to ask.

Chapter Three

"**Y**ou and I need to talk."

Gage looked up as his older brother Matt stormed into his office.

"Knock, knock. Come in," Gage said sarcastically when his brother walked straight up to his desk. It didn't take a genius to figure out Matt was pissed. Not that his brother's disposition ever stopped him from poking the bear. If Gage waited for Matt to be in a pleasant mood before making jokes, the two of them would never speak.

"I think it's time you and I had a come-to-Jesus meeting."

Gage pretended to look at his calendar. "Sorry, but I don't have the next come-to-Jesus meeting scheduled until next Tuesday at ten thirty."

"Goddammit, Gage," Matt said, sitting down in the chair across from his desk. "Can you try to be serious for a minute? We've got two issues to resolve, and I need you to listen to me and *really* hear what I'm saying."

Gage waved his hand. "Fine. What's bothering you?"

"You gotta stop shitting where you eat."

Gage sighed, suddenly aware this apparent issue they were having was the argument he'd been expecting. "Lovely expression.

People just don't use that one enough, which is a real shame. What else is on your mind?"

"I mean it, Gage. I just spent the last hour breaking up a damn cat fight between your two girlfriends."

Gage frowned. "First of all, I don't have a girlfriend, and you know it. Secondly, there was a cat fight and you didn't call me? Where's the love, bro?"

Matt lifted his gaze heavenward, as if discovering religion and foolishly believing that praying to God was going to help. "Gage," he started.

"Who was fighting?"

"Marjorie Douglas from accounting and Connie Raymond from HR, who, as far as I'm concerned, should have known better than to date the fucking boss."

Gage sighed. "I went out with Connie last week. Just for dinner and drinks. Nothing more. That woman's a billionaire hunter, which I figured out about five minutes into the evening. It was a one-and-done date, something I explained when I dropped her off that night. Didn't even kiss her good night. I haven't talked to her or replied to a single one of her fifty-seven texts since then."

"Well, she seems to think the two of you have started something really special, and Marjorie is stealing her man."

"Jesus. Went out with Marjorie a couple of nights ago. She's a sweet little thing."

"Did you sleep with her?" Matt asked.

Gage let his grin answer that question, to which Matt closed and rubbed his eyes wearily. Before his brother could say anything else, Gage let him off the hook.

"Marjorie was cool with the one-night stand. Something we established before I went back to her place."

"She alluded to the fact she wasn't planning on seeing you again, but Connie is going to be a problem if you don't intervene."

"I'll talk to her."

"And..." Matt persisted.

"No more company hookups."

Matt looked up, surprise evident in his expression. No doubt he'd expected a fight, but Gage had already made up his mind to stop putting his USB in the company computer.

It was Beaumont who'd planted the seed, made him realize he'd been flirting with disaster. He hadn't lied about not pursuing women from work, that it had been the opposite, but he was now wondering—given this morning's cat fight—if Penny hadn't been right about how a scorned woman might seek revenge. Marjorie was cool, but Connie could be potentially problematic.

"You're not just saying that?" Matt asked, suspicious that Gage was lying to escape the argument.

"Nope. I've seen the error of my ways." He raised three fingers. "Scout's honor."

Matt snorted. "Like you've ever been a Boy Scout."

"What's the second problem, Matt? I've got a meeting in half an hour."

"The second issue is the bigger one. Frost Incorporated is trying to steal Penny Beaumont."

"What the fuck are you talking about?"

"Caught wind that they've reached out to her a few times over the past month, promising Penny her own team of analysts and engineers to lead and mentor. IT is your domain, so I don't have to remind you how fucking brilliant that woman is in cybersecurity. The world is lucky she chose to use her talents for good rather than evil, because she'd make one hell of a hacker. As it stands, in just six years, she's saved—and made—this company millions with her management system on zero trust, her automation to respond to network anomalies, as well as the—"

"You don't have to list all her accolades to me. I know how valuable she is."

Matt pointed his finger at him, stressing his last point. "Find a way to make sure she stays put. Stock options, perks, flexible hours, I don't give a shit. Just figure out what she wants and give it to her."

Gage was furious. He'd just hung out with Beaumont at Rich's apartment last night for D&D. They played video games a couple times a week. And while he still couldn't believe it, he'd thought they were becoming friends—and he liked it. The idea that she'd been planning to desert the company without so much as a word had him seeing red.

"I'll deal with Beaumont."

"See that you do." Matt rose and held his gaze for a moment. Sometimes Gage got the feeling his brother always had something more he wanted to say to him, but whatever it was...it never materialized. Their conversations were strictly limited to work, neither of them seeking to discuss anything personal.

Matt had been a distant bastard for nearly a decade now, the close relationship they'd shared as kids a thing of the past. Not that Gage could assign all the blame for that to Matt. Nope. He, Matt, and his other brother, Conor, had been steadily walking away from each other ever since—

Gage shut that line of thinking down in an instant, making sure it remained locked in the vault.

"Anything else?" Gage asked.

Matt paused for a second then shook his head. "No. That's it."

He left the office, closing the door behind him.

Gage took a few moments to collect himself then turned back to his computer, pulling up the file he needed for his meeting. He clicked on the button to print it, but nothing happened. Opening the paper tray, he found it full.

He recalled Matt's information about Beaumont and picked up his phone.

"Beaumont, get to my office. Now."

He stood up, walking over to the large window that offered a breathtaking view of the Philadelphia landscape.

By the time Beaumont arrived, knocking on his door, he was cool, calm, and collected.

"Come in."

"You summoned, lord and master?" she asked, standing in the doorway, clearly annoyed by his gruff demand on the phone.

"Lord and master has a nice ring, but I thought we established Daddy as my chosen nickname from you." He grinned when her eyes narrowed.

"Hell will freeze over."

Today, she was wearing ripped jeans that looked like they'd gone through the shredder a couple of times and an ugly brown sweater with a line drawing of a cat printed on it. She was also wearing those godawful glasses that reminded him of Edna Mode from *The Incredibles*, and she had her hair pinned up in Princess Leia buns on the side of her head.

He'd actually started making it a point to run into her every day just so he could see what crazy getup she had on. Her sense of fashion—if it could be called that—was always quirky and entertaining.

Gage pointed to his printer. "My printer is broken."

Despite his annoyance about her potential desertion, he was amused by the way she shot him an irritated look.

"Seriously?"

He nodded. "Seriously. I have a meeting in twenty minutes."

Beaumont strolled over to his printer and slid the paper tray open.

"I already checked that," he grumbled.

"You say that like a lack of paper wasn't the problem previously."

"*One time*," he stressed, holding up one finger.

"I don't understand why you don't call Alex. He's the hardware guy." Even as she complained, she started pushing buttons on the machine.

"Alex takes too long to fix shit, always talking my damn ear off. I told you, I have a meeting in twenty minutes. You're quicker."

"And in the meantime, you're losing thousands while I'm here tinkering with a printer instead of doing—you know—*my job*."

Gage grinned. "Let me know when I'm losing millions and I'll worry about it."

"I'm just saying, fixing printers isn't part of my job description," Beaumont grumbled.

"Of course it is. It falls under 'other duties as assigned.'"

She shot him a dirty look as she dropped to her knees and ducked beneath his desk to check the connections.

Gage took the opportunity to check out her ass. He'd been called a lot of things in his life, but a gentleman wasn't one of them. He'd never really looked at Beaumont as someone he'd be sexually attracted to, but there was no denying...she had a great ass.

"What the hell have you been doing?" she asked. "Half your shit is unplugged."

Unable to resist, Gage joked, "Let's just say you're not the first woman to crawl under my desk today."

Beaumont peeked her head back out, piercing him with another glare. "Gross."

Gage laughed. "I'm kidding. We hired a new cleaning crew last week, and I've noticed things have been getting unplugged. Didn't think to check that."

"You need some serious cable management. Well," Beaumont said from beneath the desk. "I think it's all good now." She climbed back out and rose again. "What did you want to print?"

He pointed to the document open on the screen. She tinkered with his machine for a minute or two, clicking a bunch of buttons, then hit the print icon, and gave him a voila hand gesture when the printer started shooting out paper.

"You up for some *Warzone* tonight?" he asked.

"Really? It's Friday night. I would have figured you'd have a date."

Apart from Connie and Marjorie, Gage hadn't been doing a lot of dating in the last couple months. He hadn't lied to his brother about both women asking him out. If they hadn't, he certainly wouldn't have approached them.

Dating had grown stale, the idea of going through the whole drinks/dinner/seduction routine just to get laid, tedious. Hell, sex didn't even interest him all that much nowadays. It felt as if he'd fucked himself out. He'd done it all, and now it was just...boring. He could take care of his own business with his hand in the shower every morning and it felt just as satisfying.

How fucking sad was that?

"No date. Not tonight. So what do you say?"

"I'm not sure I'm available," she said, though he knew for a fact the woman never dated. "After all, you still owe me twenty bucks from the last time we played."

He chuckled. "I'm good for it."

Lately, the two of them had been putting small wagers on their games, the competition heating up. He and Beaumont were evenly matched.

"Actually, let's make it more interesting. Double or nothing," he added.

She paused, sinking her teeth into her lower lip, and he suddenly found himself wondering if she really needed the money. Then he considered the offer from Frost. He knew her salary here was more than decent, but maybe there was something he *didn't* know.

"I'm just kidding." He reached into his back pocket for his wallet. "I can pay up now."

Beaumont waved her hands. "No. I was thinking..."

She stopped talking, and he could tell she was suddenly nervous, something he hadn't seen from her as often in the months since they'd become friends. The silence drifted long enough that most people would have found it awkward and sought to fill it with meaningless jabber, but he knew it wasn't unusual for Beaumont to go quiet while she sorted through her thoughts.

So he waited.

"What about instead of double or nothing," she said at last, "we change the wager?"

Gage's curiosity was piqued. "What do you mean?"

Beaumont's cheeks grew pink, and once more, she fell silent.

He'd heard some of the things the guys in IT talked about—hell, he'd added his own risqué stories to his share of the conversations—and Beaumont always took it in stride. Sometimes it was easy to forget she was a woman. But now...

"Are you *blushing*?" he asked.

Her hands flew to her face. "No. I mean...it's hot in here," she lied.

"What do you want to wager, Beaumont?"

"Favors. If I win, you have to do what I ask. If you win, the same."

"Favors? Just random favors, or did you have something in mind?" It was clear there was something Beaumont wanted, but she didn't want to say. However, he wasn't the type to walk into a wager like this blind.

Beaumont shrugged. Another lie.

"I need to know the stakes before I agree."

She sighed, her gaze suddenly glued to the floor. "I have a milestone birthday coming up in a month."

"Oh yeah? About to hit the big three-oh?"

She shook her head. "No. Twenty-nine."

Gage chuckled. "Pretty sure that doesn't count as a milestone."

She lifted her eyes just in time for him to see them roll. "My brother said the same thing, but you're both wrong. This is going to be my last year in my twenties, which means I only have one more year to make this decade count. So far, the twenties have sucked."

"You want me to throw you a wild party or something? Because I could get behind—"

"No," she interjected. "I need...I want to change some things about myself."

"What things?" Gage asked, even though he was afraid to hear the answer. What if she was serious about taking the job offer from Frost? What if he couldn't change her mind?

He was ready to match their offer. No. Fuck that. He was ready to beat the other offer. She was amazing at her job, but more than that, he liked being around her and Toby and Rich. They called themselves the nerd circle, but the truth was, they were probably the coolest people Gage knew. Because they were the most real, the most genuine, the most what-you-see-is-what-you-get. On top of that, their interests matched his, and they'd welcomed him into their midst. With them, he could set his gamer, D&D side free, could shed the carefree playboy bachelor billionaire persona, and just be one of the guys.

Once again, she lowered her eyes, embarrassed by whatever she planned to say next. "I saw you with your date the other night and...well...I want you to teach me how to be like *her*."

"Like Marjorie?"

She nodded. "Yeah. I don't really have anyone else to ask."

"What about Jess? I'm sure she could give you some pointers on..." He stopped, not even certain what Beaumont was asking.

"Oh, Jess is great. And I'm definitely going to ask her for some help with hair and makeup, but she's really busy with her son and the new relationship with Tony and Rhys and—"

"She really *is* with both of them?" Gage had heard rumors, but he'd dismissed them as just that. Rumors.

Beaumont looked up again, her eyes narrowed. "Don't be a prude, Gage."

"I'm not. Forget I said anything." He'd have to think about Jess and her guys later. "Spell this thing out for me, Beaumont."

She started to look down once more, but he wasn't having

that. He stepped forward and tilted her face up with a finger under her chin. "Look at *me*. Not the floor," he demanded.

"What I need is the male perspective, and the only other guys I know are Toby and Rich, and they're not exactly killing it with the ladies. Or at least, they weren't until...*you* helped them. So I want you to help me, too. I figure you're an expert when it comes to women."

"So if you win, what exactly is it you want from me?" he asked, enthralled by this entire conversation. He was going to be late to his meeting, but he didn't give a shit. Wild horses couldn't drag him away from Beaumont right now.

"I want you to teach me how to make myself physically attractive to men. And how to flirt. And how to seduce a guy and how to be good in bed."

Gage's jaw dropped as he tried to process her request. "Wait. Are you saying you want to sleep with me?"

Beaumont tilted her head as if confused. "I'm sorry. I didn't think sex was going to be the hard part of that favor. I mean...I've never really noticed you tying any sort of morals or emotions to sex."

She wasn't wrong. He didn't. Sex was an act, not a feeling for him. Something she'd clearly gleaned from his well-earned reputation as a playboy.

Then her eyes widened, as if she'd solved her own puzzle. "Oh no, it's what I said the other night, isn't it? The work thing? I didn't even think about that! I guess I've started thinking about you less as a boss and more as a friend. That was dumb of me, because now I'm in exactly the same position as the women I tried to warn you away from."

So she really did think of him as a friend? Gage wasn't sure why such a silly, insignificant thing made him happy.

"We *are* friends, Beaumont. And it isn't the boss dynamic that has me hesitating."

"Okay. Well, I mean, if it is, I could sign something that says this was all my idea and you weren't harassing me or anything."

He shook his head. "I don't need you to sign anything. You've just caught me by surprise. I'm not sure why you want to change."

"I…" she started, but then she shook her head. "Can I just ask you to trust me when I say this is what I want? My reasons are sort of personal."

He wanted to press her on that then decided against it. For one thing, he understood wanting to keep certain aspects of his life private. For another, her reasons didn't really matter…because he'd just found a way to get what he really wanted from her.

If he lost, he would carry out his part of the deal to an extent, though he had no intention of sleeping with Beaumont. He could teach her the art of seduction without taking her to bed.

For one thing, as she'd just said, they were friends. In fact, she was his first female friend, and he didn't want to cross that line.

For another, he had no intention of losing.

"Fine. I accept the wager. If you win, I'll help you reinvent yourself." He was careful not to mention anything that might make her think he was agreeing to have sex with her.

She smiled. "Awesome. Well, I know you have a meeting, so I'll let you—"

"Aren't you going to ask what my favor will be when I win?"

"If," she corrected. "And it doesn't matter because I don't intend to lose."

"Humor me," he insisted.

Beaumont pushed up her glasses. "I'm all ears."

"When I win, you're going to sign an extended contract agreeing to work here for the next five—no—make it seven years."

Beaumont's eyes widened, then she bit her lip guiltily. "How did you know?"

Just like that, she'd confirmed that Matt's sources were accurate. "I have eyes and ears everywhere."

"I wasn't really looking to leave. They approached *me*."

"I know." Sadly, he did. He wasn't foolish enough to think headhunters wouldn't seek her out. She was too fucking talented. But he'd be damned if he'd lose her.

"It's a sweet deal," she admitted. "Like, really sweet."

He admired her moxie. "I'm willing to negotiate, discuss salary, benefits, and perks."

She hesitated. "Seven years?"

It was a long time. Almost unheard of for someone in her position. Regardless, he didn't waver. "Nonnegotiable." That was a lie, but he was curious to see how far he could push her, just how serious she was about this wager. Agreeing to it would tell him how much she wanted this favor she'd asked of him.

"Fine. You're on."

"Excellent. As you said, I'm late for my meeting. Why don't I text you later with a place and time for the competition?"

"Sounds good."

They shook on their agreement, and he watched her leave. Rather than hurry out to his meeting, he dropped down in his office chair and glanced at his computer. He laughed out loud when he realized why it had taken Beaumont so long to print his document. She'd changed his screensaver to a unicorn farting a rainbow as revenge for him making her fix the printer.

"Jesus," he murmured in amusement as he tried to figure out where the hell he went from here.

Because as much as he did *not* want Beaumont to go to work for Frost—he really didn't want that—there was another, larger part of him that wanted to help her reinvent herself, intrigued by the challenge she'd just presented.

Because he was bored with his life. Really fucking bored—and she had offered him a potentially fun distraction.

So for the first time in his competitive life, Gage wasn't so sure he wanted to win.

Chapter Four

Gage grinned when he heard a knock on the door of what used to be one of the company's conference rooms. He'd recently begun renovating it for another purpose, and today, he was unveiling it to an audience of one.

He glanced at his phone. Beaumont was right on time.

"Come in," he called out.

Beaumont stepped inside, and while her eyes widened as she looked around the room, he took a moment—as always—to check out the crazy look she'd managed to pull off. Today, her hair was pinned up in some wild waterfall style on top of her head, her jeans had colorful patches all over them, and she was wearing one of what had to be seventy-two *Good Mythical Morning* sweatshirts she owned.

As always, her big black-framed glasses were sliding down her nose and she didn't have a speck of makeup on.

She tossed the backpack she was carrying onto the table in the middle of the room then started walking around the space, her mouth hanging open, no sound coming out.

He'd rendered her speechless.

"Gage," she said after a few minutes. "Oh my God."

After the two of them had placed their wager yesterday, he'd

35

known exactly where he wanted them to hold their "battle for favors." He'd started working on creating this space a few days after his first gaming night with her and Toby. His interests had always drifted toward technology—he'd invested in several tech upstarts—but he'd wanted to expand specifically into gaming tech forever.

"What do you think?"

He had taken over this conference space in order to create a gaming room. Gage had stocked the room with six state-of-the-art computers, fully loaded with two monitors each, gaming chairs with pillows embroidered with Team Russo, several PlayStation 5 systems, and the latest in VR. The fluorescent lighting had been replaced with RGB LED lighting strips and surround sound that would really enhance the game-playing experience.

It was a gamer's paradise, and he knew it.

Beaumont shook her head in response, clearly still struggling to find her words. "I...oh my God."

He grinned. It was the highest praise he could have asked for. "I invested in a gaming start-up, Tower Games. They're based in Charlotte, North Carolina. Was thinking the nerd circle could do some testing on their products, offer insights."

Beaumont stared at him as if he'd suddenly grown wings and a halo. "Toby and Rich will flip out!"

Gage knew that. "Yeah. I can't wait to show them."

"Can I be here when you do?"

"Of course."

Beaumont spun around one more time. "I can't believe this room! It's like you snuck into my dreams and drew up the plans. It's just...*incredible*. Actually, you might want to rethink showing this to Toby and Rich, or you'll never get another second of work out of them."

Gage laughed. "Matt said the same thing. Said the first time he caught our IT department up here in the middle of the workday, he was putting an alarm on the door. Of course, I'm pretty sure he was talking about me, not you guys. Besides, I know Toby's dream is to develop his own game. This would give him that chance."

"Holy shit. This is so freaking awesome! Now I sort of hope I lose, just to ensure I can keep working here."

Gage rolled his eyes. "The outcome of this wager means nothing in regard to your job. We're not letting you quit."

"Did I mention they were offering some pretty amazing perks?" she asked with a shit-eating grin.

"There will be time for negotiations about all of that *after* I kick your ass."

Beaumont ran her hand over the expensive gaming chair. "You know...the alarm is probably a good idea because I'm not sure I can resist this place either. Maybe that will help my self-control."

Gage woke up a couple of the PCs. "I was thinking we could set up gaming nights here. Maybe even enter some e-sports tournaments together a few weekends a year. I'm calling it a team building exercise."

"I love that idea. Dibs on being team captain," she said.

Gage scowled. "Hell no. I'm team captain."

"Well, that hardly seems fair. Shouldn't we put it to a vote or something?" Beaumont asked.

"This is not a democracy. I'm the one who set all this up, footed the bill."

"Wow. Okay, Malfoy. Way to buy yourself a spot on the Quidditch team."

Gage laughed, as Beaumont went to retrieve the backpack she'd brought with her. She pulled out a pair of headphones, a big bag of Doritos, and a twenty-ounce bottle of Mountain Dew.

"What are you? A fifteen-year-old boy?" he teased.

She looked around the room and smirked. "Seems to me, a good captain would have put a snack machine in here."

"Shut up and give me some Doritos." He grabbed the bag, ripping it open and snagging a big handful.

"Hey!" she protested.

Then he added more fuel to the fire by walking over to the water cooler, grabbing a paper cup, and helping himself to half of her Mountain Dew.

The two of them got settled in front of their PCs. When he texted her the place and time last night, they'd spent a few minutes discussing which game they should play for their competition.

Gage typically came out ahead on *Grand Theft Auto*, while Beaumont consistently edged him out on *Fortnite*. So they'd agreed on *Call of Duty*, since they were most evenly matched there, with their wins and losses against each other almost fifty-fifty. They'd also decided to play the best of two out of three games.

"You ready?" Gage asked after they'd both taken some time to login to their accounts and set up their characters.

She nodded. "I'm ready."

An hour later, they were two games in and tied, one win each. Beaumont was a fierce competitor.

They stood up and stretched for a few minutes before starting the final match.

"Feel like conceding now, Beaumont? Save face?"

She tilted her head. "Never."

"Want to change the wager? Because I'm holding you to those seven years. There will be a contract, and you *will* sign it."

"You act like that's a threat. If you were hoping to scare me away, you shouldn't have shown me this room."

Gage chuckled. "Good point. You still plan to ask for the makeover favor?"

She nodded. "Absolutely."

He'd thought about her request a lot last night, trying to figure out why it bothered him. Then he'd finally landed on it. "You sure you want to trick a guy into falling for you?"

"What do you mean, trick him?" she asked.

"You're planning to change everything about yourself just to catch a guy's eye. Wouldn't it be better to find a man who likes you exactly as you are?"

Beaumont sighed, not meeting his gaze. "That man doesn't exist."

"Bullshit," Gage countered. "There's a key for every lock."

"I don't really view what I'm doing as trickery, or even changing. There are parts of myself I've never figured out how to showcase. I mean...wearing my hair in a different style doesn't mean it's not still my hair. And people change their wardrobes all the time—hence the reason every decade has 'a look.'" She fingered quoted the last two words. "Bell bottoms in the sixties, popped collars and Izod in the eighties, acid-wash jeans and flannel shirts in the nineties. How many people lived through those decades and changed their style with the times?"

"Those are broad fashion trends. I'm talking about you abandoning your unique style and adopting something that's not really you."

"They're just clothes, Gage. I don't put that much stock in them. I should think that would be pretty obvious."

"Then what about the rest?" he asked, wondering why he felt the need to push the issue. If this was what she thought she needed to do to find a boyfriend, he should just let her roll with it. His problem was...he wasn't sure he liked the idea of her changing.

"The rest of what?"

"Your hair and clothes are one thing, but you also want lessons in flirting. In seduction." He still couldn't believe she'd asked him to teach her how to be a better lover in bed. Although, of all the things she'd listed as part of her favor, that one bothered him the least. Because he didn't intend to follow through on it. At least not the way she expected.

He didn't doubt for a moment he could mold Beaumont into a genuine sex goddess if he set his mind to it. She was a blank canvas, and it was tempting to accept her challenge, to create the type of woman who would drive men crazy with lust and desire.

He was certain he could accomplish that without actually doing the deed. He'd just have to be creative.

"I'm socially awkward, Gage. You can't tell me you haven't noticed."

He didn't outwardly agree, though she'd hit the nail on the head. Russo Enterprises held an annual holiday party in December, one that Beaumont had never missed, though he wasn't entirely sure why she bothered to attend.

For six years straight, she'd parked herself at a corner table with Toby and Rich, the three of them scarfing down food, chair dancing whenever they liked a song, staring at their phones, and basically ignoring everyone else at the party.

Last year, the three of them had left the grand ballroom and spent the better part of the evening searching for *Pokémon* in and around the hotel.

"Your reason for wanting this still personal?" he asked, not wanting to admit how curious he was.

She nodded.

"So the wager stands?" he said at last, convinced he wouldn't win this argument and starting to think he didn't want to.

"It stands."

"Then to the victor go the spoils." He gestured to their chairs, and they started up the third and final game.

"Fuck," Gage said half an hour later, tossing down his controller.

Beaumont stood up, looking far too fucking smug. Gage hated to lose, regardless of the fact he didn't hate the wager. But the truth of the matter was...it was impossible for him to set his competitiveness aside, so he *had* been playing to win.

And he hadn't.

He grumbled another curse word.

"Don't be a sore loser," she said when he crossed his arms, scowling. "I beat you fair and square."

She had, but that knowledge didn't help.

"You're still not leaving Russo Enterprises," he grumbled.

Beaumont pushed her glasses up. "I never said I was. I just said I got an offer. A *good* offer."

"Your annual evaluation is next month. Tell me what Frost is offering and we'll match their offer. Fuck that, we'll beat it."

"Okay, I'll hear what you have to say," she said.

Gage considered her carefully worded answer. If not this time, at some point, another company was most likely going to swoop in with the right proposal, which was why he'd really wanted to nail her down with a long contract. "Will you promise to come to me if and when the headhunters come back? Give me a chance to match their offer?"

Beaumont seemed to consider that. "Maybe," she drawled.

"Maybe?" he asked hotly.

"You could at least attempt to sweeten the deal...by making me captain of the e-sports team."

Gage barked out a loud laugh. She was shameless. "Seriously? That's the part you want to negotiate about?"

"My life is very small, Gage. Work, games, cats. I love the idea of testing games from that upstart of yours and the weekend tournaments. For the first time in ages, I'm actually excited about something."

Sounded like they had something in common. Gage hadn't realized until that moment that Beaumont was as bored with her life as he was with his.

"So it's just the e-sports you're excited about? Not the whole reinventing-yourself project?" he asked.

"Oh, I'm super excited about that too. Especially the sex part."

His sixth sense told him her commitment to that aspect of the favor was going to become a problem down the road. Maybe this was the time to mention he'd promised his brother no more workplace hookups, and that he could teach her how to seduce a man without the two of them engaging in sex.

However, before he could broach the subject, she broke out

into some weird victory dance, something akin to the running man, and he laughed.

Penny Beaumont was an odd one, but damn if he didn't enjoy hanging out with her.

"Fine," he begrudgingly agreed. "We can be *co*-captains."

Beaumont tapped her chin, pretending to think about it. "Okay. It's a deal. We're co-captains, and I promise to tell you when someone tries to lure me away from the company so that you can match—no, *beat*—the offer. I'm not going to lie...it's starting to feel like I won three times, not just once. Co-captains, better contract, and...a big, big favor."

"We'll commence with Operation New Beaumont on Monday. But if you're serious about wanting my help, that means you do everything I say, exactly. Got it?"

She tilted her head. "Give me an example."

He stepped closer, taking note of Beaumont's height. The Russo men were tall guys, his brother Conor the shortest of the three, at six-two. He was used to looking down—way down—at his dates, but Beaumont's face wasn't that much lower.

"How tall are you?" he asked.

If his question caught her off guard, she didn't let on. "Five-ten."

He reached for the band holding her hair and pulled it free, letting her thick mass of dirty-blonde hair fall loose. He'd never seen it down. Not once in six years.

She reached up to push it back off her shoulders. He circled her, taking note that it hung halfway down her back.

"I didn't realize your hair was so long."

"It's a pain in the ass, but I'm too lazy to go to the hairdresser. Actually, I'm too lazy to make an appointment, so it's gotten out of hand. That's why I wear it up all the time. I've considered just being done with it and shaving my head, but—"

"*No.* You're not shaving your head. Most men like long hair. Gives them something to wrap their fists around when they're..." He wiggled his eyebrows, letting her fill in the blanks, and grinning at her instant blush. "It just needs a style and highlights."

"Okay," she agreed. "Although I'd intended to ask Jess's advice in regard to makeup, hair, and clothes."

He shook his head. "No. I'm in charge of all of it. My advice is the only advice you'll be taking."

She gave him a salute. "Sir, yes, sir."

Gage shook his head, thinking for the first time he might have bitten off more than he could chew. Then he took the ugly-ass glasses off, amused by the way she blinked a couple times and squinted. When her gaze focused on him, he was slightly taken aback by her bright light-blue eyes. "Ever wear contacts?"

"I tried a couple times, but it always took a few minutes to get them in, which usually made me even later to work than I already was."

Gage was aware of Beaumont's inability to arrive anywhere on time. One of Matt's biggest pet peeves was employees who were consistently tardy. To keep her out of trouble, Gage had "changed" her work hours, telling her the start time was fifteen minutes earlier than it really was. Ever since then—and unbeknownst to her—she'd been right on time, even though she constantly apologized for being late.

"You're going to try them again. And throw these Edna Mode glasses in the garbage."

She grabbed her glasses from him and slapped them back on. "I love these glasses."

"They hide half your face, Beaumont."

"That's *why* I love them."

He narrowed his eyes. "No more hiding."

She grumbled, neither agreeing nor disagreeing. Not that it mattered. He was going to get his way.

Gage reached for one of her hands. "You also have to stop biting your nails. It's a bad habit."

She sighed. "I know, but that's going to be easier said than done."

"I've got a plan for that too."

She studied his face then smirked. "You seem to have given this some thought since yesterday. Knew you were going to lose, didn't you?"

"Did you ever consider that I'm a selfless humanitarian and I threw the contest because I knew you needed my help?"

"That thought never crossed my mind."

He laughed. "Meet me at my office Monday at five p.m."

Beaumont nodded, grabbed her bag, and left.

She'd said she was excited for the first time in a long time, and Gage couldn't help but admit to himself that he felt the same way.

Chapter Five

Penny sat in the hairdresser's chair, wondering when exactly she'd crossed over into this strange alternate universe. Slipping through a portal into another world *His Dark Materials*-style was the only way Penny could make sense of her current situation.

"No," Gage insisted. "That's not what I want. No more than three inches off the back and then long layers."

"But her bone structure, the shape of her face..."

Phillippe, the hairdresser, continued to rattle on, but Penny tuned it out. Phillippe insisted on giving her a blunter cut, angled around her jaw, but Gage wasn't having it.

The debate had been going on for five full minutes, and not once had either man asked for her opinion. Not that she had one. The reason she'd requested this favor of Gage in the first place was because number one, she was clueless, and number two, she trusted him to know what would turn a man's head. There was no way her boss didn't live with a permanent case of whiplash, given his dating record.

Penny wiggled, wondering how much longer they intended to wage this battle. She'd already been here an hour, sitting and playing on her phone while Phillippe added the lighter highlights to her dirty-blonde hair. She studied her reflection in the mirror once more, shocked by how such a subtle change in coloring could make such a big difference. She loved it and couldn't wait for Jess and the other girls to see it.

"Fine," she heard Phillippe say, giving in with a heavy sigh.

Finally, she thought. She glanced at Gage through the reflection. He was standing nearby, as if daring Phillippe to stray one single strand of hair away from the script.

"You don't have to hang around if you have something else to do tonight," Penny said. "There's no reason for you to stay since this is the last part. I can pay Phillippe once he's done."

"I've already paid him," Gage said.

Penny scowled. "That wasn't part of the favor. How much was it? I'll pay you back."

Gage shook his head, dismissing her without a word.

"Gage," she started. "Seriously, I want to—"

He captured her gaze in the mirror and held it. "Not another word, Beaumont."

If anyone asked her to describe her boss in one word, she would say easygoing. However, every now and then, she caught glimpses of a different side of him. Something that was the exact opposite of laid-back. Something more...God...feral? Primal?

While Penny struggled to put a word to it, she didn't have a bit of trouble describing the way it made her feel every time he hit her with one of his infrequent deep-voiced commands.

Her stomach fluttered.

Her heart fluttered.

Her pussy fluttered.

Gage only had to give her *that* look, use *that* tone, say something wholly domineering, and *boom*. She was a fluttery mess.

She closed her mouth, the snipping of the scissors and the murmured conversations of the other people in the salon filling the silence that had fallen between her, her hairdresser, and Gage.

Forty-five minutes later, Penny ran her hands over her hair, speechless.

It was beautiful.

"Wow."

Phillippe smiled. "I must admit defeat. You were correct, Mr. Russo, to insist on this style. It is gorgeous."

Gage stared at her as she rose from the chair and turned to face him.

"I love it," she admitted. "Thank you."

Gage didn't respond, and she feared perhaps he didn't like it.

Phillippe handed Gage a large plastic bag, but before Penny could ask him what was in it, he said, "Thank you for your time, Phillippe," and gestured toward the exit.

They'd met at Gage's office right at closing time, both of them agreeing to drive their own cars here since their homes were in opposite directions, so they stopped on the sidewalk, just outside the salon.

"I wish you'd let me pay you back."

"No."

"Fine. But no more paying for anything," she insisted. "This is my makeover, my favor. The wager didn't include you shelling out money for anything."

"I'm loaded, Beaumont. Got more money than I can spend in twelve lifetimes. A haircut isn't going to break me."

"That's not the point." She paused then touched her hair once more and forced herself to ask, "Do you hate it?"

Gage seemed genuinely surprised by her question. "Fuck no. It's perfect. I can't stop looking at it."

She smiled, relieved, as she ran her fingers through it. "You realize I'll never manage to make it look like this again. That guy wielded a hairdryer like a professional gunslinger. I don't even own one."

"You do now." Gage lifted the bag and handed it to her. "And a curling iron. And all those fancy products he used. You're going to practice until you get it right. If you come to work with your hair pinned up in one of those Princess Leia hairdos again, there *will* be consequences."

Penny wanted to ask what kind of consequences, but she couldn't make herself. Because he'd used that damn tone again, setting off a nuclear explosion of fluttering inside her body.

"Okay," she said, because agreeing would ensure the quickest, easiest way out of this conversation without making an ass of herself.

"Meet me tomorrow afternoon, same time and place, for round two."

She nodded and started to turn toward the car. Before she could do so, Gage grasped her upper arm gently, twisting her to face him once more. She stood there, shell-shocked, as he ran his fingers through her hair, then closed his fist around it.

For a moment, she thought he was going to use that grip to pull her closer, to—ohmigod—kiss her, but then he released his grip.

"Nothing like having something to hold on to when you take a woman from behind, driving in deep and hard."

"Oh…" she breathed.

He studied her too intently for her comfort. "You'd like having your hair pulled, wouldn't you?" he murmured.

His words drew a picture of just such a thing in her mind, leaving Penny too flustered to respond.

"Perfect. Goodbye, Beaumont."

She gave him a little wave, the slightest fluttering of her fingers, to match the same sensations he'd just fired off…everywhere else.

On Friday afternoon, Penny stood outside Gage's office door, just as she had every single day this week, preparing herself for whatever the hell round five might consist of. Gage had clearly made a list, and they were systematically working their way through it.

The entire week had been a lot of fun, though she couldn't quite believe Gage's commitment to honoring the bet, touched by his willingness to spend hours with her every evening after work to give her what she'd asked for.

Of course, her favorite part of each night came at the end, when Gage explained—in dirty detail—how the changes they'd made would attract men. Every comment had fed her fantasies, ensuring her vibrator was getting one hell of a workout this week.

Tuesday's excursion to the optometrist led to the contacts she was currently wearing and still trying to adjust to. Gage had allowed her to keep the glasses but informed her she couldn't wear them to work anymore.

Then he'd leaned in close, running his lips over the side of her face, his beard tickling her cheek, his breath hot in her ear. "No glasses in the way. Gives a man unobstructed access to kiss every part of your face and to look deep into those pretty blue eyes of yours when you come on his cock."

On Wednesday, she'd spent two and a half hours getting a tutorial on how to apply makeup from a professional makeup artist Gage had hired for the lesson. Then he had dropped an ungodly amount of money buying her all the makeup, despite her argument that she had money and could afford it.

After the lesson, they'd stood on the sidewalk once again, something that had become part of their daily ritual. He reserved his comments about her changing looks until they were alone. Gage had reached for her, only he didn't grip her hair or kiss her face. Instead, he'd run his thumb over her lips, while she'd prayed the man would kiss her.

He hadn't. Dammit.

He'd pulled his thumb away to show her that the lipstick hadn't smeared. "Can't decide if that's good or bad," he'd mused. "It sucks when a woman's lipstick smears when you're kissing her, but I do like the look of it staining my cock after she goes down on me."

He'd followed that pronouncement up with a wink, chuckling when she blushed.

Then, yesterday, she'd been treated to her very first mani-pedi, and Gage had indeed found a way to stop her from biting her nails, given the acrylics they'd applied. After the manicure, he'd taken her hand, led her to the sidewalk, pulled her close—oh-so close—and whispered in her ear that a man loved the feel of a woman's nails scratching his back, or using them to tickle their way down his chest to fist his cock.

She glanced down and admitted to herself that she loved the way her hands looked, though she was going to have to ask about making the nails a bit shorter. Typing on her keyboard had been a bitch today, and she wondered how in the hell women with long nails ever got a damn thing done on the computer.

Her frustration and constant cursing whenever she hit the wrong key had led Toby to ask why she was trying to look like a girl all of a sudden. Four days in, and that was the first time any of the guys in her department acknowledged the changes she'd made in her appearance. She'd simply looked at him and reminded him she *was* a fucking girl.

Last night, she'd been wondering if all the effort was even worth it...until she'd gotten home the same time as her new neighbor, David, who'd not only made eye contact but introduced himself! And Penny, for the first time ever, had managed to string together three whole sentences without sounding like a fool. David was new to Philly, single, a lawyer, and he now knew she was also single, worked in cybersecurity, and was available to answer any questions he might have about the city.

Score one for Operation New Beaumont.

She didn't have a clue what today would bring. Gage had told her not to bring her car to work because he'd be driving her home, so she'd taken the El.

Knocking on the door, she entered after he called out, "Come in."

He smiled when he saw her. "You've perfected the hair and the makeup."

She was pleased by his compliment and thrilled with the way she looked. But damn if it didn't take a lot of work. She'd had to set her alarm an hour earlier every day this week and she'd still been late. "Thanks, but these nails have to go."

Gage frowned. "Why?"

"Because I can't type with them. Today was an experiment in torture. I nearly ripped them off at lunchtime, but…"

He crossed his arms. "Nearly, or you tried to?"

"Fuckers are on there tight."

He narrowed his eyes. "No ripping off the nails. You can go back to the salon this weekend and ask them to file them shorter. Okay?"

"Okay," she muttered. "But you know it's not just the typing. I nearly gouged my eyes out this morning, trying to put the contacts in with these claws."

Gage chuckled. "Never considered how treacherous life is for women until this experiment with you."

"Very funny. What's on the agenda for today?"

Gage stepped closer, walking around her as he took in her outfit. "Wardrobe. You need a new one."

She shook her head. "Not a whole wardrobe. I have plenty of clothes."

"Are any of them sexy?"

She looked down at her mom jeans and faded black men's T-shirt that said, "IT. I'm just in it for the cache."

"I'm going to go out on a limb and say no. Probably not."

Gage laughed. "Good answer."

"I just need a couple sexy outfits," she insisted.

"Mm-hmm." He was totally ignoring her. "Come on." He placed his hand on the small of her back and led her out of his office, closing and locking the door behind them. His hand remained on her back the entire ride down in the elevator to the parking garage beneath the building.

Part of her "favor" had included sex, but so far, with the exception of Gage's too-brief touches at the end of each night, he hadn't mentioned when they might move forward with those particular lessons.

She hoped it was sooner rather than later because her girl parts were hungry. Starving.

Gage hit the button to unlock the doors on his Audi A8 then opened the passenger door for her. "Your chariot, my lady," he teased.

She rolled her eyes, but only to try to hide how charmed she was by his old-fashioned, gentlemanly gesture. They talked about work stuff until they arrived at his destination, an upscale boutique on Rittenhouse Row. Rather than open her door to get out, Penny reached across the console, grasping Gage's forearm.

"No more paying for stuff," she said. She'd fought—and lost—this same argument every single day, but this time she was determined to win. "I'm not getting out of this car until you promise you'll let me pay for whatever I pick out."

"Fine. You can pay for whatever you pick out." He removed her hand from his arm, got out of the car, then met her on the sidewalk.

Penny hadn't expected the quick concession, so, of course, she was instantly suspicious.

Gage guided her into a small but swanky boutique, and she knew two steps over the threshold the place was going to be way out of her price range. "You know, they have really nice clothes at Target."

Gage shook his head. "No. Part of our deal was that you follow my advice to the letter."

Penny lifted a tag to peek, her eyes widening. "Jesus H. Christ," she exclaimed. "This basic white T-shirt costs seventy-four dollars. I'm not buying anything in here."

"You don't have to. But I am."

"But you said—"

He cut her off. "I said you could pay for whatever *you* picked out. I never said you could pay for what *I* pick out."

"You knew what I meant!"

He pulled one of those classic little-black-dress numbers from one of the racks, looking at her and then the dress. "And I know what I promised," he said in a tone that let her know that, once again, she'd lost the argument.

An attractive salesclerk approached them, her gaze slowly sliding down Penny, her brow furrowed because, clearly, she knew the same thing Penny did. She didn't belong here. In truth, the clerk fit in better with her silky blouse, pencil skirt, practical heels, and elegant updo. There wasn't a single hair out of place on the woman.

The clerk recovered quickly when she shifted her gaze away from Penny and saw Gage, who, in his bespoke suit, pretty much screamed money.

"Can I help you find something?" she asked Gage.

"I'm helping my friend update her wardrobe. Actually, we're replacing it completely."

The woman's eyes widened just enough that Penny suspected she either owned this high-priced boutique or worked on commission. "I can definitely help you with that." She pointed to the dress Gage still held. "That's a wonderful choice. Would you like me to put it in one of the dressing rooms?"

"One thing," Penny muttered to Gage. "You can buy me one thing, so choose wisely."

Gage handed the salesclerk the dress. "Follow her and go try this on while I look around."

"How do you know that dress is the right size?" Penny asked.

"It is," he replied smugly, reminding her he was an expert when it came to women's bodies.

Penny glared at Gage, who smiled back, apparently amused by the fact she was annoyed with him. She held up one finger, silently making her point once more, before trailing behind the clerk. The woman unlocked a door, revealing a dressing room that was big enough to hold a damn dance party. She handed her the dress. "Do you need any delicates as well?"

Penny considered the ratty sports bra and granny panties she was wearing as she eyed the tight-fitting, low-cut dress. "Um... yeah...maybe."

"Wonderful. I'll be right back."

Like Gage, the clerk didn't bother to ask her size, but damned if both of them hadn't guessed right the first time.

Penny was down to her shabby undergarments by the time the clerk arrived. No doubt the woman was wondering how in the hell someone like Penny had shown up on Gage's radar.

She heard the woman complimenting another of Gage's selections, suggesting a sweater that would pair with whatever he'd picked out.

Penny stripped then slipped on the lacy bra, refusing to look at the price tag before sliding on the bikini briefs. Both items were soft and comfy and fit her like a second skin. The balconette bra pushed her breasts up, showcasing them, making them look...sexy.

Reaching for the dress, she pulled it on, then turned to study her reflection in the mirror. Penny gasped, her mouth falling open.

Holy shit!

She certainly felt sexy.

Of course, she also felt naked and awkward and certain there was no way in hell she could ever go out in public with so much of her body showing.

There was a brusque knock on the dressing room door.

"You got it on yet?" He sounded impatient.

"Yeah. I don't think—"

"Open the door."

"Gage, seriously. I—"

"Open it *now*."

Damn him and that deep, sexy, commanding voice. She walked barefoot over to the door and opened it.

"Jesus, Beaumont," Gage said, his tone matching her feelings exactly. "I'm buying that dress."

"You think it's not too..." She waved her arms over her body, searching for the word. "I mean, I'm not really leaving much to the imagination here."

She expected Gage to laugh.

He didn't. He just kept looking at her...as if she was...

"Beautiful."

He said the word, and for the first time in her life, Penny felt like it fit her.

She'd been lazy. That was the first thing she thought as Gage looked at her so appreciatively. Considering her current morning routine consisted of putting on her glasses, throwing on whatever clothes she grabbed first—either from the closet or the floor, she wasn't fussy—tossing her hair up on top of her head, and leaving the house, she could probably stand to add a few extra minutes to make an effort.

No, more than that. She *wanted* to make an effort. She liked the way she looked right now. A lot. She'd never figured out how to do this on her own. Back in high school, she'd asked her mom a couple of times, but...well, as much as she loved her mother, she was no fashion plate either, her clothing monochromatic and super conservative.

Okay, boring.

"Really?" she couldn't help but ask. She was new to this whole beautiful shit.

His gaze lifted to hers. "Really."

"Okay. Then I'll buy this. Let me just change back into my other clothes and we can—"

Gage cut her off. "Here's what happens next. Tish and I—"

"Tish?"

"The salesclerk."

She snorted. The clerk was lovely and elegant, so of *course* Gage had already gotten her name. Hell, he probably had her number and a date lined up already too. After all, she'd left him alone for almost ten minutes. "Ask her out yet?"

Gage frowned, confused. "No. I'm here with you."

Penny didn't know how to respond to that, but he didn't give her a chance.

"We're going to bring in outfits, you're going to put them on, then give me a fashion show. We're going to *Pretty Woman* the shit out of this place."

"*Pretty Woman*?"

Gage looked surprised. "You've never seen the movie?"

"Of course I have. I have a mother. I'm just shocked that *you* have."

Penny wasn't sure what to make of Gage's frozen expression. For a split second, she thought she saw the shimmer of something...sad...flash in his eyes before he went unnaturally still. "I had a mother too," he said finally, the words gruff.

Had.

Shit. Penny knew both of Gage's parents had passed away. It was why their three sons had taken over Russo Enterprises when they were still quite young, only in their early to mid-twenties.

Whatever sadness she'd seen was gone in an instant when Gage—clearly a master of controlling his emotions—turned around with a wicked grin and said, "You ready to do this thing, Tish?"

Tish, who'd looked so prim and proper when they'd first arrived, was standing there, grinning from ear to ear, armed with so many clothes, Penny considered making a break for it. Did they expect her to try on every damn thing in the store?

Then she decided to hell with it. This was an adventure, a once-in-a-lifetime experience, and she was going to have fun with it.

"What size shoes do you wear?" Gage asked, looking down at her freshly painted toenails.

"Ten." She grimaced. "Not exactly dainty, huh?"

"We're not going for dainty, Beaumont. We're going for sexy, remember?"

She nodded.

"And for the record...you're nailing it."

Penny was smiling like a giant buffoon, falling for Gage's charms just like every other woman he'd ever met, but she didn't care. After all, his mad skills with the ladies were the reason she was here, why she'd sought him out to help her to begin with. "*We're* nailing it," she corrected. "I could never have pulled half of this off without you."

He seemed pleased by her compliment, stepping out of the way so Tish could deliver the first of what appeared to be seven hundred outfits. Tish had found an armchair somewhere and moved it outside her dressing room so Gage could sit there and watch ala Richard Gere style. The quiet classical music that had been playing since their arrival was switched to an upbeat Dua Lipa number, the volume cranked.

Tish paired every ensemble with shoes—too many of which were out of Penny's comfort zone heel-wise. So while she'd attempted to give Gage her impersonation of a supermodel strutting on the catwalk—she watched *RuPaul's Drag Race*, after all— the best she could pull off was the newborn foal look as she wobbled in and out of the dressing room, risking a sprained ankle with every step she took.

So much for fucking *Pretty Woman*.

Two hours later, Penny's sense of adventure was gone. She was getting seriously hangry.

She stepped out of the dressing room in a pair of painted-on jeans that she had to admit she loved and some frou-frou sweater she hated. Not that her opinion had counted for much as they'd worked their way through the mountain of clothes now in two distinct piles. Gage was the one who'd determined the yesses and the noes.

Fortunately, she agreed with pretty much all his choices. The clothing was truly lovely, but not a lot of fun. Most of it was basic, nondescript, with solid earthy colors or muted patterns. Nowhere near as flashy or silly as her usual style, which was probably a good thing.

Though, she was going to have to work her way up to leaving the house in some of the more revealing outfits.

She didn't bother putting shoes on with this outfit as she basically stomped out of the dressing room and threw her arms up in a "so?" gesture.

Gage stood up and walked over to her. "Those jeans were made for you, but I'm not a fan of the sweater."

"Oh, you sure? I mean," she said, plucking at the frills, trying to think of something positive to say about it.

"It doesn't work with those jeans," he insisted.

"Okay. Um. Can this be the last outfit? I'm getting hungry."

"Yeah. We're almost there." Gage reached for something hanging from the arm of his chair and pushed her backwards into the dressing room, following her in, the door swinging closed behind them. Penny glanced over his shoulder, suddenly aware Tish was nowhere to be seen.

"What are you doing?"

"I think this shirt would look better with those jeans." Gage held the soft cotton out to her. "But don't tell Tish I said so."

She held it up and grinned. "Gage. Wow." The pale-blue shirt looked like it had been made for her.

"I noticed you like cats on your clothes."

She laughed. There was an adorable small black cat stitched on one side that was whimsical and fun and so her. "Was this actually here?"

Gage nodded. "Can you believe it? Found it buried on a sale rack."

"I love it."

"I knew you would. *Now* we can leave. I'll settle up on the purchases while you get dressed."

"I want to keep waging the battle to pay, but the truth is, I can't even afford these jeans and this—" She glanced down at the tag on the cat shirt, her eyes widening when she saw the price. "This was on the sale rack?!"

She'd purposely stopped looking at the price tags after the first shirt, but now...

"Maybe we should put some of the clothes ba—"

"Say thank you, Beaumont."

"Gage," she started, guilt setting in at the thought he was most likely dropping thousands on her tonight. *Thousands.*

He lifted one eyebrow. "Two words. Give them to me."

"Thank you," she said, sincerely, more grateful to him for his help than she could ever express.

He smiled and tapped a knuckle under her chin. "Good girl."

Holy shit. *His* two words packed a punch.

"Of course, if you added Daddy to the end, I'd really feel your appreciation."

She narrowed her eyes. "Go away."

Gage laughed as he left the dressing room, completely oblivious to the state he'd had left her in. Hot and bothered didn't even touch the way she felt right now.

When she came out of the dressing room, back in her normal clothes, which didn't feel as right as they had when they'd arrived earlier, Gage was outside, loading too many bags into the trunk of his car. She understood now why he'd insisted on driving. There was no way all those things would have fit in her Smart ForTwo Electric car.

They listened to music as Gage drove her to her apartment then together, they lugged all their purchases upstairs. All four of her cats greeted them at the door. They were hungry too. She introduced Gage to all of them, surprised when he lifted Hermione—the tiniest one—and cradled her in his arms.

"Tell me why you want the makeover," Gage pressed. It wasn't the first time he'd asked. Hell, it wasn't the fifth time.

She kept giving him some bullshit line about her reasons being personal, but the truth was, she'd been too embarrassed to tell him. It wasn't easy telling her sexy-as-sin, never-sleeps-alone boss that she was lonely. But after this week, after all the time, money, and effort he'd invested in helping her, she felt like he deserved to know.

"I don't want to be single anymore."

He waited for her to expound on that.

"I'm lonely," she confessed. "And I refuse to turn thirty and still be...the nerdy, geeky loser living alone with a bunch of cats."

Gage scowled. "You're not a loser."

She shrugged because his simply saying so didn't mean she didn't feel that way.

"I notice you didn't say anything about me not being a nerd or a geek," she added, with a grin, hoping to dispel his sudden anger.

"You're not those either."

"Want to order a pizza?" she asked, trying to change the subject. "My treat. I've got some PBR in the fridge. We could play *BeatSaber* or something."

For a second, it looked like Gage wanted to continue their argument, but then he shook his head. "No. I have a couple of errands to run before I head home."

"Okay," she said, gesturing to the pile of bags at their feet. "Today...this whole week...it's been...um..."

Ugh. Here came the stammering again. She thought she'd overcome this with him, but standing here in her apartment—Gage Russo was actually *in* her apartment, voluntarily—she couldn't help but consider the other part of the favor, wondering when they could move on from the makeover stuff and on to the good shit.

"Stage two starts tomorrow," he announced, as if he could read her mind.

"Okay," she said again, though this time it was too breathy, too...holy shit.

"You have a couple girlfriends you can call?"

The fuck?

"What?"

"Tomorrow is the grand unveiling of Beaumont 2.0. You're going dancing, but you need a couple of girlfriends—wingmen—to go with you."

"Oh."

"Maybe Jess," he suggested.

Penny shook her head. "No. Rhys and Tony would want to come too, and the last thing I need is my overprotective big brother and an equally overprotective Moretti hovering."

"Good call."

Penny considered who to invite. Sadly, a few months ago, her list of friends wasn't much larger than Toby and Rich. But now... "I'll invite Tony's cousin, Liza, and some other friends, Keeley and Gianna."

"Perfect. I want you to put on that little black dress—the first one you tried on—and those strappy fuck-me heels."

"You mean the fuck-me-up heels. I can't walk on those."

Gage crossed his arms. "You have all day tomorrow to practice. Make sure to do your hair just like Phillippe showed you and do the darker evening look the makeup artist taught you."

"Where am I going?"

"Enigma. Ten o'clock. It's one of my brother Conor's nightclubs, and it's the perfect place for you to spread your wings. You're going to dance with your girlfriends, and I promise, before the end of the night, you'll have your choice of every man there."

She liked his confidence, even if she didn't exactly share it. Changing her looks hadn't really changed her personality, but Gage seemed really excited about the experiment, so she nodded.

"Sounds great."

Chapter Six

Gage sat alone at a table in the corner, sipping his top-shelf bourbon, and forced himself to acknowledge he'd made a mistake.

A big one.

Penny had arrived an hour earlier, though she hadn't seen him. He'd chosen his position carefully, wanting to watch her without her realizing his presence.

She had followed his instructions to the letter—and he hadn't been able to take his eyes off her since she'd walked into Enigma.

She was hands-down the most gorgeous woman in the club tonight. That went without question.

But that still wasn't going to help her.

When he'd first accepted this silly wager of hers, he'd viewed the opportunity to reinvent quirky Penny Beaumont as something to break up the monotony of his day-to-day life, as well as something that would offer him a fun, unique challenge. He'd considered her his own personal video game, one where he would have to fight his way through all the levels in order to win.

Last night, he'd foolishly thought he'd completed the game, beaten the main story, seen the goddamn credits. Tonight was supposed to be his victory lap. The part where Penny picked up a guy, took him back home, and forgot all about the second part of her favor...the part he had no intention of following through on.

Or at least...he *hadn't*.

After spending the last week with her, it occurred to him that he'd been wrong to think he wasn't attracted to the woman, that she wasn't his type. And the real kicker of that realization was that his sudden desire had fuck-all to do with her changed looks and everything to do with the fact that she was awesome. Funny and honest, with interests that matched his almost right down the line.

Last night, he'd found himself getting more and more out of sorts as she modeled her new clothing, because none of it was *her*. He'd had to bite his tongue more than once, determined to give her what she wanted. After all, that was the point of the whole damn wager. To turn her into...every other woman he'd ever dated.

Seemed simple at first, but now it rubbed against the grain.

When she walked out of the dressing room for the last time in that godawful, frilly gray sweater the last seven women he'd dated would have loved, he'd hit his limit, demanding she buy the cute cat shirt instead. He didn't give a shit if that meant he was taking her two steps backwards from her goal by encouraging her to be herself.

To add insult to injury, he'd been pissed as shit when she'd called herself a loser. Not at *her*. But at himself. Had he perpetuated those feelings by referring to her and Toby and Rich as the nerd circle? Her comment had felt like a punch to the stomach, and he'd gone home feeling like the world's biggest dick.

And tonight...dammit...he'd jumped the gun and set her even further back.

"Gage?"

Gage looked up, resisting the urge to grimace when he saw his brother, Matt, standing next to his table. He'd made his brother a promise about workplace romances, and while he didn't intend to sleep with Penny, he wasn't so sure he didn't want to. *Fuck.*

He'd dropped Penny in the middle of quicksand with nothing to grab onto, and now he was resigned to the fact that he needed to use tonight to analyze and regroup. He'd have to adjust his game plan for helping her.

And if he was secretly pleased that this meant spending more time with her, he managed not to dwell on or attempt to analyze that emotion too hard.

Just like he was trying not to figure out when he'd started thinking of her as Penny and not Beaumont.

"Hey, bro. What are you doing here?"

"Had a late meeting with Conor. He was showing me the plans for a new restaurant he hopes to invest in with Harper Branson."

Gage whistled. "The supermodel?"

Matt nodded. "Apparently, rather than spending her millions lying on the beach on some tropical island after retiring from modeling, Harper attended culinary school. She's graduated and looking to open up her own restaurant here in Philly."

"Good for Conor."

Matt smirked. "You would think so, but you know Conor. All work, no play. He views her past career as an ace in the hole as far as making the venture lucrative. Not sure he's even given a thought to how breathtakingly beautiful the woman is."

"Yeah. I guess that would require looking up from the ledgers. Poor bastard's missing out."

"Not really. Conor has a nose for business and he's not wrong about this investment. I wager it will make him a fortune in the end."

Gage considered using the old "pot calling the kettle black" line on his big brother, but he let it slide since Matt was actually out on a Saturday night. He gestured to the empty seat at the table. "Join me?"

Matt, to his surprise, nodded and sat. A waitress stopped by to take his order, and Matt asked for the same thing Gage was having. "Drinking alone, or are you meeting someone later?"

"I'm alone."

That confession appeared to shock his brother as much as Matt's willingness to hang out surprised him. It had been far too long since the two of them had gone out for a drink that wasn't tied to some business deal or meeting.

Perhaps it was time one of them extended an olive branch. After listening to Penny affectionately mention her brother several times this week, he'd found himself longing for...family.

"Any plans tomorrow?" Gage asked, tempted to invite his brother over to watch the golf match on TV.

"I'm going into the office to catch up on some paperwork. Did you manage to take care of the Penny Beaumont issue?" Matt asked.

So much for that idea. Matt had a one-track mind. All business.

"We're renegotiating her contract next month during her annual review. She was being headhunted, not looking to leave the company."

"Fucking headhunters," Matt muttered, as the waitress delivered his drink. They drank in silence—not awkward but not exactly companionable either.

Gage's gaze drifted back to the dance floor, and he grinned before he could school his features.

"Something amusing?" Matt asked, following his gaze.

"Just taking in the show." He gestured toward the dance floor. Matt had been out of town this week on business, only returning home late this afternoon. As such, Gage knew for a fact his brother hadn't seen the new Penny, and he was curious to hear what Matt thought.

"Just a bunch of people bumping and grinding," Matt said, starting to turn away. Gage could tell the moment his brother spotted her. "Is that...?"

"Beaumont."

Matt studied her for a moment. "She looks..."

"Beautiful," Gage supplied, when his brother failed to fill in the blank.

"Yes. But...what the hell is she doing?"

Gage couldn't help it. He laughed. The aghast tone of Matt's voice perfectly matched Gage's initial response when he saw Penny dancing.

"If I had to venture a guess, I'd say she was working her way through all the *Fortnite* dances."

"Jesus," Matt murmured, his gaze locked on their IT girl. "I can't decide if it's a train wreck or not. She's really good. It's just so...*much*."

Penny had entertained him with her wicked flossing moves and disco fever. She'd also ridden the pony, and she was currently doing one hell of an awesome robot. Her girlfriends weren't helping much, laughing, cheering her on, and attempting to follow her lead.

They were having a hell of a lot of fun, though none of their moves were sexy, and none of the men he'd anticipated bumping and grinding their way into the circle of attractive women had appeared. Probably because, despite the silliness, Penny was an intimidatingly good dancer. And also flailing around so much, no one was willing to risk her putting their eye out.

The song ended, and the three women started to leave the dance floor, intent on heading to the bar for a drink.

Gage stood up quickly.

"What are you doing?" Matt asked.

"Asking Beaumont to dance."

His brother narrowed his eyes. "You promised no more work-place affairs."

"This isn't an affair. I lost a bet."

Matt scowled. "What the hell does that mean?"

Gage grinned, not bothering to explain. He intercepted Penny and her friends halfway across the floor.

"Oh, Gage," Penny said when she saw him. "I didn't know you were here." She turned to her girlfriends to offer introductions. "Gage, this is Liza Moretti and Keeley Gallo." Then she told her friends, "This is my boss, Gage Russo."

Gage didn't miss the slight narrowing of Liza's eyes when she heard his name, but unlike her male relatives, she managed not to scowl or give him the evil eye.

"I was wondering if I could steal Beaumont from you for a few minutes," he said to the other women.

Keeley nodded. "Sure. We'll get you a drink and meet you back at our table, Penny. Probably shouldn't have left our stuff there for so long, but that music was kicking."

"Back in a flash." Penny accepted his outstretched hand without hesitation, the two of them completely at ease with each other after a week of evenings spent together.

He guided her back to the dance floor, resisting the urge to glance toward the table he'd just vacated. He didn't have to look in that direction to feel the heat of his brother's glare.

"Missing a girlfriend?" He recalled her mentioning three names.

"Gianna has a boyfriend and apparently tonight was date night," she explained.

A club remix of Ludacris's "Stand Up" was playing, the perfect beat for this lesson.

He gripped her hips, keeping her close, splitting their legs, so one of his feet was between hers.

Penny stiffened, her arms hanging loosely at her sides. "What are you doing?"

"We're dancing."

"I...um...I don't know how to dance like this."

It sounded as if she was confessing she'd never danced with a guy before...then he recalled her admitting a few nights earlier that she'd never gone to prom in high school.

He'd learned countless things about her this week, each new tidbit drawing the picture of an awkward, lonely girl who'd grown up to be an awkward, lonely woman. She'd come to him for help breaking the mold, convinced that by doing so, she'd find some Mario to fawn over her newly discovered Princess Peach side.

"Just follow my lead, okay?"

He started to roll his body, swaying in time to the beat, and she mimicked the motion. Penny was a quick learner.

"I'm afraid I haven't had much luck on the guy front," she admitted. "But I'm having a blast. This place is great."

"I should have explained club dancing to you. That's my fault."

She tilted her head as if confused, then her eyes traveled around the dance floor. He recognized the second the light went on. "Oh. Shit."

"You're a good dancer, Beaumont, but I need you to repeat after me. Sexy at the club. Not silly. You can pull out all those moves you were just doing at a family wedding, okay?"

She crinkled her nose. "I made an ass of myself, didn't I?"

He shook his head. "No. This is on me. I made an assumption. I won't do that again." He lowered his hands, skirting the line between gripping her hips and her ass, pulling her closer until her breasts were flush against his chest. Her hands were landing everywhere and nowhere all at once, as she tried to figure out where they were supposed to be.

"Put your hands on my thighs," he instructed. "Just loose. Let your fingers glide in time with the motion."

She did as he asked, her touch sensual enough that he had to start doing multiplication tables in his head to keep his cock from getting hard.

Or, well, *harder*.

He hadn't had sex since Marjorie. That hadn't been a conscious decision—just something that happened. He'd been too busy with other things—okay, the nerd circle and Penny's favor—to date.

Fuck. No. He wasn't calling them the nerd circle anymore. He was calling them what they were. His friends.

He stopped swaying, changing to a hip thrust so he could lean closer, his lips brushing the shell of her ear.

"This is how you dance in a club," he said. "You and your girl-friends in a circle, but not too tight. You're dancing slow, sexy, shaking that hot ass of yours."

"Hot ass?" she breathed.

"So hot. You look around at the guys on the floor, let them know you're interested. Eventually, a man will come closer, start dancing next you. Check him out. If you're not attracted to him, move closer to your girlfriends or leave the floor. If you like him, smile, bat those long eyelashes. Give him a little encouragement. You hold all the power in this."

Penny lifted her face, giving him an up-close glimpse of her gorgeous blue eyes. Her eyelids fluttered dramatically, an adorable grin crossing her face. "Like this?"

He suspected she meant her words as a joke, but it fell short. All the math in the world wouldn't help him beat back this hard-on.

"Are you interested?" he asked, not entirely sure his question was merely part of the lesson.

"Yes," she whispered.

He used his hands on her hips to spin her around, her back to him. He pulled her close, the two of them moving in time with the music, bumping and grinding together like horny teenagers at the homecoming dance. There was no way Penny couldn't feel what she was doing to him. However, rather than pull away, she pressed her ass harder against his crotch.

Fuck. He wasn't sure who the teacher and who the student was at this point.

He spun her to face him once more and she lifted her hands to his shoulders, her eyes cast downward, as if she was embarrassed.

"Look at me."

She did as he asked, and he shifted closer, his gaze lowering to her lips. She ran her tongue over the lower one, wetting it.

Gage was a second away from taking her up on that unspoken

invitation to kiss when a drunk woman bumped into them, roughly pushing them apart.

"Ssshit," the woman slurred. "I'm so fucking s-sorry. Too much tequila." She burst into hysterical laughter, as if tequila was the funniest thing on the planet.

The moment ruined, Penny looked a little lost. He'd let this go way too far.

Time to retreat. He gestured toward the bar, indicating he was ready to leave the dance floor. He didn't dare touch her back or take her hand, for fear he wouldn't lead her to her girlfriends but rather to his apartment.

"You got it now?" he asked, fighting like the devil to return them to solid ground. A lesson. It was just another lesson. Nothing else.

"I do. Though it's not really dancing, is it? I mean, it's just sort of bouncing in place."

He laughed. "Yeah. It is, but dance like that, and the men will start swarming likes bees to honey."

"Okay. Thanks, Gage. You're a great teacher."

He winked, and then she turned to find her friends while he returned to his table. Mercifully, Matt was gone. Gage didn't fool himself into thinking he'd escaped the third degree he was going to receive from his brother. At most, he'd just delayed it. But at least it would give him some time to figure out how to explain something to his brother that he no longer understood himself.

He took a sip of his bourbon, then—because he couldn't help himself—he looked for Penny.

"Damn," he murmured when he spotted her. A couple of guys were at the table she was sharing with her friends. The men had made their move on Liza and Keeley while Gage was teaching her how to dance.

Of course, the deejay picked that moment to play a slow song. The guys asked Liza and Keeley to dance, and Penny waved them away, encouraging them to go.

He was tempted to cross the room to ask her to dance, but

he'd already interfered too much. Penny needed more experience when it came to meeting people in a club. She was serious about her desire to find a guy, and while Gage might be interested for the moment, he was never going to be anyone's boyfriend.

Penny sipped her drink then pulled her phone out of the pocket of her jacket. She messed around with it for a few minutes, and Gage couldn't help but wonder with some amusement if she was hunting for *Pokémon* or *Candy Crush*-ing it.

When the slow song ended, a faster one beginning, Liza dashed over to the table to drag Penny out to join them.

She was one hell of a student, as she'd already mastered his dance lesson. Her hips swayed in a slow, sensuous motion that was pure sin, and the erection he'd managed to will away started to emerge again.

Penny hung in there for three more songs, but it was obvious she was the odd guy out, and as the men moved closer to her friends, he could see her confidence wavering.

Fuck this.

Time to intervene.

He started to stand, but his view of the dance floor was suddenly blocked by a pair of double D's barely confined in a low-cut sequined top.

"Hey, Gage. I didn't expect to see you here."

He barely restrained his groan when he looked up to see Connie standing next to his table. "Connie," he said, hoping his less than friendly tone would penetrate. Matt had told him to set things right with their barracuda HR woman, but he'd failed to do so.

Forgotten was the more accurate word. Ten minutes after his brother issued that order, Penny had walked in, asked for a favor, and this past week had taken on a life of its own.

"Were you here for the meeting with Conor as well?" she asked.

Interesting. Connie knew Matt's schedule? It was starting to look like Connie wasn't setting her sights just on Gage but any Russo brother she could land.

"No."

"You looked good out there on the dance floor."

Gage narrowed his eyes. The last thing he wanted was for Connie to fuck with Penny, but before he could warn her away, she looked over her shoulder, toward the dance floor, and mused, "That woman looks so familiar, but I can't place how I know her."

It was more than likely Connie and Penny rarely crossed paths at work. HR was on the eighth floor of the Russo Enterprises building, while the IT department was on the third floor. Penny joked she used the stairs every day instead of the elevator because it was her cardio workout, so it was unlikely they ever ran into each other.

"Connie, I think I need to reiterate a few things to you."

His ploy to draw her attention away from Penny and back to him worked.

"I know what you're going to say, Gage, and I'm very sorry about the Marjorie incident. I don't know what came over me, but you don't have to worry. It won't happen again."

The perfect canned response courtesy of Human Resources.

"I hope that it won't."

"I'd love to buy you a drink—just as friends," she hastened to add. "As an apology."

He shook his head. "No. That's not necessary."

She hovered for a second longer, obviously trying to find another excuse to stick around. He was anxious to check on Penny, but he didn't want to draw Connie's attention back to her.

"Good night, Connie," he said dismissively.

She nodded once then executed a perfect spin, making sure he'd not only gotten a front row seat to her tits but a parting glimpse at her ass in the shortest, tightest miniskirt ever designed.

She'd wasted her time. She wasn't two steps away from the table before he was searching the dance floor for Penny again.

When he found her, he didn't like what he saw. The song was winding down, so Penny fanned herself before pointing to the table. It was an excuse, a way to make her escape from the two couples, and it worked. At the table, she pulled her phone out once more then stifled a yawn.

He recognized the second she decided to pack it in. She headed back to the dance floor to say goodbye to her friends.

He threw cash down on the table to pay for his drink then caught up to her at the exit. "Leaving so soon?"

"Yeah. I'm kind of tired and my feet are killing me. Not used to heels. Besides, I think my window of opportunity closed. I'm just going to get an Uber home and try this again another night."

"Forget the Uber. I'll drive you home. It's my fault that window closed."

"No, it wasn't. I needed the lesson in bouncing...I mean dancing," she joked. Even though he could see how disappointed she was, she didn't lose her sense of humor.

"Come on, Beaumont. I'm taking you home."

She didn't put up an argument, and he realized why when she ripped off her shoes the second they pulled out of the parking lot.

"Sweet mother of God," she said, sighing in relief. "How much did those shoes cost?"

"Why?" He wasn't about to get into another argument over her paying for shit.

"It'll determine how guilty I feel when I throw them away."

He chuckled. "Toss them in the back of your closet and forget about them until you decide you're ready to give them another try."

She mumbled something indecipherable—probably cursing him and the shoes—but then she said, "Fine."

When they pulled up in front of her apartment, she hesitated. Gage knew in an instant what her problem was when she shot a dirty look at the heels.

"Stay there." He walked around the front of his Audi and

opened the passenger door. Penny started—reluctantly—to put the heels back on.

"No." He stopped her, reaching down and tugging her out of the car. Before she read his intent, he bent down, tossing her over his shoulder fireman style.

"What the fuck?"

He closed the car door and carried her to her apartment that way. Spinning when they reached the entry, he turned his back so she could enter the building code upside down, giggling the entire time.

Once they were inside, she tapped on his ass. "You can put me down now, you lunatic. This dress is so short, I've probably just mooned the whole neighborhood."

The apartment building was carpeted, clean, and well-maintained, so he helped her slide back to her feet. Then he took her hand and the two of them walked to the elevator.

"You don't have to come all the way up," she said, even as the elevator doors slid shut.

"I know." They disembarked on the third floor, and he walked her to her door.

"Want to come in?" she asked. "It's still kind of early."

"Yeah. I'd like that."

She tossed the shoes by the door and set her clutch on a table, walking toward the kitchen. "Want a drink? I think I have some beer or a bottle of Chardonnay."

"I'll have whatever you're having," he said, walking into the living room, looking around. He'd only been here a few minutes yesterday when they'd carried in all the clothes they'd bought, so he hadn't taken in much.

The apartment fit her. It was clean but not exactly tidy. There were a couple pairs of shoes near the couch, where she'd obviously slipped them off after work. There was an empty glass on a coaster next to a pile of remotes and game controllers on the end table. Her Nintendo Switch was on the coffee table, along with an empty Chinese container. He grinned when he spotted part of a bra peeking beneath a chair. She struck him as one of those women whose first order of business after getting home from work was stripping off the bra immediately.

Penny came back in with a couple glasses of wine. He took one from her and tapped it against hers before taking a sip.

"How are your feet?" he asked.

She grinned. "A little better, but I think it'll take some time for them to forgive me. I'm going barefoot for the rest of the weekend, just to make it up to them."

"So what did you think of the club?"

She shrugged. "It was pretty much what I expected. Bit of a meat market, right?"

"Oh yeah," he agreed.

"It's a shame no one really dances. That would make it a lot more fun."

"You're missing the point of the bump and grind," Gage said. "It's not about having fun. It's about hooking up."

"I guess. It's just...I like to dance. Might sound silly, but I dance a lot around the apartment. I thought tonight... well...whatever."

Gage was amused by her disappointed tone. She looked like a kid who'd had their favorite toy taken away.

"Put some dance music on," he said.

She gave him a funny look but then hit some buttons on her phone, hooking the Bluetooth to her speakers. She scrolled through a list of songs until she found one with a great beat. Then she turned to face him and rolled her eyes as if bored, while bouncing in place, her arms stiff by her sides.

He laughed, even as he shook his head. "Not like that. I want you to show me some of those sweet *Fortnite* moves."

She lit up like a Christmas tree. "Really?"

He nodded.

Penny quickly moved toward him and said, "Let's start with Fresh. It's a classic."

Gage mimicked her moves, making her laugh as he did his best Carlton impersonation.

For the next hour, the two of them laughed their asses off as they worked their way through her extensive repertoire of dance moves, including Groove Jam, Disco Fever, and even the Flapper.

He cried uncle first and, exhausted, the two of them dropped down to her couch, both trying to catch their breath for a few minutes.

"Sorry about tonight," he said. "I threw you in the deep end without really preparing you. I'll do better next time."

Penny twisted to face him. "You're a good teacher, Gage. I've never...I mean, I've always been on the outside of a lot of this stuff, looking in and trying to figure out how to get where everyone else is. Tonight was really fun, and I think next time I'll have a better idea of how to act, how to fit in."

Gage hated the idea of her conforming, taming down her dancing, or trying to make herself...less.

Less of what made her Penny.

But she was dead set on this course, determined that this was the path to finding a guy. So who was he to try to change her mind? She was tired of being alone and wanted someone in her life. Her end goal had him starting to wonder if he'd made a mistake by eschewing relationships, by confining himself to sex without strings.

He dismissed that thought the second it landed.

He wasn't wrong.

Rising, he said, "I should probably head home."

Penny stood as well and walked him to the door. "Thanks again, for everything."

He nodded and started to reach for the doorknob. Then, before he could think too much about it, he turned back to her. "How about one last lesson?"

Gripping her shoulders, Gage pulled her toward him and kissed her.

His lying side said this would be a platonic kiss, sweet and short, and he'd decided to let that voice guide him.

Until his lips touched hers.

Then he admitted to himself—in no uncertain terms—*exactly* how he was going to kiss her.

He slid his hands around her back, pulling her tight against him, as he pushed her lips open, driving his tongue inside her mouth, plundering, possessing.

She tasted like the wine, sweet, tangy, offering him everything he silently demanded. He could get drunk off her kisses.

Her hands were on his waist, her fingers gripping his shirt. He wanted the clothing gone, wanted to feel her fingers on his bare skin, wanted to hear the soft moan she just gave him in the bedroom, wanted to turn the volume up on it until it became a scream as his cock sank deep in—

Gage broke the kiss, lifting his hand to touch her flushed cheek. Penny's closed eyes opened slowly, and she blinked a couple of times.

"How did I do?" she whispered.

Fuck.

Lesson.

Mentor.

"Good," he said, clearing his throat when his word came out too gruff, too husky. "Very good."

"Maybe we should practice some more." If those words had come from anyone beside Penny, he'd think them the ultimate in flirtation, but it was obvious her request was sincere.

He was tempted—too fucking tempted—to take her up on it.

He wanted her.

Jesus Christ. He wanted Penny Beaumont.

Time to put on the brakes.

"Good night, Pe—" He paused then quickly corrected himself. "Beaumont."

"Good night, Gage."

Chapter Seven

Penny took a sip of her Malbec and tried to listen as her girlfriends chatted at the table. She'd been surprised but pleased when Keeley called her up to invite her to happy hour with her, Gianna, Liza, and Jess this afternoon.

Apparently, Penny had opened the door to genuine friendship when she'd asked them to go to the club with her last weekend. She'd been nervous as hell making that call because their transition to girlfriends had still been pretty new, and restricted to times when Jess initiated the get-togethers.

But she hadn't wanted to admit to Gage she didn't have any girlfriends, so she'd gathered her courage and issued the invitation.

And now...she was at happy hour. With girls who really did feel like friends.

She would have been happier about that if this past week hadn't sucked so much. She'd had a total blast the entire previous week, recreating herself with Gage's help. She had foolishly anticipated that would continue.

After all, they hadn't accomplished every aspect of the favor.

She was still reeling from that good-night kiss last Saturday, and she couldn't wait to expand on that part of the lessons.

Unfortunately, it seemed she'd monopolized too much of

Gage's time—even though he'd planned all the outings—because this week had been one big fat bust. She'd fabricated a couple of work excuses so that she could drop by his office, but apart from answering her questions, he hadn't mentioned getting together again.

Today, she'd finally gathered enough courage to ask him point blank if he wanted to come by her place this weekend to continue her lessons. He'd told her he had plans and wouldn't be able to. She'd waited for a moment, hoping he'd give her some indication of when—or at this point, she was starting to wonder, *if*—they could meet again.

He'd said nothing. Worse than that, she got that stonewall expression she'd seen too many times when a guy she liked was trying to give her the brush-off. While she was a dating disaster, she was an expert when it came to picking up on "I'm not interested" vibes.

Not that Gage had ever been interested. He'd only been hanging out with her because he'd lost a bet.

Fuck, that was depressing.

She realized she'd fallen too deep into her thoughts when she heard Jess say her name and it occurred to her, it wasn't the first time.

"Earth to Penny." Jess waved a hand in front of her face.

"Sorry," Penny said sheepishly.

"Where do you go when you drift away like that?" Jess asked.

Penny shrugged, dismissing the question. "What were you saying?"

"I was saying I absolutely love your hair like this."

Penny smiled. Today was the first time she'd seen Jess since she'd basically changed everything about herself.

"And that shirt is so cute. Is it new?"

Penny nodded. "It is." She was wearing the blue cat shirt Gage had bought for her. It was her favorite piece of clothing out of all the new things he'd purchased.

Jess took a sip of her wine. "You look absolutely stunning. By the way, the birthday party is still on. Three weeks from tomorrow. We're going to have it at Divine, the restaurant Rafe's grandfather left him."

Rafe Baros was one of the seemingly countless hot guys who'd gone to high school and remained friends with the Moretti brothers. It had taken Penny quite a few years before she could string more than a couple words together anytime Rhys invited her along to Moretti outings, be they family celebrations or summer picnics, because she was too intimidated by the endless parade of sexy men.

Now, as was her forever curse, all of the hotties had placed her solidly in an untouchable category, although in this case, it was the "little sisters are off-limits" one, rather than the "just friends" one.

Rafe's grandfather had owned several properties before his death a month or so earlier. Since then, Rafe had basically uprooted his life, quitting his job to take over running three different businesses. In addition to Divine, his grandfather left him a nightclub and a small pub famous for serving unique flavors of micro brewed beer.

"It's nice of Rafe to let us hold it there," Penny said.

"He's been working too hard lately, trying to get his grandfather's estate in order while moving into the old guy's legit Gothic mansion. You should see that place. It's like something out of an Edgar Allen Poe story. He's completely overwhelmed, even if the stubborn ass won't admit it," Keeley explained. "I told him I was giving him a few more weeks to get his shit together and then he was taking a night off. I promised to take care of everything for the party if he'd just supply the place and come. He needed a fun night and you needed a kick-ass birthday! Two stones and all that."

Penny still wasn't looking forward to the party, but she managed to give Keeley a fake "I'm so excited" smile. It was the least she could do after all the trouble everyone was going to on her behalf.

"Did you give more thought to inviting that hot neighbor?" Jess asked.

"Hot neighbor?" Gianna asked, leaning closer. "Do tell."

"Nothing to tell," Penny said sadly. After the successful conversation on the elevator, she hadn't seen David again.

"No worries." Jess was apparently armed with an arsenal of single men. "If that doesn't pan out, you could always ask Gio or Luca to be your date for the party. Neither one of the twins is dating anyone right now."

Penny didn't even bother to consider that suggestion. The Moretti brothers, like Gage, were a million miles out of her league. Besides, she was Rhys's quirky kid sister, and the Morettis definitely had that unspoken bond with their friends about dating sisters, even if Jess didn't want to admit it.

"I thought Gio was dating someone," Keeley said.

Jess shook her head. "No. No one since Jill Patrick. And even that wasn't too serious. I kind of think she was his booty call for a few months."

"Why did I think she was Rafe's booty call?" Keeley mused.

Keeley, like Penny, fell into that off-limits category. Her big brother, Kayden, had been friends with the Moretti brothers since preschool. After their parents' untimely deaths in a plane crash when Keeley was just fifteen, Kayden had stepped in and raised her. Keeley was probably the most off-limits of all the kid sisters. Not that she seemed to care. Keeley was a free-spirit and online dating aficionado, much to her brother's dismay.

"I'm bummed I couldn't go to Enigma with you all," Gianna said. "Date night was a bust because Sam wound up working late, so by the time he got to my place, all he wanted to do was stay in, order pizza, and watch baseball. I hate baseball so much."

"What happened the other night...with those guys you were dancing with at club?" Penny asked.

Liza and Keeley looked at each other and groaned in unison.

Jess laughed. "Oh my God. Were they that bad?"

Liza shook her head. "No. They were okay. I mean, we were

having a good time dancing, and it's not like we were going home with them or anything, but..."

"But?" Jess prompted.

Keeley took over. "But the night took a turn when our brothers showed up. They evil-eyed the poor guys until they finally melted away."

"Which brother?" Gianna asked Liza.

Liza grimaced. "Aldo. Bruno's got his hands full with his three kids—they are holy terrors, but damn if I don't love them—and Elio is out of town for off-season training with the team."

Liza's brother, Elio, was a professional hockey player. Something Penny would have found cool if she gave a shit about the game...which she didn't. *Rocket League* was her preferred sport.

"They just happened to show up at Enigma? The club Conor Russo owns?" Jess asked. "That doesn't seem like the kind of place Aldo and Kayden would hang out."

"It's not," Keeley said, her tone dripping with annoyance.

"Did you tell them you were going to be there?" Gianna asked.

Keeley shook her head. "Of course not. I'm not new here."

"Apparently you are," Liza said, grinning. "Or you'd stop sharing your location with Kayden on Find My Friends."

"I know, I know. I always swear I'm going to delete that app, but...well, he worries about me. I'm all he has, and he's all I have," Keeley said.

"I think that's sweet," Penny said.

"Me too," Jess added.

Keeley sighed. "Yeah. It's sweet. And annoying as fuck. Kayden refuses to acknowledge that I've grown up. It doesn't help that he's a cop. High school was a nightmare. Guys would show up to pick me up for a date, and by some ridiculous coincidence, Kayden always managed to be wearing his uniform and cleaning his gun at the same time."

Keeley's brother was a big guy, like super big, so Penny could just imagine how intimidating that must have been. While she'd gotten to know him, and had discovered Kayden was basically a big teddy bear, Penny didn't doubt for a moment he could also be one scary motherfucker if the situation called for it.

"Your boss is cute," Liza said to Penny. "Even if he is a Russo."

"Boss?" Jess asked.

"Gage. He was at the club," Penny said.

"So was his brother, Matt," Liza chimed in. "He and Gage were sitting together when we were all on the dance floor, watching us. I swear to God, Matt Russo must be the most miserable man on the planet. The dude never smiles."

Penny was surprised by Liza's comment. She hadn't realized Gage was there until he'd approached them, and she hadn't seen Matt at all.

"Matt doesn't really strike me as the clubbing type," Keeley added.

"Me either, though it's not really surprising that he and Gage would be there. Since Conor owns it," Jess said.

Liza nodded. "Maybe that explains why Matt was watching me so closely. Probably making sure there was no Moretti threat."

"He was watching you?" Gianna asked.

"Yeah. It felt a little bit like a schoolyard stare-down for a minute or two. I thought he'd look away when I made it clear I saw him watching, but he didn't blink, just held my gaze. It was..." Liza shrugged and dropped the subject. "Anyway, how goes the job search, Keeley?"

After that, the conversation drifted away from the Russos and on to work things. Penny sort of mentally checked out, though she was careful to listen just enough to nod at the appropriate times. And even though she sucked at small talk, she was still disappointed when they asked for the bill. Unlike the other women—who all had plans for the evening—Penny was going home alone, with nothing more exciting on her schedule than her annual re-watch of the entire *Bones* series.

She walked out of the bar and waved as her friends left. Standing on the sidewalk, Penny fought back a wave of melancholy. She'd felt lonely for months, but it was stronger tonight, more potent, painful.

Shaking it off as best she could, she headed toward her apartment. The bar the girls had chosen for happy hour wasn't far from her place, so Penny had opted to walk.

She passed several restaurants, the area starting to come alive with people out and about, ready to kick off their weekend in style. She debated stopping at the Greek place to order takeout for dinner, but as she glanced through the front window, she spotted Gage inside.

He was sitting with a gorgeous brunette, laughing and talking and giving her that charming smile that Penny saw every time she closed her eyes.

She stared for several minutes, trying not to fall apart, wishing she wasn't suddenly awash in...agony.

Seeing him with another woman hurt.

It hurt bad.

She was the world's biggest idiot.

Gage lost a bet.

Gage wasn't interested in her.

Gage was just a friend.

He wasn't her boyfriend, and he could date whomever he wanted.

The problem was, he was charming, sexy, and funny, and he'd kissed her like she mattered, like she was as vital to his life as air.

More than that, he told her she was beautiful—and made her believe it.

It had gotten into her head, made her long for something she couldn't have. Worst of all, she was looking at her loneliness from a different perspective because she now knew exactly what she was missing out on. Things like companionship, fun, someone to eat with, talk to, kiss good night.

She sniffled, wondering for the millionth time in her life what was wrong with her?

Why not *her*?

Turning, she continued toward home, thoughts of grabbing dinner gone.

Fuck it, she thought miserably, exhaustion setting in.

Fuck it all.

* * *

Penny waited for the elevator, the smell of her Chinese takeout causing her stomach to growl. She'd skipped dinner last night. And breakfast this morning. And lunch this afternoon.

Food had taken a backseat to the pity party she'd been holding for herself since seeing Gage out with that woman last night.

However, her stomach finally put its foot down tonight, demanding sustenance. So she'd put on a bra but hadn't bothered to change out of the tatty T-shirt and yoga pants she'd worn all day. She also hadn't bothered with a shower or her hair or her makeup or her contacts.

Which meant Murphy's Law dictated disaster. Because when the elevator doors slid open, David was there.

And he wasn't alone.

He had his arm wrapped around Audrey's waist. Audrey lived on the fourth floor, and she had definitely been one of those "we wear pink on Wednesdays" girls back in high school.

"Hey, Penny," Audrey said in a cheerful tone that felt less friendly, and more "OMG look at the freak show."

"Hey," she said lamely.

David smiled, but it was forced, and just like that, any progress she'd made with him a week earlier vanished in an instant.

"David invited me out to dinner and a movie," Audrey said, leaning closer to the man, her flirting so natural, so flawless. How the fuck did she do that? "Though I'm hoping I can talk him into skipping the movie to take me dancing instead."

David chuckled. "I think I could be persuaded."

Audrey smiled and batted her eyelashes, looking at David like he'd just promised to name a planet after her or something. "Enjoy your Chinese," Audrey said, as the two of them stepped off the elevator, linked hands, and headed out for their date.

Penny got on the elevator and closed her eyes tightly, determined not to cry.

Fuck it, she thought.

Fuck it all.

Chapter Eight

Penny bolted upright at the unexpected sound of someone knocking on her door, and Luna—who'd been curled up next to her—darted out of the room like she'd gotten an electric shock.

Penny had been lying on the couch the better part of the last two days, only getting up for food or drinks or when nature called. She hadn't showered, so she looked like utter dog shit.

There was no way she was answering the door.

Another knock. This one louder.

"I'm not leaving until you open the door, Beaumont."

Gage. Of course, it was fucking Gage. She could lube a car with the amount of grease in her unwashed hair right now. And she was getting a zit on her forehead. When in the hell was she going to outgrow the damn zits?

"Go away," she yelled. She'd called in sick to work today, so maybe he'd just assume she was too ill to answer and leave her alone.

"No," he yelled back.

Fine.

What the hell did it matter how she looked? It wasn't like *he* was looking.

She stomped to the door and flung it open. "What?"

"Damn," he said, his gaze missing nothing as his eyes slid from her bedhead hair to her baggy T-shirt and yoga pants—the same ones she'd worn the past two days—and her bare feet.

"What are you doing here?" she asked.

"You called in sick."

"I know."

"You haven't called in sick once in six years. I looked it up."

Any annoyance she harbored toward him vanished when she realized he'd come because he was worried. "Oh. I guess I have a hearty constitution."

She stepped aside, a silent invitation for him to come in, before shutting the door.

He studied her face. "To be honest, you don't look sick."

She shrugged. Maybe she didn't have a cold or the flu, but she still felt like shit. She was calling this a mental health day. Not that it had done a damn thing to improve her mental health. The pity party she'd thrown for herself had morphed into a misery marathon that showed no signs of ending soon.

"I just needed a day off," she said, turning toward the kitchen. "Want something to drink?"

"Sure." Gage followed her, his nose crinkling. "What the hell is that smell?"

Penny gestured toward the pan on the stove. "I burned my lunch."

He glanced at the charred remnants in the pan. "What were you making?"

"Hard-boiled eggs."

He looked at her with one eyebrow raised.

"I can't cook," she said by way of explanation.

"That's not cooking. That's literally just boiling water."

"I got distracted."

Gage chuckled. "Video game?"

She shook her head. "*Bones* binge watch."

"That's a great show. You know, now that I think about it, you sort of remind me of Brennan."

Penny wasn't sure if she should take that as a compliment or not, regardless of the fact she loved the show because she connected with the lead character. She opened the fridge. "I have PBR or Yoo-Hoo."

Gage paused. "That's a surprisingly difficult decision. I love Yoo-Hoo."

"Who doesn't?" she asked, grabbing each of them a bottle of the chocolate drink.

The two of them walked to the living room, sitting on opposite ends of the couch. He'd only been in her apartment twice, but he seemed at ease here. Almost like he fit. Especially when Forrest jumped onto his lap, purring loudly as he settled.

"Why is his name different from the others?" Gage asked. "You strayed from your Harry Potter theme."

She glanced around the room at her cats, two of whom—Harry and Hermione—were dozing on the cat tree, while Luna lurked in the doorway, still leery after being woken up from her nap. "I called him Ron originally, but...well...he's not exactly the brightest bulb in the lamp. One morning, I was brushing my teeth, and Forrest was sitting beside the bathtub, head tilted to one side, just looking at it. I swear there was nothing to see. He still does it. Every morning. It's so random and weird. Anyway, I started calling him Forrest Gump and it stuck."

He took in her appearance, looking at her a little more closely than she cared for, considering she'd done a complete one-eighty and reverted to Penny 1.0—pre-Gage-makeover.

"You know..." he started. "I don't hate those glasses as much as I thought. They're sort of growing on me."

Of all the things she'd expected him to say, that wasn't it.

"But that shirt sucks. What size is it?"

"Two-X," she replied. A lot of her tees and sweatshirts were that size.

"You're nowhere near a 2X. Why do you buy your clothes so big?"

She had no idea where all these questions were coming from, but she decided to just roll with it. "They're more comfortable."

"You sure you're not hiding?"

"Hiding?" she asked, then she considered his question seriously. Was she hiding? "I don't know. Maybe. When I was younger, it took me a little longer to lose my baby fat and a lot longer to develop my..." She held her hands out in front of her chest. "In middle school, I was the chubby girl. Believe me, you don't want to be the chubby girl amongst a bunch of vicious thirteen-year-old girls, whose boobs came in right on time and perfectly." Then she added, "Of course, you don't want to be with boys that age either. They're kind of ruthless dicks. Took me ages to shed the nickname Pancake."

Gage gave her a quizzical look.

"I was flat and round."

"Middle school kids suck. But, Beaumont, you're gorgeous now. You see that, right?"

"I'm still kind of round," she said, aware that perhaps Gage was right about her hiding. But what she hadn't told him was the hated Pancake nickname had followed her right up through high school graduation, even after she'd stopped being flat and round. What was it about high school abuse that made it linger longer and cut deeper than insults lobbed during adulthood?

"You're curvy in all the right places, which is what every fucking man in the world loves."

She smiled halfheartedly. The first smile in days. "Thanks."

"What's wrong, Beaumont? Why the sick day?"

She considered lying but decided, what the hell? It wasn't Gage's fault his kiss had blurred some lines for her, created feelings she had no business feeling.

After all, she'd asked him to teach her the art of seduction as part of a favor, a bet. He was—or at least he had been—playing by rules she'd set. Now it felt like he considered the bet paid.

In truth, it was overpaid. She'd asked for too much, but... well...when he agreed to all of it, she thought maybe King of the Playboys wouldn't mind having sex with her. "I don't think the new look is working."

"Why do you say that?" he asked.

She couldn't tell Gage she was catching feelings for him. There was no way in hell she could say that. She might be clueless when it came to flirting and other girlie shit, but even she knew you didn't tell the confirmed bachelor who was only with you because he lost a bet that you had the hots for him. So she picked the safer route. "There's this guy," she started.

Gage scowled. "What guy?"

"When I asked you to help me, it was because I was hoping it would help me attract the attention of my new neighbor, David. He's super cute, and he seems nice. He looked through the old me, so I thought if I changed some stuff..."

"What happened?"

"I ran into him Saturday night. He had his arm wrapped around Audrey from upstairs. Needless to say, Audrey is fucking gorgeous. Perfect."

Gage shook his head. "I doubt that."

"He asked *her* out. Even after all the changes I made to myself, he didn't see me. Didn't..." She stopped abruptly, unable to admit that David didn't want her. Just like Gage didn't want her. It was either stop talking or start crying, and she refused to look so pathetic.

"Beaumont," Gage started, and she instantly hated the pity in his tone.

So she doubled down, reached for something that sounded less broken, less weak. "I wouldn't mind," she said, forcing a smirk, "but Audrey's kind of a bitch."

Gage chuckled. "Maybe so, but the guy sounds like a grade-A douchebag. He's a blind asshole, and if Audrey is a bitch, then he deserves what he gets. You're too good for him."

"Said no one ever," she added in a shitty attempt at a joke.

"I just said it." Gage looked at her like he dared her to contradict him again.

Then she recalled the beautiful woman she'd seen him with on Friday. "What did you do this weekend?" She looked at him closely, wondering if he'd tell her the truth or if he'd lie.

Gage sighed. "Had a date Friday night."

"How did it go?" she forced herself to ask, even though it would kill her to hear him brag about one of his sexual conquests. She was going to have to find a way to make herself scarce from now on whenever Gage came down to the IT department to entertain the guys with all the dirty details about his hookups.

"Fine. Meredith's a flight attendant from L.A. Whenever she has a layover in Philly, she gives me a call."

"Oh."

Gage tilted his head, now looking at *her* far too closely. "We had dinner and then I took her back to her hotel."

Penny raised her hand. "I don't need the play by play. Save that for Toby and Rich. I can fill in the blanks just fine."

Gage shook his head. "No. I mean, I took her back, dropped her off, and said good night. Told her it was probably for the best if she didn't call again. Whatever attraction we'd shared in the past had clearly evaporated. She felt it the same as I did."

"Oh," Penny said again, not sure how to respond to that. She'd seen the flight attendant. The woman had been a knockout. If Gage didn't feel any attraction to *her*...what chance did Penny stand?

Gage looked at her for a long time, and she feared he was searching for a way to tell her he'd helped her as much as he was willing to. Apart from the kiss, he hadn't even mentioned the part of her favor that included sex.

The silence drifted into the uncomfortable range, and Penny decided to cut her losses. The lessons were over and she didn't need to hear him say it. In fact, that would probably make her feel even worse than she did now.

"I'm going to go get a shower," she said. "I'll be at work

tomorrow and life can resume as normal. Promise." She stood up and he followed suit. She ignored the two-ton weight that landed on her chest when she realized this was it.

She started down the hall, deciding he was a big boy. He could see himself out. She didn't have it in her to say an awkward good-bye. "See you tomorrow," she called over her shoulder, escaping into her bedroom.

Shutting the door, she leaned against it, then decided to get a shower, hoping it would make her feel better.

Thirty minutes later, she gave her hair a quick fluff after towel drying it. She'd treated herself to the longest, hottest shower in history, taking time to shave all the pertinents and scrub her skin with her pomegranate-and-lemon body wash.

She'd been right. She felt a million times better.

And even though she was alone, she popped her contacts in and swiped on some mascara, just because. Then she went back into her bedroom and threw on a pair of clean yoga pants. She started to reach for one of her too-large T-shirts then changed her mind and grabbed ladies-cut medium one instead.

She jerked with surprised when she heard Gage's voice, calling out from the living room.

"Penny," she heard him call. "Pizza's here."

Pizza?

What the hell? He was still here? Why hadn't he gone home?

Then she considered the other thing he'd said.

Gage just called her Penny for the first time ever.

What did that mean?

She walked down the hall, breathing in the delicious scent of pepperoni and cheese. Detouring by the kitchen, she grabbed them each a PBR, and a roll of paper towels to use as plates and napkins.

"You're still here," she said, when she returned to the living room and found him sitting on her couch.

"Yeah, I am."

"Why?"

He stared at her for a moment then gave her a non-answer. "I was hungry. Figured you might be too. Feel better?"

She nodded, though it felt a bit like a lie. She'd felt much better before she realized he was still here. Now she was confused and stressed out about what his continued presence here meant. What if he'd stuck around to tell her the bet was paid in full.

"You sure?" he asked again, and she wondered what he saw on her face.

Time to get a grip. She was a grown-up. She could do this. "Yeah. I let the pity party run into overtime. I shouldn't have done that. Sorry about missing work."

Gage rolled his eyes. "I didn't come over here tonight to yell at you as your boss. I was worried about you."

She smiled then dug deep to put them back on firm foundation. If she could find a way to take them back to the way they were before the makeover, maybe she'd manage to shake these feelings for him. "Thanks. Wanna watch *Bones* with me?"

Gage opened the pizza box, grabbing a slice for her then one for him. Penny hit play where she'd left off on her *Bones* binge, and they ate and drank and talked about the show.

Penny had always struggled with social interaction, but Gage was surprisingly easy for her to hang out with. She didn't feel like she had to measure every word, and while she hadn't gone Full Monty on the hair and makeup, Gage still looked at her like she was pretty, and not some oddity pulled out of the cast of *The Greatest Showman*.

When the show ended, she reached for the remote, ready to fire up the next episode, but Gage took it from her hand and turned the television off.

"Come here," he said in that deep, sexy voice.

"What?" She was already sitting next to him, so she wasn't entirely sure—

Gage removed all free will when he reached out, pulling her toward him until her face was only an inch away from his. Sitting this close, she could see the flecks of green in his light-brown eyes.

And before she could stop herself, she reached up to brush back the lock of brown hair that fell over his forehead.

He blinked a couple of times, her affectionate, familiar action obviously catching him off guard.

"We're going to pick up where we left off."

"Where we left off?" she asked stupidly, his close proximity causing a complete system failure as far as her brain was concerned.

"The lessons, Penny."

Again, he said her first name. A million people in her life had called her Penny, but when Gage said it...she melted inside.

"The kissing lesson?" she whispered.

"Among other things."

He closed the scant distance between them, true to his word.

Penny had spent the last nine days trying to convince herself that Gage's kiss wasn't as amazing as she remembered.

She was right.

Because that first mind-blowing kiss paled in comparison to this one.

She loved the roughness of his beard against her face. His fingers found their way to her hair, his hands closing around two fistfuls, using it to hold her close, to tilt her head to the left so he could kiss her more deeply. She recalled his comment about men liking long hair.

When Gage released her hair, he lowered his hands to her waist and lifted, never breaking the union of their lips as he pulled her over his lap. She straddled his thighs and draped her hands around his neck.

And that was when she felt it. Evidence of Gage's attraction.

To *her*!

She pressed her pussy closer, the hard ridge of his erection right there beneath his pants.

He was hard. *For her!*

He'd come straight to her apartment from work, so while he'd taken off his suit jacket, he was still wearing his dress shirt, though he'd loosened his tie. She toyed with the knot.

Gage broke the kiss. "Take it off."

She looked at him.

"My tie," he added. "Take it off."

She slid the silk knot free then pulled it from the collar with one long, slow glide.

"Unbutton my shirt," he commanded.

Penny was helpless to resist that sexy tone, and she'd spent a little too much—okay, a lot too much—time imagining him shirtless.

Okay, naked.

Completely naked.

She unbuttoned his shirt, her gaze locked on the progress of her fingers. She bit her lower lip nervously then opened the shirt completely. Gage took over, untucking the shirt and shrugging it over his broad, muscular shoulders.

Penny ran her fingers over his bare rock-hard chest. Gage took advantage of the company's gym on the second floor. He let her explore—with her hands and her eyes—for several minutes before taking control once more, drawing her face back to his to resume their kiss.

She went in too hot, too anxious for more, and their front teeth clacked together.

"Ouch," she said, pulling back. "Sorry."

Gage merely gripped her cheeks, guiding her back more slowly, this kiss lasting longer than the previous one.

She gasped when his fingers drifted beneath her T-shirt, stroking her skin for a moment before pulling the shirt off in one quick motion.

Penny felt her face flush with heat—*desire*—as she sat on Gage's lap with only her bra to shield her breasts from his gaze.

No man had ever seen her naked. Not like this.

She would have expected to be embarrassed, but there was no

chance of that. Not when she saw the hungry, appreciative look in Gage's eyes.

"Jesus, Penny," he murmured, before leaning forward and sucking on one of her tight nipples, right through the bra. It was wet and hot and so arousing, Penny felt light-headed. She was a fan of hair as well, she thought vaguely, as she gripped his, using it to hold his mouth against her breast.

Gage sucked harder, and her back arched. He moved to her other breast and did the same, then back again.

Penny writhed on his lap, desperate for something...*more*. She pressed herself against his erection, rolling her hips up and back in the same motion he'd shown her on the dance floor.

Gage groaned, his breath hot. So fucking hot.

Then she felt her bra loosen, and she realized he'd unhooked it in one well-practiced playboy move.

She would have made a joke about it, but she was struggling to catch her breath, to keep up. Every nerve ending in her body was flashing as bright as sparklers on the Fourth of July.

One second her bra was there, the next it was gone.

Then Gage was there again, but there was nothing between his mouth and her nipple.

"God!" she cried, gripping his hair tighter. Too tight.

Gage winced, releasing her nipple with a soft pop so he could gently pry her fingers loose. "Easy there, tiger. I'm too vain to be bald."

"Gage," she whispered, intent on apologizing. Before she could offer it, he lifted her off his lap, twisting until her back landed on the couch, Gage above her.

"Oh," she breathed, her heart racing. With arousal...and nerves.

This was going so fast. And while she wanted this more than she wanted her next breath...it was...it was going *so* fast. She was struggling to keep up.

Her breathing was ragged, and for a moment, she wondered if she was having a panic attack.

"Penny. Look at me."

Until he spoke, she didn't realize her gaze had been firmly locked on his left shoulder.

She lifted her eyes, and her breath came to a full stop. She'd waited a lifetime for this, to lay beneath a man who looked at her like Gage was looking at her right now.

Gage.

Jesus.

She was lying under her gorgeous, totally out-of-her-league boss.

How did I get here?

What do I do next?

Her phone rang, the sound of Flight of The Conchords' "Hiphopopotamus vs. Rhymenoceros" coming through loud and clear. Penny jerked upright at the unexpected sound, her nerves getting the better of her, and her forehead collided with Gage's, the impact hard and painful enough that she saw stars.

"Shit! *Fuck*," she cried out, grabbing her head. "Dammit, that hurt."

Gage rubbed his own forehead, his eyes closed for a second, as if he was trying to shake off his own pain.

She'd hurt him. Again.

Then—dammit—he pushed himself off her, reclaiming the other side of the couch.

The phone stopped ringing—actually, it stopped singing "I'm the hiphopopotamus. My lyrics are bottomless"—as she lay there, feeling stupid. So far, she'd managed to nearly knock out his teeth, rip out a couple handfuls of hair, and give him a minor concussion.

Soooo...this was going well.

"Didn't realize making out with you was going to be a full-contact sport," he joked. "I might have to consider taking up taekwondo."

She sat up and reached for her shirt, suddenly feeling exposed. She pulled it on quickly.

Gage narrowed his eyes as if upset with her for covering up. Surely, he didn't want to continue? Hadn't she just proven she was as much a disaster sexually as she'd been on the dance floor?

Her phone rang again. And once again, she ignored it, staring at Gage and feeling so fucking awkward.

"Sounds like someone's trying hard to get in touch with you," he said, once it stopped ringing. "Maybe you should check who it is."

She reached for her phone, frowning when she saw two missed calls from Jess.

"It was Jess. She wouldn't call twice in a row unless—" Before Penny could finish her comment, the phone started ringing again. This time, she answered. "Jess?"

"Hey, Penny. I'm so sorry to call like this, but I need a favor. Were you in the shower or something?"

"No. I, um, had my headphones on. Didn't hear the phone," she lied.

She could hear the grin in Jess's voice. "Thought that was probably it. That's why I kept trying. I know how you are when you get in the zone."

"What's going on?"

"Aunt Berta fell down the steps a few minutes ago when she was going back to her apartment."

"Oh my God! Is she okay?"

Gage frowned and leaned closer.

"She's fine...mostly. Her wrist is quite swollen. Rhys was on call at the hospital tonight, so we contacted him right away. He wants me to bring her in for X-rays. Tony is driving back from Pittsburgh as we speak—he had a late meeting—but he's still a couple hours away. He said he'll meet us at the hospital if we're still there.

"I was wondering if you could come watch Jasper while I drive her to the ER. I'd just put him to bed when she fell. I would wake him up, but it's a school night and I have no idea how long this is going to take. I hate to ask you, but Aunt Berta expressly forbid me from telling anyone in the family that she fell. Said she doesn't want anyone making a fuss."

"That sounds like Aunt Berta. Of course I'll watch him." Penny loved Jasper and Aunt Berta and Jess, but damn if this wasn't the worst timing ever.

Or maybe the best.

Her insides were still quivering, but she couldn't figure out if all that internal shaking was based on desire or anxiety. Maybe she was smarter to walk away from this tonight, so she could regroup, gather her wits, and find some way to do this with Gage without looking like a complete idiot. She'd mastered the dancing after a bit of practice, so she was certain she could crack the code on this as well.

She looked over at Gage apologetically. He winked at her, having heard enough to figure out their sexy fun time was over. Maybe he was glad for the reprieve, the chance to escape relatively unscathed.

Or...*oh my God.*

Maybe this was her one and only chance with him, and she'd just royally fucked it up.

Too many maybes.

She really needed to find a way to shut her brain down at times like this.

He stood up and put his shirt back on, tucking his tie in the pocket of his suit jacket, which he draped over his arm. There should be a law against covering up a chest like his. She'd write her congressman in the morning to suggest drafting a bill.

"I can be there in about twenty minutes," she choked out, recalling Jess was still on the other end of the phone.

"Perfect. Thanks again, Penny."

Penny hung up and stood. "Sorry. Aunt Berta fell. Jess needs someone to watch Jasper."

"I figured that out." Gage reached for her, pulling her toward him with his hands on her waist. He stole a quick, hard kiss. "Friday night."

"What?"

"Friday night is the next lesson. We're going to go on a practice date—dinner, drinks, and what comes after. Beginning to end."

"Beginning to end?"

Gage nodded. "Yeah. You sure this is still what you want?"

Dammit. He was too astute. He'd obviously recognized her nervousness for what it was.

"Yes," she said without hesitation, suddenly realizing it was the truth. Nerves be damned. She wanted to sleep with Gage Russo and—halle-fucking-lujah—he still wanted to be with her too.

She walked him to the door, surprised when he pulled her back into his arms to steal yet another kiss.

"Sweet dreams, Penny."

She closed the door behind him, leaning on it.

Sweet dreams indeed.

Chapter Nine

Gage sat in his car outside Penny's apartment, trying to figure out what the hell he was doing here. The past three weeks had done a number on his head.

The first week after losing the bet to Penny had been a lot of fun. He'd enjoyed helping her with her "makeover" and spending time with her. Sometimes it was hard to reconcile the woman he'd come to know lately with the quirky, awkward IT girl, who'd been relegated to someone just there, hovering in the background of his life for the last six years.

More and more of the real Penny had emerged after that first game night a few months earlier, and now he considered her a friend, a real and true friend.

Or...at least, he had.

That friendship line had gotten a bit blurry since the night at Enigma. That night, he'd started looking deeper, seeing more of who Penny was beneath the surface, underneath her crazy outfits and hairstyles.

What he saw...well, it shook him up.

Between her vulnerability, her sense of humor, and her intelligence, he'd begun to feel an attraction he hadn't expected. Which made things problematic for him.

At first, he hadn't been one hundred percent on board with her desire to change herself to land a guy because he'd viewed it as trickery, but after hearing that she'd been bullied about her looks growing up, he'd started to understand that what Penny was doing was less about recreating herself, and more about unveiling the woman she'd been all along. The one she'd chosen to hide away for fear of ridicule or rejection. That sort of revelation, he could get behind.

But he'd miscalculated. Because he'd genuinely thought he could buy her some new clothes and makeup, help her fix her hair, and that would be enough to satisfy the bet. And as the makeover progressed, each day unveiling more and more of Penny's natural beauty, that belief had been solidified. After all, what man could look at her and *not* want her?

That's why he figured the trip to Enigma would seal the deal. She'd find a guy, hook up, and his debt would be cleared. Problem was...he appeared to be the only man who "saw" her.

So he'd taken her home—and made the mother of all mistakes by kissing her good night.

That kiss.

Fuck.

That was what had *really* shaken him up. Because he hadn't been able to stop thinking about it. Or the fact he'd wanted to do a lot more than just kiss her that night.

When Meredith had called to ask him out, he'd considered it the answer to a prayer. A chance to get back to life as normal.

So much for that.

He'd been bored out of his mind within five minutes of picking her up, but he'd tried to push through, determined that if he could just get the meal over with, they could get down to the good stuff back at her hotel room.

Pushing through failed spectacularly, because that involved spending the entire dinner comparing Meredith to Penny, and finding the sexy flight attendant seriously lacking. So, instead of fucking his desire to be with Penny out of his system with another woman, he'd given Meredith the heave-ho and spent the rest of the weekend alone with his hand...fantasizing about an IT girl. In big glasses. And mom jeans.

Penny Beaumont, unbeknownst to her, had accomplished the one thing no other woman had ever managed to do. She'd gotten under his skin. And so far, she'd stayed there.

He'd spent the entire previous week avoiding her, struggling to find a way to tell her that the wager was paid in full. It wasn't like she could bitch about him not giving her what she'd asked for. He'd dropped thousands on her makeover, when the first bet had only been for a lousy twenty bucks. She'd gotten way more than the original wager was worth, so he didn't feel any guilt about not carrying on.

Or so he pretended.

By Monday, he'd felt downright invincible, proud of himself for resisting her for eight whole days. Then she'd called in sick, and all his hard work flew right out the window as he spent the entire day worrying that she really *was* sick.

Or worse...that she'd met some guy. What if she'd used his lessons, landed a guy, and indulged in a sex-filled weekend? One so hot that she'd needed a day off to recover?

The idea of Penny with another man had driven him past the breaking point.

Which meant that as soon as five o'clock hit, instead of going home as he'd intended, he turned the steering wheel the opposite direction and headed straight to her place.

To make matters worse, she'd given him the perfect opportunity to bail on the rest of the wager Monday night. All he'd had to do was walk out the door when she left to take the shower. Just walk out and guide them back to business as usual.

All he'd had to do was leave.

Just leave.

Instead, he'd picked up the phone and ordered a pizza, settled in with Forrest on his lap, and then... If Jess hadn't called, he didn't doubt for a second, he would have taken Penny right there on her damn couch with the entire cast of Harry Potter cats watching them.

Even now, as he sat outside her apartment, he was lying to himself. Pretending he could take her out for a "practice" date then bring her home while offering her nothing more than another lesson on good-night kisses.

He was full of shit.

Because if tonight went like every other night he'd spent in Penny's presence recently, he was going to level up in the game— and the next level included taking her to bed.

She claimed to need lessons in seduction, but as far as he could tell, she was already an expert. God knew she'd been seducing him for weeks. Maybe even months.

Gage climbed out of the car then took the elevator up to her place, casting a glance at the closed door of her neighbor's apartment across the hall, the man who'd apparently been the impetus for Penny's makeover. He tried to pretend the sudden rush of anger he felt toward the man was based on the fact he'd hurt Penny's feelings by asking out another neighbor, not jealousy.

He kept walking and knocked on her door. Penny answered it within two seconds, as if she was hovering right behind it, waiting for him.

He considered instructing her to wait a minute or two before answering the door, that it would look better if she didn't appear so eager.

But he didn't, because he *liked* the idea of her being excited to see him.

Her smile was wide and infectious. "Hey," she said cheerfully.

"Hey," he said back.

"You want to come in for a minute?"

He shook his head. If he followed her into her apartment now, chances were slim the two of them would make it for their dinner reservation. She was wearing one of his favorite purchases from the boutique in Rittenhouse Row. The electric-blue cocktail dress brought out the blue in her eyes. The flared chiffon skirt ended just above her knees, while the plunging neckline ensured he was about to spend the next few hours issuing his cock the old "down boy" command.

"We need to go now; we have reservations at XIX Nineteen."

"Seriously? I've always wanted to eat there." She paused. "But you know, we could have gone anywhere tonight. Chili's or Outback or Cheesecake Factory would have been fine. It's just the dating experience I need. I hate that—once again—you're spending a fortune."

Gage reached for her hand and pulled her toward him, nabbing a quick kiss. "We're not going to Cheesecake Factory. You're beautiful, Penny, and I want to show you off."

Her face flushed, clearly pleased by his compliment. It bothered him that she'd gotten so few of those in the past that her immediate reaction was an embarrassed blush. He was going to break her of that, telling her over and over how beautiful she was until she believed it.

Dinner with Penny was a much different affair than it had been with Meredith. The conversation was entertaining and nonstop, the two of them laughing throughout most of the meal. They had so many shared interests, it felt seamless as they bounced from one topic to the next, while polishing off a delicious dinner and bottle of champagne on the rooftop bar that overlooked the city.

They'd gotten into a humorous discussion involving their favorite fonts, with Gage confiding he wouldn't read anything if it was in Comic Sans. He fucking hated Comic Sans. Of course, Penny found that hilarious and promised that henceforth, all her emails would be in that font, which prompted him to threaten to fire her.

A threat that had been a mistake when the cheeky woman reminded him she had another job offer. He really needed to find a way to lock her into a long-term contract. When he suggested a second wager over a game of *Mario Kart*, Penny demanded he finish fulfilling the terms of the current bet first.

Which sent his mind straight to the gutter in terms of all the ways he planned to *fulfill* her.

"Although," Penny said, completely oblivious to the kinky places his thoughts had landed, "I have to admit I'm proud of how forward-thinking we are. I mean, how many grown-ups allow *Call of Duty* and *Mario Kart* to drive all their important life and business decisions?"

Gage chuckled. "The world would be a happier place if everyone adopted that practice."

Penny took another sip of her champagne and looked around once more. She'd done so constantly. "It's so beautiful here," she mused for the tenth time.

Friends with the manager, Gage had managed to swing it so that he and Penny had the entire balcony to themselves. Dining by candlelight, under the stars, with the Philadelphia skyline as their view, created for a romantic—and yes, beautiful—atmosphere. Not that Gage had taken more than a cursory glance. He was too busy looking at her.

After he paid the bill, they held hands, sharing sweet, almost innocent kisses while they waited for the valet to return with his Audi.

The ride back to her place was sexually charged, the air practically humming from the electricity sparking between them.

He stole a few more kisses in the elevator then walked her to her door.

"Invite me in," he demanded. A gentleman would let the decision be hers, but the beast she'd unleashed when she opened the door in that gorgeous dress was fighting hard to break the chains barely tethering him and keeping him from kicking down the door and carrying her straight to her bed.

"Come in," she whispered, the words so sensual, so packed with hunger and need, he lost all patience. He took her key from her hand, unlocked the door, ushered her in, then shut it behind them. Penny shuddered when he threw the dead bolt.

"Gage," was all she managed to say before he pushed her back against the closed door, kissing her like the plane was going down.

Penny wrapped her arms around his neck, returning his kiss... with interest. On Monday, he thought he'd detected some nervousness in her, but none of that was present right now.

She'd asked him to teach her how to seduce a man, how to be better in bed. That request had hovered in the back of his brain all week as he relived their far-too-brief make-out session on her couch. It was obvious she lacked experience. He was curious about her past lovers, wondering how many men had come before him.

They broke apart, the two of them gasping for air, and he found himself asking the question that kept popping into his head. "Why do you think you're bad in bed?"

Penny blinked a couple times, and he grinned at the way it took her a few moments to focus. He'd kissed her senseless, and he liked it. Considered trying to keep her that way for the entire night.

"What?" she asked.

"Did some guy tell you that you were bad in bed?" If that was what had prompted her request for sex lessons, his next question would be more of a demand—for the guy's name and address. He wasn't usually violent, but the idea of some asshole hurting her that way had him seeing red.

"No. No one said that."

Gage was confused. "Then why do you need lessons on how to be better in bed?"

"That's not what I asked for. I said I want to be *good* in bed."

Gage rolled his eyes. "Semantics."

Penny shook her head. "No, it's not. It's not a question of thinking I'm bad. Just inexperienced. I don't really know *how* good or bad a lover I am. I've never done it."

Gage's hands, which had been resting on her waist, fell away. "Wait. *What?* Are you telling me you're a virgin?"

Penny shrugged. "Well, not physically, I guess. I mean, I'm

sure the hymen is gone. I have a vibrator and a dildo, and they get a workout, believe me. But...technically, yes. I'm a virgin. You knew that though. I told you."

Gage took a step back, his vision going gray around the edges. "No. You never told me you were a virgin."

Penny frowned. "Why the hell would I ask for sex lessons otherwise?"

Gage ran a hand through his hair, trying to get control of himself. He'd literally been minutes away from taking...*Jesus*... from taking Penny's virginity.

He'd never slept with a virgin. Ever. Not even in high school. He'd lost his own virginity when he was fourteen...to a senior girl who'd initiated him into sex in fucking style. After that, he knew exactly what type of woman he wanted in bed, and she sure as fuck wasn't innocent.

Gage wasn't that kind of lover. He didn't do gentle or sweet or patient or anything that came even close to making love. He fucked hard and fast, rough and raw. He took experienced lovers to his bed because he knew what he wanted and how. He made demands—kinky, challenging demands—and he expected them to be followed. Period.

"You should have been a hell of a lot more specific when you laid down the terms of the wager. Because there's no way I would have agreed to take your virginity."

Penny crossed her arms, and he was tempted to pull them down, away from her body. Right now, all they were doing was drawing attention to her gorgeous D cups and making it hard for him to be the stand-up guy he needed to be.

Because regardless of this new information, Gage's dick was still honed in on Penny Beaumont, virgin or not.

He expected her to launch into an argument, to demand he satisfy the terms. If she'd done so, he probably would have stood a fighting chance because if there's one thing he could win, it was a heated debate.

What he couldn't defeat was her very simple, very softly spoken, "Gage, please."

"Penny," he said, too aware of the almost pleading tone in his voice. "Be practical. Logical. Don't you want your first time to be with someone special, someone you…" He swallowed deeply before forcing himself to say the word he'd scrubbed from his vocabulary a long time ago. "Love?"

Penny rolled her eyes in outright frustration.

Nope. Wrong emotion. This was full-blown *anger*. As was evident when she threw her hands up and exploded. "Jesus Christ, Gage! I'm not a fucking nun. It's not like I've been saving myself all these years. I haven't had sex because no one's asked! If a guy had even looked my way twice back in high school, I would have been in the backseat of his car so fast, it would make your head spin."

She wrapped her arms around herself now, her anger starting to wane as she continued her confession. "But no one looked."

And he realized every word she was saying was the truth. Because Penny didn't have it in her to lie. Right from the start, no matter how embarrassing or painful, she'd laid open old wounds, showing him exactly who she was without pretense.

Typically, her eyes were downcast when it was hard for her to admit something, but this time, tonight, she held his gaze, let him see it all.

"Not in high school. Not in college. Not at work. I mean, to be fair, I wasn't really putting myself out there. It's hard to be seen when you're hiding under big clothes, hunkered down in your bedroom or some fellow nerd's basement twenty-four seven because it's easier to live as some video game character than in your own skin."

"Penny," he murmured.

"I'm going to be thirty soon. And I've never really *lived*. I want to have sex. I want to be good at it—and I want *you* to be the one to teach me how. Now. Tonight."

He swallowed deeply, searching for his no.

It didn't exist.

"Take me to your bedroom." Gage's voice sounded rusty, rough, and even after he spoke, he couldn't find a way to resist this, to do the right thing, to step aside and insist she find someone else.

Despite his protests, just the *idea* of her with another man drove him nuts, raised his blood pressure.

So when Penny took his hand and led him down the hallway to her bedroom, he let himself make the monumental mistake of following.

Because he'd fallen for Penny Beaumont, the quirky, adorable, nerdy IT girl. And even as he admitted that to himself, he knew it wasn't going to be enough.

He was going to hurt her.

Badly.

That was inevitable.

Chapter Ten

Penny stepped across the threshold to her bedroom, waiting for those damn fluttering nerves, a panic attack, anything to kick in.

But for the first time...there was no hesitation standing in her way.

She felt confident, happy, excited.

She was exactly where she wanted to be.

Then she looked at Gage and thought for a second, she saw a glimmer of resistance...reticence?

If so, the master of controlling his emotions shut it down quickly, because one moment, she was looking at him and the next, Gage had twisted her away from him, his fingers slowly lowering the zipper of her dress.

Her head tilted to the left when Gage's lips landed on the side of her neck, his soft kisses hot, wet.

Then he slid the dress over her shoulders, letting it fall to a heap at her feet.

"I don't sleep with virgins," he whispered in her ear.

For a moment, she panicked, thought he was going to back out. Dear God, she'd spontaneously combust if he left her alone now.

"Gage—" she started, trying to turn around to stop him if he tried to leave.

"Shhh," he cut her off. "I don't sleep with them because my desires, my needs, run too dark, too strong for an innocent woman to handle."

"I can handle it," she insisted. She might be inexperienced, but she wasn't young and she wasn't naïve. Her porn preferences included bondage and spanking and capture. When she played with her toys, it was never gentle and easy, her fantasies always starring one of the dark heroes from the erotic mafia or motorcycle club romances she was addicted to. She was a sucker for the dirty-talking bad boy in those books, the more dominant the better.

Gage turned her back around so that she faced him. His eyes slid to her breasts, in obvious hunger, before he captured her gaze and held it. "I hope you can. Because I can't give you easy."

She didn't look away, didn't falter when she said, "I don't want easy. Actually, I would hate that."

"Show me your toys."

She frowned. "What?"

"You said your hymen's gone. Said you have a vibrator and a dildo. Is that all you have?"

Heat suffused her cheeks as she debated whether to answer that question with the truth. Gage took the decision away from her.

"Don't lie to me. I'll know. And I'll punish you for it."

Holy Mother of Mary. That deep, sexy voice was back.

"I have...others."

Gage's lips quirked. "I see. What?"

She bit her lower lip, unable to answer.

"So you can play with them, but you can't tell me what they are?"

It was a dare. It hadn't taken Gage long to figure out she was helpless to resist a challenge.

"I also have a butt plug and...well...I don't know what the official name of it is, but I have one I call my clit tickler."

Gage didn't smile, didn't comment. Instead, he gripped the back of her neck and yanked her forward roughly, kissing her until she was light-headed from the lack of air. Then she felt his hands wrap around her and, once again, her bra was unfastened in record speed.

"I can't get *myself* out of my bra as quickly as you can," she teased, falling back on the humor they shared, unfamiliar with this too serious, too intense Gage.

He pulled the straps over her shoulders in response, dropping the bra next to her dress on the floor. Then, he knelt before her, pulling her panties down, tapping her ankle, silently telling her to lift her foot so he could discard them as well.

When he rose, she resisted the urge to lift her hands to cover herself. After all, she was totally nude and he was completely dressed, a state he didn't seem in a hurry to change.

She ran her palms over her thighs, then her stomach, back to her thighs, all while trying not to wiggle like a worm on a hook under his gaze.

"Put your hands behind your head. Lock your fingers. Hold that position until I tell you to stop."

She blinked a few times, trying to decide if she'd heard him say what she thought he said. Was he being serious?

Gage responded to her indecision with a stern look. "Now, Penny."

She lifted her hands, locked her fingers.

He stepped closer, drawing his finger down the middle of her chest, through the valley between her breasts.

"Breathe," he murmured, and air flew from her lungs in a whoosh.

"I know your first instinct is to cover yourself, to shield yourself with your hands. Don't *ever* do that."

"It's just so har—"

He didn't let her finish, didn't let her make an excuse. "You've learned how to do the hair, the makeup. You thought those things would be hard too, but you practiced and you got it. So you're going to practice this too. You're going to look at yourself in the mirror every damn morning, and I mean *really* look. At every single inch of yourself—your face, your body, your hair, the zits, the parts you hate, the parts you don't hate—until you see it."

"See it?"

"How perfect you are. *Just* the way you are."

"Oh." It was all she could say. The only sound she could squeeze through a throat that was rapidly closing with tears. Not bad tears. Not necessarily good ones either. Just...tears.

She'd spent a lifetime studying the flaws, let a cruel nickname from school sink too deep, let it define how she carried herself. She wrapped her awkwardness around her—not like a shield but like a cloak of invisibility. Distracting people with the quirkiness so they didn't look closer to see the real faults.

Gage stripped that cloak off, forced her to take a hard look at herself, and what she found...God, she liked what she'd found. Really liked it. He was teaching her how to love herself, something she'd never truly mastered.

"You say you want a lesson in seduction."

She nodded, even though his words weren't a question.

"All you have to do is look at a man with those big blue eyes and flash him one of those sweet, sexy grins of yours, and he'll follow you to the ends of the earth."

As he spoke, he touched her, stroked her, circled her. His eyes taking in every part of her.

"All you have to do is be yourself. Your funny, intelligent, interesting self."

Once he'd made a complete circuit, he stopped right in front of her.

"You're beautiful, Penny. You can put your hands down now."

She lowered her arms, but this time they hung naturally by her side. The familiar heat that colored her cheeks whenever he told her she was pretty struck. And now, as always, Gage noticed, running his knuckles down the side of her face.

No one had ever said such wonderful things to her before. Gage was a playboy, a charmer. Women fell into his bed with just one crook of his finger.

She knew all that, and yet, there wasn't a doubt in her mind that he meant every word he was saying to her.

But perhaps what meant even more was the knowledge that it didn't matter if it was a line or not. It only mattered that she believed it, felt it.

And she did.

"Gage," she whispered.

"You've seduced *me*, Penny. Every minute we've spent together, you've been seducing me, drawing me in, making me want you. You never needed that lesson."

She swallowed deeply.

"So we'll skip that. Move on to the other one. Get your toys."

"Why?"

Gage moved closer, his lips brushing the shell of her ear. "Because I'm going to use them to teach you how to please me —*Men*."

Penny noticed the quick change, but Gage didn't give her time to process his misspoken word.

"And then...I'm taking your virginity. Claiming it as mine."

Once again, she struggled to pull air into her lungs.

"Breathe," he murmured again.

She took several deep, slow breaths, apparently enough that Gage decided she was ready.

"Toys," he reminded her.

Penny turned toward her bed, reaching beneath it to pull out a rectangular box. Gage followed, watching as she removed the lid.

She wasn't bold enough to look at him, to see his reaction to her collection.

"Lay down on the bed. On your back," he commanded.

She started to put the lid back on the box, but Gage took it from her, tossed it to the floor. She assumed the position he requested—demanded—then resisted the urge to cover herself. He wasn't wrong. It was going to take practice before she would feel at ease lying naked with a fully dressed man looking at her.

Gage reached into her box and pulled out her clit tickler. He studied it for a moment before handing it to her. "Show me how you use this."

Jesus.

Penny's masturbation was restricted to the middle of the night...under the mantle of darkness.

What Gage was asking to see...it was personal, private.

Gage crossed his arms and waited, letting her know with just one stern expression that they weren't doing anything else until she gave him what he wanted.

Penny pressed the tiny vibrator to her clit then pushed the button. She was surprised to realize she was quite wet already. Usually it took a few minutes with the clit tickler to get her wet enough to slide the dildo in. And even then, she sometimes relied on KY Jelly as well.

She gasped when the first rapid vibrations hit her clit and her legs fell open. This was by far her favorite toy, the one that pushed her over the edge time after time.

Gage watched as she stroked herself with the tiny vibrating nub, her hips rising and falling, her breathing growing more rapid.

Somewhere along the line, her eyes drifted closed. So she was surprised when Gage took the vibrator from her, bent toward her, and took over, pressing it more firmly against her clit.

"God," she cried out. "Gage!"

"Open your eyes and look at me."

Penny did as he asked, blinking several times to try to focus. She was close to coming. Like, ridiculously close.

For the first time since entering her room, Penny got a glimpse of her easygoing boss when Gage's lips tipped up in a smile. However, it was brief, a blink-and-you-missed-it grin.

Keeping the vibrator against her clit, he slipped two fingers inside her pussy.

One thrust and she was done for.

Penny's back arched as she came hard, her orgasm crashing down like an avalanche, starting slow but gaining power and strength as Gage began to pump his fingers inside her, drawing it out longer and—God help her—longer.

She tried to shove the hand wielding the vibrator away from her clit. It was too much. The pleasure so white hot, it burned.

"Please," she begged, but Gage wasn't finished making her suffer. He kept the vibrator against her clit, kept fucking her with his fingers until all that remained of her was a quivering, trembling heap of bones and skin.

Gage turned the vibrator off then slowly slid his fingers out.

Penny watched with hooded eyelids as he pushed his fingers, wet with her arousal, into her mouth. She sucked them in, loving the way Gage growled when she ran her tongue along the pads of his fingertips.

"Jesus," he murmured, withdrawing them slowly. Then he reached back into her box of toys and pulled out her dildo.

She honestly wasn't sure she could take much more. She was a one-and-done girl. She'd bring herself to climax then sleep the sleep of the righteous. She'd never lapped the bases twice in one night.

She started to say as much, but words failed her when Gage pressed the dildo to her opening. She was still wet—too wet, even —from her first orgasm, so it slid in easily. It wasn't a particularly large toy, but it got the job done. Especially when she paired it with her magic clit tickler.

Gage thrust the toy in and out several times, then pushed it all the way in and left it there. He glanced back down at the box. "Is this your biggest toy?"

She nodded.

"I'm tempted to fill your ass with the butt plug too, but..." Gage paused, staring too intently at her pussy stuffed with the dildo. "But I can't wait, can't..." He unbuttoned his shirt, shrugging it off.

Penny took her time admiring his chiseled abs, muscular arms. "You're beautiful," she whispered.

This time, his grin lasted longer. "Hope you still feel that way in a minute." He unfastened his belt and slid it through the loops. Then...he unbuttoned his pants.

Moment of truth.

Penny had felt his cock through his pants a few times, so she knew he wasn't exactly a small man. However, those brief touches hadn't prepared her for...*that*.

"Oh."

He chuckled but didn't stop undressing, shedding his pants, boxers, shoes and socks with quick efficiency.

"Still beautiful?" he asked, a teasing lilt in his voice.

Penny's gaze was locked on his cock, his question about whether or not she had bigger toys now making sense.

Gage stepped back to the bed and reached down. She thought he was going to pull the dildo out, so she let out a squeak when he gripped the bottom of it and pounded it in and out of her pussy with a surprising amount of force.

He'd warned her, told her he wasn't the gentle type. And she'd assured him she didn't want that.

She'd been right. The powerful thrusting of the dildo ramming inside her sent her to the brink more quickly than she could have imagined. One second, she'd thought herself too done-in to come again, the next, she was crying out Gage's name, as he drove her to a second orgasm, this one shorter, more pronounced.

Penny thrashed her way through it, insensible to her surroundings. She hadn't even realized Gage had taken the dildo out until she heard it hit the floor. Then the mattress sank under his weight.

When she managed to pry her eyes open, Gage was right there above her, caging her beneath him.

His thick, long cock brushed against her stomach. Somewhere along the line, he'd donned a condom. How had she missed that?

"You still want this?"

She nodded. "So much," she said, her voice hoarse from her cries.

She felt raw inside, her body a live wire waiting to spark... again and again. And he hadn't even fucked her yet.

How the hell was she going to survive this?

Gage lowered his head and kissed her. It was sweet and gentle, comforting.

When he broke the union of their lips, he studied her face, and she got the sense he wanted to say something. Perhaps to warn her again. She could see the tension by his eyes, in the lines in his forehead.

"Do it, Gage. I don't need soft, don't need easy. I just need you."

Her words appeared to have released whatever final restraint remained. Gripping his dick, he guided it to her opening. And then, he set the beast free.

Gage slammed to the hilt in one brutal thrust, and she screamed. Pain and pleasure morphed together until she didn't know whether to laugh or cry.

He stretched her to her limit...no, maybe more, filling her in a way that should hurt. It didn't. She lifted her legs, wrapping them around his waist, using his body as leverage so that she could tilt her hips, move toward his fierce pounding.

He'd promised hard and fast.

He delivered.

Penny came again—Jesus Christ, a *third* time—her ravaged body sparking, sizzling. She screamed, fisting the sheets beneath her.

Gage shifted, lifting her legs until they were thrown over his shoulders, opening her up to more of his glorious assault. He drove deeper as Penny shook her head.

"Too much!" she yelled at him.

"No, it's not."

"I...God, I can't..." She gasped for air. "Can't. Again. Too. Much."

"Take it. Dammit, Penny. Take...me. Fuck!"

She flew apart at the seams. And so did he.

Did she seriously think she'd come before? Those were only preambles to this one.

This one that shook her to her very core. Gage thrust just one more time, calling out her name as his face contorted with his own painful pleasure.

They lay there, connected, together, frozen, as if they were sculpted from stone. Then, slowly, he came back to life.

He pressed his forehead to hers. "Tell me I didn't hurt you." There was a tension in his tone that she hated.

"You didn't hurt me. Gage...I've never...I didn't know it could be like that. I think I understand now how people can become sex addicts. Little worried about how I'm going to be able to go about life as usual after that."

Gage laughed. "God, Penny. You're good for my ego."

She rolled her eyes. "I never noticed your ego suffering."

He gave her a quick kiss on the cheek and rolled over, lying on his back next to her for just a few moments. Then he rose and walked to the bathroom.

Penny listened to his progress, aware he was getting rid of the condom, washing up. She was too boneless to move herself. As she lay there, she tried to take stock. Her pussy was sore, not in genuine pain but more in a used-a-muscle-I-didn't-know-I-had way.

Then, it all began to really sink in.

She'd lost her virginity.

To Gage.

This was the best night of her life.

But even as she thought that, she knew...it was going to end.

So she was surprised when Gage returned to the bed, lying down once more. She'd expected him to get dressed and go home.

Gage was silent, but she didn't mistake the quietness for him falling asleep. Obviously, he was searching for a way out that wouldn't hurt her feelings.

"You don't have to stay," she whispered.

"What?"

"I know you don't do sleepovers. You don't have to come up with an excuse to leave. You can just go. I don't…" She paused. "I don't want you to give me an excuse that will end up on Toby and Rich's list. We're friends, and we don't lie to each other. So…let's don't start here."

She kept her gaze locked on the ceiling, refusing to glance in Gage's direction for fear of what she might see. He shifted, and she expected to feel the mattress lift without his weight as he climbed out of bed.

What she didn't expect was Gage's arm wrapping around her waist, tugging until her back was snug against his chest.

He was spooning her.

Why was he spooning her?

"Penny," he murmured, his voice gruff, close to sleep.

"Hmm?"

"I'm not leaving. Now go to sleep."

She huffed out a breathy laugh.

But then, she did as he said, sleep coming to claim her quicker than it ever had before.

Chapter Eleven

Gage opened his eyes, blinking in the dark, unfamiliar room. It took him a few moments to figure out where the hell he was. And when he did...he grinned.

Lying on his side, he looked down to discover that instead of spooning Penny, he was curled up with Forrest, who was purring contently against Gage's chest. Penny was equally flanked, both girl cats snuggled next to her, the three females all sharing the same pillow in a way that was pretty fucking adorable. Only Harry appeared to be missing, and Gage wondered if perhaps he'd stolen the big-ass cat's spot.

Gage lifted himself up, resting his weight on his elbow, fighting like the devil to figure out how in the name of God he'd ended up in Penny Beaumont's bed.

More than that, he was struggling to believe how much he liked being there.

Forrest lifted his head, clearly disturbed by Gage's movements. He rose, did that arched-back cat stretch, then hopped off the bed.

One down, two to go.

He'd woken up with a hard-on, one he should ignore. After all, he'd just taken Penny's virginity a few hours earlier.

It didn't matter. He was drawn to her like the tide to the moon.

He wanted her again, needed her.

Which was an uncomfortable realization that he flat-out refused to think about.

As he inched closer, Luna gave him the once-over, then, like Forrest, she gave way, leaving the bed. Hermione must have thought she was missing some midnight cat party, because she jumped off the bed as well to follow the other two.

Penny, still asleep, turned over, facing away from him. Her back was bare, the sheet pooling around her waist. He slowly tugged it down until he was treated to a sneak peek of her curvy, perfectly rounded ass.

Reaching for her, he wrapped his arm around her, resuming the position he'd claimed when they'd first fallen asleep.

Penny stirred a little but settled quickly, still lost in the throes of sleep.

Gage lay there for several minutes, just listening to her breathing.

What the fuck was wrong with him?

He had no business being here. It was one thing to teach Penny about sex. If he really tried, he could probably convince himself he was just fulfilling the terms of the wager. He could call himself a mentor, feel justified in providing an inexperienced woman tutoring in the ways of sex.

That's what he *should* be doing. Putting this into context. Making it fit his well-ordered lifestyle.

Not...this.

He hadn't spent the night in a woman's bed since he was twenty-one. Not since the year his entire life crumbled to the ground.

The year he'd lost...everything. Including himself.

He closed his eyes, tried to shut it down, lock it out. For over a decade, he'd managed to hold it all at bay by simply sealing the vault and walking away.

Penny shifted in her sleep, snuggling closer, as if unconsciously seeking his body heat to keep her warm. The intimacy meant his hard cock was *this close* to being nestled between the cheeks of her ass.

Slowly, gently, he inched his lower body away, so that he could angle his dick downwards, sliding it into the valley between her legs, burying it between her folds.

It wouldn't take more than one quick change in position, bending her forward, to allow him to slip his cock back inside her liquid heat.

Penny didn't stir, and he couldn't stop himself from grinning.

He'd worn his girl out.

His...girl.

Fuck.

Too many thoughts slammed home at once, crashing in on him in a way he hadn't allowed in so many fucking years.

Penny hadn't just unlocked the vault. She'd swung the door open and shoved him inside, forcing him to face what he'd hidden away.

How had he let this happen?

He needed to leave. Now.

Gage lifted his arm from her waist, but he wasn't quick enough.

"Mmm." Penny wiggled her bottom, rousing slowly.

The movement rendered him incapable of reasonable thought.

"Don't move," he whispered, cursing silently for putting himself in this position in the first place. Penny had given him the green light to leave earlier. Offered him an easy out. Why hadn't he taken that opportunity?

Penny, still not fully awake, wiggled again.

Gage reacted, letting impulse guide him. He twisted her facedown beneath him in one quick, smooth motion. One second he was spooning her, the next, he was sliding inside her body, Penny's hips in his hands. Seated to the hilt, he held steady, clenching his teeth, overwhelmed by how fucking good she felt.

Penny, awake now, didn't realize how close he was to the brink, didn't understand that she was luring the bear from his cave when her pussy tightened around him.

"Gage," she whispered, his name nothing more than a plea.

That was when his brain engaged, and he understood why she felt like heaven on earth.

There was nothing between them.

"I need to get a condom."

Penny's pussy clenched again. She wasn't making this fucking easy.

"I'm on birth control. And obviously clean. But if you want to put on a condom—"

Gage didn't give her a chance to finish that statement. Just like he didn't give himself a chance to think about what the hell he was doing.

He lifted her hips higher, sliding out, then he slammed back in, both of them grunting at the sheer force of impact.

"I'm clean too."

Penny's fingers tightened in the sheet, seeking purchase, something to hold on to as he took her with the force of a freight train. This was going to be over quickly if he didn't find a way to maintain control, so he slowed his roll.

Because he wanted this to last.

It was just...he'd never fucked a woman without a condom.

More than that, he'd vowed he never would. Primarily because he'd never trusted any of the women he'd slept with enough to risk pregnancy. So...what did it mean...why was he...with *her*...

She said she was on birth control, and he believed her. Knew she wouldn't lie, wouldn't try to trap him—and his billions—with a pregnancy.

"God, Penny!"

She shoved her ass backwards, catching his inward thrust, driving him in deeper, harder.

He was struggling to keep up, the feel of her overwhelming. Reaching down, he grasped a handful of her gorgeous blonde waves, using it to pull her body toward him, away from the bed.

Still inside her, the two of them moved together, one of his hands gripping her hair, the other wrapping around her waist, seeking out her self-destruct button.

He knew the secret to a lot of women's orgasms didn't rely on the pounding of his cock inside them so much as the pressure applied to that one tiny nub.

Penny gasped and jerked when he hit paydirt, stroking her with the same speed and force as her beloved clit tickler.

It had taken everything Gage had to hold still as she'd played with herself earlier. He'd intended to watch her bring herself to orgasm, to study what made her purr, what made her come, but that plan changed quickly. Because he hadn't been able to look at her without touching. So he'd grabbed her toy and taken over, finger fucking her until she exploded.

He'd never seen anything more beautiful.

Penny's bouncing on his dick became more frantic, her pussy quivering. She was close. She started to fall forward, but he held her up with an unyielding fist in her hair. He was pulling it hard, and he suspected it stung. He could also tell Penny liked it.

Her hands, resting on his thighs, tightened, and he felt her nails scoring his skin.

"Gage," she cried out, coming loudly, her body trembling against his. "God!"

Gage released her hair, using both arms to hold her against his chest, to keep her pressed close. He started reciting the Greek alphabet, determined to hold his own climax at bay. He wasn't finished with her. Not by a long shot.

Tonight was all he was going to give himself.

He wouldn't—*couldn't*—come back here again.

So he'd steal every second, cram a lifetime of memories into this one perfect night.

As Penny's orgasm began to wane, she seemed to become

aware of the fact he hadn't come as well. She looked over her shoulder at him, her expression somewhere between confused and nervous.

He gave her a malevolent grin that erased the confusion and pushed her all the way into the "oh shit" realm.

"I don't think I can—"

He cut her off, nipping her shoulder until she squeaked with pain.

"You're going to keep coming until I tell you to stop. You don't get to decide when that is."

"My insides feel like jelly."

"Does your pussy hurt? Is it too sore?"

She shook her head, the perfect honest woman. He'd just given her an out as well. And like him, she didn't take it.

"No. It's not that," she admitted. "It's just, damn...I didn't think too much pleasure could be a bad thing, but...it's like I'm boneless right now, shaky as a newborn foal."

They were having this conversation with his unsheathed dick still inside her, but it didn't feel awkward or strange. It just felt like...them.

"Penny," he said.

"Yeah?"

"You're gonna get a lot shakier before I'm finished with you."

She blew out a long breath. "You are ridiculously hot."

He laughed. Then he pushed her back down on the bed. "Keep your ass up, head down."

She obeyed without question, without any further complaint, and it occurred to him that—despite her inexperience—she was far and away the best lover he'd ever had.

Their bodies fit, her pussy gloving his cock like it was made just for him. Her breasts filling his hands exactly right. Even their heights matched, all the important parts lined up perfectly without a lot of bending or squatting to hit just the right spot.

Gage ran his hand over her soft ass cheeks, his cock filling her but not moving.

Penny seemed to think that meant the job fell to her. She started to shift forward, but he stopped her with hard hands on her hips.

"Don't move."

"But—" she started.

Gage lifted his hand and brought it down on her ass, spanking her with enough force to make it sting.

She gasped. "Ouch!"

Then he lifted his other hand, striking the other cheek. She wiggled forward, attempting to get away. He spanked her again, then again.

Penny's face was buried in a pillow, muting her cries, but he didn't need to hear her to know what she was feeling. Her inner muscles clenched with every blow, so much so, he was in danger of erupting. Penny was fucking him, and she didn't even realize it.

He ran his finger along her spine, his gentle caress after the stronger blows catching her off guard. "More?"

He hadn't brought up the subject of safe words, hadn't explained that she held all the power, ultimately. Perhaps because this didn't feel like that to him. Being with Penny wasn't a game. It wasn't even him paying a bet.

He was with her because he wanted her. It was as simple—and as difficult—as that.

Penny lifted her head from the pillow and glanced at him over her shoulder. "Yes," she breathed. "I want more. I...I like that. So much. Oooo, does this mean I'm kinky?"

He chuckled, amused by her delight over that idea. Then, because he felt compelled to make sure she understood she could set limits, he said, "You can always tell me to stop, and I will."

The puzzled look she gave him proved she felt the exact same way he did. "I know that. I trust you."

Three words.

She'd just unwittingly gutted him. With only three words.

Trust.

Suddenly, he understood how she'd managed to open that vault. She'd found the very key he'd thrown away.

Gage sucked in a ragged breath, fighting with everything he had to shut his fucking brain down.

Stop thinking.

Start fucking.

The words began to play themselves over and over like a mantra as he began to thrust his hips, slamming into her.

Harder. Faster.

Penny came again, crying out loudly, shaking just as hard as he'd promised she would.

But he didn't stop. He couldn't. If he stopped, the thoughts came back. He had to hold them at bay. It was the only way he'd survive this. Survive *her*.

Pulling out, he gripped her waist and flipped her to her back. She flopped over with little finesse, as boneless as she'd claimed.

He lifted her legs, her knees resting within the crooks of his elbows, as he shoved inside her again.

Penny groaned but didn't protest. Didn't ask him to stop.

He fucked her like a man possessed, and when her third orgasm struck, it sucker punched him right into completion, and he came, jet after jet of come erupting inside her, and for a split second—just one—he let himself imagine what it would feel like if she weren't protected, if she *did* get pregnant.

Gage didn't expect the—fuck him—warmth that flooded him at the idea.

And that was when he knew he'd let this go way too far.

He withdrew, dropping next to her on the bed, gasping for air, telling himself his labored breathing was due to exertion, not panic.

Penny didn't stir and when he looked over, he saw she'd fallen asleep.

He watched her for several minutes, too many thoughts warring for supremacy in his fucked-up brain.

Only one yelled loud enough to be heard over the din. The one that told him he had to get the hell out of there. Right now.

Gage rose slowly from the bed, dressing quietly, keeping his gaze resolutely away from the bed. He couldn't look at her without wanting to climb back in, without pulling her body beneath his and taking her again and again, until both of them were shaky, boneless masses.

Picking up his shoes, he left her bedroom, drifting down the hallway to the living room. There, he put his shoes on and retrieved his jacket.

He glanced down when he felt Forrest rubbing around his ankles. Bending, he petted the cat.

"Take care of our girl," he instructed the furry beast, who merely purred in response.

Gage took one last look around, steeled his resolve, and then left.

Chapter Twelve

Penny stood outside the door to the gaming room, silently giving herself a pep talk. It was just before four. The company had only just recently started allowing people to work flexible hours, so this was quitting time for some of the employees. As such, a few of the offices had begun to clear out.

Unable to sleep all week, she'd been at the office by seven every day—a Festivus miracle if there ever was one. She'd skipped lunch today so she could have left an hour ago, but it had taken her all damn day to build up her nerve.

She could do this. She *had* to do this.

It had been six days. Six long-ass, brutal days since Gage Russo had taken her virginity, ruined her for all other men forever —she'd always thought it would be wonderful to feel that way, but now she knew it sucked—and then snuck out of her apartment like a thief in the night.

Honestly, if she was the only one getting hurt, she could deal with it. After all, that was what she'd signed up for. Sex lessons with her playboy boss. She wasn't so foolish that she believed Gage would fall in love with her.

Because there was a big difference between what she wanted and what she expected to get.

And—as always—she got what she expected, not what she hoped for.

While she lacked bedroom experience, she was the number one seed when it came to dashed hopes, so she was well versed enough in disappointment to mask her emotions.

But the thing was…she wasn't the only person who was upset right now. And that was what she needed to fix.

Taking a deep breath, she opened the door. His assistant had told her he would be here, and the woman hadn't lied.

Gage didn't hear her enter, didn't hear her lock the door. His back was to her, and he was lost in a video game, headphones blocking all sound. She walked closer and looked over his shoulder, studying the game. It wasn't one she recognized, and she wondered if he was testing a new one from the gaming company he'd purchased.

The fact that he was doing that without her, Toby, and Rich meant she was doubly pissed off now.

"New game?"

Gage wasn't startled by her presence, and she wondered now if her arrival really had gone unnoticed. He paused the game and took off the headphones.

"It is," he replied.

"You don't seem surprised to see me."

Gage gestured to his cellphone lying next to the keyboard. "My assistant just texted. Said you were on your way. What's up?"

While his words were casual, his tone was anything but. He seemed distant and cold, two words she used to describe his brother, Matt, but never Gage.

"You haven't been down to IT this week."

Gage lifted one shoulder. "Been busy."

"Yeah. The thing is, I'm pretty sure that's a lie. You've managed to stop by the office three or four times a week, every single week, for the last six years. So I know you're lying low because of me. Because of," she swallowed heavily, "last Friday."

"Penny—" he started, but she'd practiced what she wanted to say all damn day, so she forged on.

"I'm not mad," she hastened to say. "About you leaving, I mean. I told you that you could, so if you're thinking I'm upset, I'm not."

He nodded. "Okay."

"Toby said you bailed on D&D for tonight."

He opened his mouth, but she waved away whatever excuse he intended to offer. "I'll skip it so you can go."

He frowned. "What?"

"It's obvious what we did sort of screwed up the friendship we had going. I asked you for too much, and I shouldn't have. That's on me. But your absence this week hasn't gone unnoticed and, well, the guys miss you. They're thinking *they* did something wrong, and they can't figure out what, and I hate that. Hate that they've become collateral damage in something that I did."

Gage sighed—a long, heavy sigh—then he stood up and walked over to her. To her surprise, he reached out and drew her in. Her head spun as Gage wrapped her in his embrace and held her there.

"I'm not avoiding you," he said at last, even as he continued to hug her. "Work really is kicking my ass, and I thought you might like some space, some time to yourself. I didn't realize Toby and Rich would notice my absence, let alone miss me."

Penny snorted. "You're kidding, right? You're the coolest friend they've ever had."

Gage released her, but he didn't move away. "You always say that, but the truth is, I'm more comfortable with you guys than I've ever been with my frat brothers in college, other work colleagues, or even my brothers."

"So what I'm hearing you say is you're a big old nerd too," she teased. Penny dug deep, fighting to maintain this easy-breezy disposition. It felt like the years of practice, honing her "I'm okay with this" skills, had all been for this moment.

"I'm sorry I left the other night."

She shook her head. "You don't have to—"

"Let me say it, Penny. I said I was trying to give you space this week, but the truth is, *I* was the one who needed space."

"Why?"

Gage looked away. "That's a hard question to answer."

She waited, then realized he didn't intend to try.

Time to finish her speech and get out. "Okay. Well. I'm letting you off the hook for the rest of the lessons. I just wanted to let you know so—"

"The rest of what lessons?" he interjected.

"The sex lessons."

"We covered that part of the wager," he insisted.

Penny shrugged. "Not really. I said I wanted to be good in bed."

"Jesus Christ. Let's get something clear. You're good in bed. You're fucking *awesome* in bed."

Now she frowned. "We only went over two positions. Everybody's probably good at missionary and doggie style. They're like, super basic."

Gage put his hands on his hips and leaned in until his face was close to hers. "The terms of the wager have been fulfilled. Paid in full."

"Not really, but—"

"Dammit, Penny. You can't keep adding to the terms of the bet."

"I'm not. The wager was for sex lessons, *plural*. Obviously, it's implied—"

"Implied, like your virginity was implied?"

She ignored his outburst. "Implied that we'd cover all the positions."

"All?"

"Well, okay, maybe not all, but a hell of a lot more than two. That's practically nothing."

Gage crossed his arms and shook his head. "Nothing," he

muttered, clearly talking to himself. "She thinks the other night was *nothing*."

"That's not what I said," she answered, even though he wasn't talking to her. "Friday night was incredible. Mind-blowing. And it just...well, it whetted my appetite for more. But since the lessons are over, I guess it's time to put them to the test."

Gage's eyes narrowed, and she got the immediate sense he was angry. "How?"

"I'm thinking I should ask David out for a date."

"The fucking neighbor?" he barked.

She frowned again. "Why not? I mean, he seems like an easy place to start. Jess keeps telling me I should go out with Gio but—"

"Moretti?" Gage threw his hands in the air. "Put that idea out of your mind. You're too sweet. That guy would chew you up and spit you out."

Penny scoffed. "No, he wouldn't. I know your family has some Hatfield and McCoy thing going with the Morettis, but Gio is really nice. All those guys are."

"Stay away from the Morettis, Penny."

"No," she said, her temper piqued.

"No?!" he all but shouted at her.

"*No*. What the hell was this whole makeover thing about if I don't actually get out there and try to find a guy?"

Gage ran his hands through his hair, frustration rife in his expression. He turned away from her, walking over to the window to look down on the city.

The silence lingered, but neither one of them sought to end it. Penny was trying to calm down, trying to figure out which part of what she'd said had upset him so much. It was obvious he considered the bet paid in full, so why should it matter to him *who* she tried to date?

"New wager," he said after a few minutes.

"What?"

"I want a new bet."

"What are the terms?"

"If you win, I'll give you one more week of lessons. Sex lessons. But that's it. No changing the terms of the bet or adding *implied* things when the week is over. Oh—and I decide what the sex lessons are."

Of all the things she'd expected him to say, that wasn't even on the list.

So she didn't have a clue how to reply. Because what he was offering was dangerous. Too dangerous.

If she agreed, her desire for Gage's love would only grow stronger.

She was a fool. An optimistic fool.

But it didn't matter. Because she knew she was taking the bet.

"And if you win?" Penny quietly asked.

Gage cursed himself.

He was a fool. A jealous fool.

Regardless, he pushed on.

"You sign that seven-year contract to continue working here." Then, because he was a stupid prick, he added, "And you stay the hell away from Gio Moretti."

"What's the game?" she asked.

He pointed to his computer. "That one. The one I'm testing. It's an RPG. Pretty challenging."

"You have an unfair advantage. You've played it. I haven't."

"I only just opened the file a few minutes before you walked in here. We'll take half an hour to familiarize ourselves with it and then we'll start the contest. Person who reaches the highest level before getting killed wins."

"You really just opened it?"

He nodded. "I swear. So is it a bet?"

She bit her lower lip, and for a moment, he feared she'd reject the offer. He wasn't sure what he'd do if she said no. The idea of Penny going out with her tool of a neighbor or—God forbid—

Gio Moretti, drove him out of his mind, making him do insane things.

Penny held out her hand. "It's a bet."

He took her hand then used his grip against her, pulling her toward him. They weren't sealing this deal with a handshake. He gave her a hard kiss that lingered. He'd meant to end it quickly, but her lips were soft and warm and—

No. No more of that.

He broke off the kiss, and the two of them took their seats. For thirty minutes, they explored the game.

"Wow. I love this so much!" Penny gushed as the half hour wound down. "You're going to make a fortune from this game. I bet it's bigger than *Elden Ring*."

Gage was pleased by her comment, then he realized if Penny liked it, chances were good his company *did* have a hit on his hands. She was an extremely discerning gamer. He'd run the game by Toby and Rich tomorrow to see what they thought.

"Ready to start?" he asked.

She nodded.

And...they were off on their digital adventure.

They'd been at it for nearly an hour when Gage glanced over to watch her play. She was wholly immersed in the game. She was biting her lower lip, a nervous habit that seemed to come out more when she was playing to win. Like him, she was competitive almost to a fault.

Except for now.

Because for the first time ever, Gage threw the game.

"Damn. I'm dead," he said.

Penny barely spared him a glance as she fought valiantly to advance to the next level. She just had to get there without dying...

His ego was on the fence in regard to the lack of attention she was paying him, because he couldn't tell if she was that desperate to win another week in bed with him or more interested in the game.

With Penny, it could go either way.

His question was answered when she defeated the beast and moved into the next realm. She tossed down her controller with a smug smile. "I win."

She was wrong.

He'd won.

"Come here."

She stood up somewhat hesitantly. After all, they'd been sitting right next to each other.

He gripped her hips so that she was standing right in front of him. He hadn't bothered to rise from the gaming chair. He had something else in mind.

"Are we starting now?"

He shook his head. "Right now doesn't count. The clock on the wager starts tomorrow."

"So what are we doing now?"

"You're taking your victory lap," he explained, as he unfastened her jeans, pushing them and her lace panties off so that she was naked from the waist down. He ran his fingers along her slit, grinning when he discovered she was already very, *very* wet.

Penny reached out to cup his cheek, the gesture so affectionate it took him aback. When he'd initiated this second wager, he'd only been thinking of himself. He'd convinced himself he could handle just one more week with her, that he'd fuck her out of his system and move on.

He hadn't considered Penny's feelings.

Now...

"Don't fall in love with me," he said quietly.

Penny's fingers, which had been stroking his beard, stilled, then her hand fell away. "I won't," she whispered.

It was the first lie Penny Beaumont had ever told him.

And he pretended to believe it was the truth.

Gage unfastened his own pants, lifting his hips to draw them down. "Straddle my lap."

She placed her knees next to his legs, a tight fit in the chair, then she lowered her ass to his thighs.

Gage gripped the back of her neck and pulled her toward him for a kiss. He should really stop kissing her, because it added a level of intimacy that continued to blur the lines, make things confusing...for both of them.

But *should* wasn't a strong enough word for him, not when he stole a taste. Penny kissed like she played video games—all in.

Her hands drifted around his shoulders, her lips parted, her tongue met his halfway.

Kissing had never been part of his foreplay routine. It had always felt too tame, too boring. His erection, which had been riding at half-mast since she'd walked into the room, disagreed. It thickened, making the last leg of the journey to rock hard.

Penny lowered one of her hands, grasping his dick, running her fist along his flesh. It was an innocent touch, too gentle.

Gage broke the kiss. "Grip it hard."

She did as he requested, but he shook his head. "Harder," he said.

"I don't want to hurt you."

He cupped her jaw, forced her gaze from where it rested on his cock to his face. Holding it, he said, "Do as I say."

Penny tightened her grip, but her stroke was still too slow.

"Add your other hand. And increase the speed."

She did as he said, and he closed his eyes, cursing himself for a fool. Penny had revealed herself to be a quick study in most things, so he didn't know why he thought this would be any different.

Especially when she slid off his lap, kneeling on the floor before the chair.

He followed her lead, shifting until his ass was on the edge of the seat, Penny tucked beneath his outstretched legs.

He ran his finger over her mouth, pushing his thumb inside. Her eyes met his as she began to suck.

"Virgin mouth?"

She nodded, increasing the suction.

"I'm going to be so selfish, Penny. This week, I'm claiming all your innocence. *All of it*," he stressed, making sure she understood exactly how far he'd push her if she held resolute on receiving sex lessons from him.

Her eyes drifted closed, not from fear but desire.

He pulled his thumb free from her mouth. "Open up," he commanded. "Take me in."

"You're too big."

"Do as I say," he repeated, amazed how those four tiny words seemed to be some sort of trigger for her.

She leaned in, taking the head of his cock inside her mouth. He gave her time to adjust to his girth. He wasn't surprised that she was clever enough to understand she couldn't fit it all inside. As such, her hands continued to stroke the base of his dick, her fists still gripping tight.

Soon, she found her rhythm, adding suction or the stroke of her tongue along his dripping slit. Gage saw stars, his vision going gray around the edges.

She was a novice, and yet, she had him on the verge of blowing after just a few short minutes.

Gage considered doing just that, but this wasn't *his* victory lap. It was hers.

He grasped her hair, pulling her head away until his dick popped free. Standing, he shoved the keyboard aside then lifted her until her ass was perched on the edge of the gaming desk.

"Open your legs," he instructed as he reclaimed his seat on the chair. Rolling it between her legs, he lowered his head, giving her as good as she'd just given him.

Penny's hands closed in his hair as she cried out his name.

"Holy shit! Gage…"

He sucked and nipped her clit, pressed the flat of his tongue against it, gave her some of those "tickles" she enjoyed so much.

"So good," she said, so breathlessly, he knew it was time to level up.

He pushed his tongue inside her, tightening his grip on her thighs to keep her from slipping off the desk.

"Ohmigod! Ohmigod!" she chanted, her hips rolling toward him with each thrust of his tongue. She was so close, he decided to close the deal.

Gage shoved three fingers inside her while sucking on her clit.

Penny went off like a bottle rocket, and he was suddenly grateful he'd taken over the conference room at the end of the hallway for his gaming space. If anyone happened to be outside, there would be no mistaking what was happening in here.

Gage lifted his head when Penny's fingers went slack in his hair. Standing, he kissed her, letting her have a taste of herself on his lips.

"You're fucking sexy when you come," he growled.

She returned his kiss tenfold. "I warned you. Now it's happened." He frowned, confused, until she added, "I'm officially a sex addict."

He chuckled. "If I were a good boss, I'd offer to make sure treatment for that affliction is added to our health care benefits. But the truth is...I don't want you cured."

"Misery loves company?" she teased.

"Something like that." He resumed his seat on the gaming chair then crooked his finger.

Penny's gaze slid down to his still-too-hard cock, and she gave him a sultry smile.

Fuck it. His patience was in tatters.

He reached for her, refusing to wait the few seconds for her to come to him. One second she was on the desk, the next she was straddling his lap, sliding down his cock, as he put the chair in the prone position and lowered it so her feet could touch the floor.

"Jesus, Penny," he murmured when he was completely inside. "Ride me, Beaumont."

"Hard and fast?" she asked with a grin.

"Is there any other way?"

She moved her hips and gave him everything he asked for and more. They hadn't bothered with a condom. Apparently, that was no longer a conversation. Though taking Penny bare made him feel like a fucking novice as well. The sensations, no longer muted by latex, were too sharp, too damn powerful.

Good. Great. *Amazing.*

He tilted his hips slightly, the new position allowing him to slide in at just the right angle.

Found it.

Penny trembled when his cock stroked her G-spot on the next thrust, and the next and the next.

Within seconds, she was coming again, and Gage didn't even bother to hold back. She rode it out, his cock seated to the hilt, as jet after jet filled her.

Penny remained on his lap, even as his dick began to soften, falling forward and resting her head on his shoulder, the two of them struggling to catch their breath.

He'd bought himself another week. Seven days.

He did the mental calculations. That gave him one hundred and sixty-eight hours to take Penny in all the ways he wanted.

One hundred and sixty-eight hours.

It was a big number.

It also wasn't going to be enough.

They remained there, locked together for several minutes. Penny was the first to stir.

She lifted her head and gave him one of her adorable after-sex smiles. Then she stood up gingerly, her muscles clearly stiff after that workout.

He helped her put her pants back on then refastened himself. They looked ruffled and Penny's cheeks were flushed. He ran his hands through his hair in attempt to straighten it, then he did the same for her, finger-combing her long blonde locks.

Yeah, that didn't help. It still looked like they'd just had sex.

His only consolation was the fact it was late, and most folks had probably cleared out by now.

"Want to grab a burger together before we head over to Toby's?" he asked. She'd offered to skip D&D, but the game wouldn't be nearly as much fun without her. Plus, it was her night to be Dungeon Master, and she was a *brilliant* Dungeon Master.

She blushed. "I think I should probably run home, grab a quick shower."

"That's an even better idea. We'll swing through a drive-thru then shower at your place before the game."

"You want to take a shower with me?"

He nodded. He loved being her first in all things.

"Okay," she said cheerfully. "But Toby will be pissed if we're late."

"Start working on your apology, because we're definitely going to be late," he assured her. "Come on. You can text him while I drive."

They left the gaming room, walking toward the elevator together. Gage was pleased that they'd dodged a bullet, the corridor empty of employees.

Of course, the moment he sent that thought out into the universe, karma decided to kick back.

Like an idiot, he placed his arm around her back, tugging her toward him playfully as they waited for the elevator.

The doors slid open at that very moment. With one occupant inside.

Connie.

Gage quickly released Penny, but the damage was done.

"Hey," Penny said, as they entered the elevator.

"Hello," Connie said. "You're both working late."

While Penny's smile was genuine, Connie's resembled that of a shark circling a baby on a life raft.

"The boss is a slave driver," Penny joked, completely oblivious to the underlying tension.

Connie laughed, but the sound couldn't be described as anything less than forced.

It was a quick ride to the first floor, where Connie disembarked. He and Penny were headed to the garage below the building, where his car was parked.

Connie glanced over her shoulder at them, and Penny waved goodbye just before the doors closed. Gage was starting to understand Penny's issues with teasing in school. The woman didn't have a malevolent bone in her body—except for when she went all Trevor Phillips on someone's ass in *Grand Theft Auto*—so she didn't seem to recognize it in others.

Connie had been fine since their chat at Enigma, so he was probably just buying trouble. Or at least he hoped so.

Once they were alone in the elevator, Gage stole a quick kiss, putting the other woman out of his mind. "Ready for this week?"

She nodded enthusiastically. "So ready."

Game on.

Chapter Thirteen

Penny grinned when she heard the knock on her apartment door. It was Monday night and Gage had promised to bring dinner with him. He'd had a late meeting over drinks with a client, so she'd headed home on her own, anxious to tidy up her place and change the sheets after their marathon sexcapades this past weekend.

Gage was taking his role as tutor very, *very* seriously.

She opened the door then frowned at the bags in his hands. "I thought you were bringing dinner. That looks like groceries."

Gage shook his head, obviously disappointed in her reaction. "It *is* groceries," he said, walking into the apartment and straight past her. He headed to the kitchen. "I'm going to teach you how to cook."

Penny groaned as she followed him. "I know how to cook. I just don't like it. Too much standing around."

"That's obvious." He opened her refrigerator and pointed inside. "Two pizza boxes, four cartons of Chinese and half a sandwich leftover from the night we got takeout from the deli. The only thing in here that you bought at the grocery store besides beer and Yoo-hoo is condiments."

"That's not true." She opened the freezer. "I have fudgesicles."

Gage, clearly not finished making his point, forged on as if she hadn't spoken at all. "You burned hardboiled eggs."

"That wasn't because I didn't know how to make them. I told you. I got distracted."

Gage started unpacking the groceries on the counter. "Fine. Tonight, we'll cook without distractions."

She snorted. "You're like the biggest distraction in the world. You realize that, right?"

Gage reached out for her, giving her a quick kiss. She loved his kisses—all the variations. The long, soft, wet, open-mouthed ones. The rough, passionate, hard-enough-to-leave bruises ones. And even these fast, closed-mouth, almost platonic ones. Every kiss he gave her made her head spin, her heart race, and her pussy clench.

"Even bigger than Rhett and Link?" he asked.

"Even bigger."

"Bigger than *Warzone*?"

She tilted her head. "Way bigger."

"Damn. I think I like that."

She rolled her eyes then looked at his purchases. "Wait. Aren't you Italian?"

"You know I am," he replied.

"Isn't it like some sort of cardinal sin to cook spaghetti with sauce from a jar or pasta from a box?"

He chuckled. "Probably. But given your reputation in the kitchen, I thought we should work our way up to the fancy stuff. Besides, it's getting late and I'm hungry."

"Me too. So...what do you want me to do?"

"I'd ask you to fill a pan of water and bring it to a boil for the pasta, but I'm afraid that might be too advanced for you," he teased, bending down and pulling out two pans, one for the pasta and one for the sauce.

He'd been here every night since last Thursday, four nights—

she was keeping count—and it surprised her how well he fit in her tiny one-bedroom apartment. It was very easy for her to forget he was seriously loaded, basically born with a silver spoon in his mouth.

He opened the jar of sauce, poured it in a pan, turned on the burner, and handed her a wooden spoon. "Stir."

She did as he asked, half-heartedly, watching while he filled the larger pot with water and set it to boil. He continued to work with quiet skill, preparing the rest of their meal. Then he grabbed the corkscrew and opened a bottle of red wine, pouring each of them a glass.

"Here. You can have a drink while we cook. Maybe that'll make you less grumpy about me forcing you to stand in the kitchen."

He clinked his glass against hers, took a sip, then set it down so he could finish prepping their meal. He'd bought a pre-made salad and a box of frozen garlic bread.

"You seem very at ease in the kitchen," she mused. "With all your money, I would have expected you to have a full-time house-keeper and personal chef."

Gage shook his head as he salted the water. "Nope. My bach-elor pad is just that. A home for one. I don't always have a lot of time to cook during the week, but on the weekends, I typically spend a few hours doing meal prep, stuff like that. I like being in the kitchen."

She crinkled her nose, letting him know what she thought of that. He laughed and bopped the look away by tapping the tip of her nose with his finger. Then he grabbed his cell from his back pants pocket, opening the phone. Flipping the screen for a selfie, he turned so that both he and Penny were in the shot. He faked a horrified look of her wielding the spoon, and she laughed as he snapped it.

"Smart-ass," she muttered, still grinning. "So who taught you to cook?"

Gage didn't respond right away as he bent down and opened

the drawer beneath the oven. He pulled out a cookie sheet for the bread and put it in the preheated oven.

"You probably grew up with a full kitchen staff or something, am I right?" she pressed on. Gage was very closemouthed when it came to his family. Every time she broached the subject, he clammed up.

"We had a cook growing up who prepared the meals for our family. Dad was one of those old-school types, who liked to conduct business over a meal, so it wasn't unusual for him to invite potential clients or investors to dinner at our house."

"That sounds...really boring."

Gage didn't laugh as she expected. Instead, he looked at her like she understood something no one else did. "It was. But Dad had trained his trick ponies well. My brothers and I knew we were to sit quietly, eat politely, speak only when spoken to. My mom was there to look pretty and entertain the client's wife or girlfriend or—sometimes—mistress with small talk."

Penny waited for a moment, wondering if he'd say more. She didn't miss the vein of resentment in his tone. When he fell silent again, she decided to lead by example. Maybe if she opened up, he would too.

"My family rarely sat at the dining room table. In fact, most of the time we couldn't. It was the place where all the shit ended up, bookbags, mail, folded laundry. So instead, we usually sat in the living room with our plates on our laps, watching repeats of old sitcoms like *Cheers* and *Seinfeld*. My dad loves *Seinfeld*. He can work a quote from the show into pretty much every conversation he has."

Gage took another sip of his wine. "I think I would have liked eating dinner that way. We never ate anywhere besides the dining room. And I've never been able to break that habit. Even when it's just me at home alone, I eat at the kitchen table."

"Really?"

He nodded.

She continued with her family story. "Don't get me wrong. I

know all that research out there says dinnertime should be sacred, spent around the table. But...when I look back, some of my favorite times with my parents were sitting on the couch, laughing at Kramer and Elaine and George. Besides, my parents didn't need a set mealtime to talk to me or Rhys. They talked to us all the time, about school and grades, our friends."

"You're close with your parents."

She nodded. Gage had been here when her dad called last night for his weekly chat. She'd promised to keep it short before she answered, but Gage told her not to do that, to take her time. Then he'd gone to the kitchen to make coffee so she'd have privacy.

"Very. Were you? Close to yours?" she added.

Gage hesitated, and once again, she thought he might brush off her question. She was shocked when instead, he answered her.

"It was my mom who taught me how to cook. Monday was the chef's day off, so after school on those days, I'd meet her in the kitchen, and we'd make dinner together."

Gage's tone when he spoke about his mother was the polar opposite of the one reserved for his dad. It was the first time he'd given her any insight into his mom.

"Was she Italian too? All homemade sauces and pastas and shit?"

He chuckled. "She was. But she liked to experiment in the kitchen, try different things. Her favorite thing to make was Indian cuisine."

"Wow. That sounds way above my skill level."

Gage bumped his hip against hers as they stood side by side in front of the stove. "We'll work up to it."

She caught the slight wince when he realized what he said. It wasn't the first time he'd slipped up, alluded to some future plan that wasn't going to happen.

"How old were you when she died?"

And just like that, the lightheartedness of the moment vanished, a sudden tension filling the air. "Twenty-one," he said, and she could tell that was the last thing he intended to say on the subject.

Penny wanted to kick her own ass for bringing up such a sad topic, especially after finally getting him to open up. She had a million more questions she wanted to ask about his mother, his brothers, and his dad, but she knew she wouldn't get answers. So she fought to bring back the fun.

"You know. As much as I appreciate this lesson, I'm pretty content with my current cooking routine."

Gage took the escape she provided, smirking at her. "Your current routine can't be called cooking. Takeout, delivery, and bowls of cereal are not cooking."

"Maybe not, but once or twice a month, I give Aunt Berta money for groceries, and she makes me a couple of casseroles that I can reheat in the microwave. That's sort of cooking."

Gage shook his head. "Not even close."

The timer went off, and Gage checked the spaghetti noodles. Confident they were done, he strained the water. "Want to grab the garlic bread from the oven?"

"Are you sure you trust me?"

"Just do it," he said with a laugh, loading their plates with a small helping of salad, the spaghetti, then grabbing a slice of bread from the tray.

Penny refilled their wine glasses, grabbed forks and napkins.

Gage started for her small kitchen table.

"Want to eat in front of the TV?" she offered.

He gave her a bemused look. "You seriously ate spaghetti on your lap?"

She nodded. "And steak and fried chicken. I'm a master when it comes to balancing plates full of food on my lap."

"How about a compromise?" He left the kitchen with their plates, setting them on the coffee table before grabbing two pillows from the couch and tossing them to the floor. "A table *and* TV."

"Perfect." They both took a seat on the floor next to each

other, while she grabbed the remote and started channel surfing. "Ooo. *RuPaul's Drag Race?*"

"Pass."

She clicked for a minute more before finding *Seinfeld*. She looked in his direction for approval, and he nodded.

"Yeah. Leave it there."

They ate as they watched, cracking up at the classic lines, referring to themselves in third person after "The Jimmy" episode.

"Penny wants more wine," she announced after they'd finished eating.

Gage stopped her before she could stand up. "Gage wants Penny. Naked."

"Penny likes Gage's idea better," she joked.

Gage rose then held his hand down to her. "Bedroom."

They raced each other to her room, tripping and shoving each other out of the way in their attempt to get there first. They were laughing, out of control by the time they got there.

"I win!" she announced.

Gage lifted her up and tossed her on the bed, coming down on top of her. "Nope. I do."

He lowered his head and kissed her.

She wrapped her arms around his shoulders, sinking into his kiss, certain no future dates or—God, please—boyfriends would ever kiss as good as Gage. He tasted delicious, like tomatoes, garlic, wine.

He'd definitely followed through on her request to try "all" the positions. They'd spent the weekend working their way through his own personal Kama Sutra list, including everything from sixty-nine to sex against the wall to several variations of missionary and doggie style where he bent her like a pretzel.

She'd discovered she had muscles in places she didn't even know existed.

After several minutes, he lifted his head and looked at her. She got a sense he was thinking about what happened next, so she remained quiet, curious about what tonight would bring.

He pushed himself off the bed then held his hand out to help her stand as well.

"Take your clothes off, Penny," he commanded as he began to strip off his own.

She did as he asked, anxious to get down to the good stuff. Any shyness she'd felt around him initially was long gone. They'd spent more time together naked than dressed over the past few days.

Once they were bare, she started to climb back on the bed, but he stopped her, gripping her upper arm.

"Get your butt plug. And lube."

Penny's heart skipped several beats. He'd mentioned claiming every drop of her virginity, but so far, anal play hadn't made an appearance.

She bent down to pull her box of toys out from under the bed. She grabbed what he asked for, tossing them on the mattress.

She could feel the weight of his gaze on her, just as she could feel the heat creeping to her face. No doubt she was as red as a beet at the moment.

"You look nervous."

She shook her head but still didn't establish eye contact.

"Look at me, Penny."

She sighed, but he wasn't inclined to wait for her to comply. He cupped her chin and pulled her face up. "You *have* played with the plug before, haven't you?"

She nodded.

"And you enjoyed it?"

She'd loved it. Rather than admit that aloud, she merely nodded again.

"Then why are you nervous?"

Penny considered lying but realized that would only hurt her in the long run. "You're a hell of a lot bigger than that plug, and believe me, just taking that in was a challenge."

He reached out and pulled her into his embrace and she rested her head on his chest. "Tonight, we're just going to play with the plug."

She lifted her head. "But you said—"

"I know what I said. But if that scares you, then it's off the table. These lessons are for you, remember?"

She considered that, hating the way he continued to refer to what they were doing as lessons, even though there was no denying that's exactly what they were.

Because at the end of every "lesson," he got dressed and left, never once spending the night again. No more near misses like the first time, when he fell asleep with her initially, only to cut and run in the middle of the night.

At least he'd honored her request by not offering her lame excuses or lies.

Nope.

Instead, they'd lay together for a few minutes, catch their breath, and then he'd offer the dreaded, "I should head home" line. That was it. And because she was her, she always said, "Okay. Good night," as she walked him to the door without requesting more.

Longing for more from Gage was a one-way ticket to Broken Heartsville.

"Okay," she said stupidly, aware he was waiting for an answer. She was drifting back into that bad habit of getting lost in her own head.

He studied her face a moment longer, looking at her in that way that sometimes had her worrying that he could read her mind. Could he tell she was catching feelings for him? Had she somehow let the mask slip?

Her concerns eased when he said, "Get on the bed. Hands and knees."

She quickly assumed the position because it meant he couldn't see her face, couldn't see her struggle to keep her emotions out of what was happening between them.

Gage ran his hand over her bare butt cheek then playfully smacked it. She wiggled her ass, encouraging him to do more. He accepted the dare, smacking her again, harder. She'd never considered herself the type of person to get turned on by a spanking, but she couldn't deny she liked the heat and the...well...the psychology behind it.

It made her feel naughty and wicked and wanton—all sexy words for a very awkward girl. She liked it.

Gage peppered her ass a few more times, though he wasn't hitting her particularly hard. Then he ran his hands over the freshly spanked skin. "So warm," he mused.

She was tempted to go for broke and ask him to turn up the heat—to take her from warm to hot, but she forgot the request the moment something a lot less hot touched her.

Gage had opened the lube, placing some around her anus.

"Breathe, Penny," he reminded her. Something he had to do quite a lot. She'd heard the word *breathtaking* a million times in her life, but with Gage, it wasn't a cliché. It was a problem. He'd touch her, and instinctual things like breathing suddenly became impossible.

She tensed up when the tip of his finger breached the tight hole.

"Don't do that," he said. "Just relax."

"Turn around and let me stick my finger up your ass. Then we'll see how relaxed *you* are."

Gage chuckled. "We'll save that for next time."

She glanced at him over her shoulder. "Seriously? You'd let me do that?"

"I'm not saying it's one of my turn-ons, but if you wanted to explore that way, I'd be game."

She shook her head. "I don't think I'm going to crack the Gage code. Every time I think I'm getting close, you say something that doesn't...fit."

He leaned down and bit her ass cheek.

"Ouch!" she said, though it didn't hurt so much as surprise her.

"Penny."

"Hmmm?"

"Don't stop trying to crack the code."

She didn't know what to make of that request, but it wasn't like he was giving her a lot of time to think about stuff. His finger returned, only this time, it sank two knuckles deep.

She groaned, dropping down from her hands to her elbows, resting her forehead against the mattress as Gage slowly—oh-so slowly—walked her through anal play. She had no idea how much time had passed as he added lube, then another finger, then found a rhythm—not too easy but not too fast—that had her toes curling with pleasure.

When she experimented with the plug on her own, she'd been a bit too reticent in testing her own limits. Gage wasn't giving her that option. He pushed her to, and then beyond, what she thought she could handle.

By the time she felt the tip of the plug against her ass, her arousal was off the charts.

"Please," she whispered, when he simply held the toy there. She thought perhaps he was waiting for permission, but when he failed to move, she realized that wasn't it.

Lifting her head, she looked back at him. First at his face, and then lower.

She wasn't the only one impacted by the eroticism of their play. She'd never seen his cock so erect, so thick and hard.

"Gage?"

"Roll over on your back, Penny. I want to see your face when I slide this in."

Damn. That was hot.

But also, a lot.

Gage never let her hide her feelings about the things they did. It was as if her reactions fueled his own arousal.

She paused...for a second or two too long.

"Do as I say."

She had no idea what it was about those words, but when he said them to her, she was moving before her brain could consider her actions.

Instantly, she twisted on the mattress, lying on her back, her legs outstretched.

He lifted her ankles, resting them on his shoulders, then lost no time taking them right back to where they'd left off. Except this time, he didn't stop just before breaching her tight hole. He pushed the well-lubed toy inside. And he didn't work it in slowly, like she did to herself.

Gage preferred the straight-forward method, pushing it in with one powerful thrust.

She winced slightly when the widest flared point penetrated then released a long sigh when it was fully lodged inside.

"Okay?" he asked.

She nodded. "So okay."

"Good. Because we're not done."

"What do you—"

Gage crawled over her, caging her beneath him, then placed his dick at the opening of her pussy and—

"Wait!" was all she got out before Gage slammed into her soaking-wet pussy with the same relentless, take-no-prisoners thrust he'd used for the plug.

She was stretched beyond full, so she'd expected pain.

What she hadn't expected was the orgasm.

It ripped through her like a tornado, razing everything in its path. Penny arched up, crying out his name along with her entire repertoire of curse words.

"Motherfucker! Goddammit. Holy shit. Gage! *Gage.*"

He didn't move. Not a single muscle. Instead, he remained there, buried inside her, riding out the storm.

When she returned to earth, he was looking down at her with something like...

She didn't know. Wonder? Adoration?

There was one word tugging at her consciousness, but she wouldn't let herself think it. Wouldn't let herself feel it.

Oh, who the fuck was she kidding?

She *felt* it. She felt it with every fiber of her being.

Love.

And for a split second...she thought she'd seen the same emotion reflected in his eyes.

But only for a second.

Because then...it was on like *Donkey Kong*.

Gage began to thrust—deep—driving her to the brink again. The second orgasm was gentler, though it still packed a punch. She lay boneless beneath him, something that didn't escape Gage's notice.

He chuckled then kissed her cheek. "Still with me?"

She shook her head, her eyelids too heavy to lift. "Nope. I'm a goner, no hope for me. Leave me here and save yourself."

"Penny."

It was at that moment—and probably because of the tone in his voice—that she realized he was no longer moving.

She squinted up at him with one eye.

"You're no quitter," he said, dangling that challenge in front of her again. How the hell did this man get her so completely?

"Dammit."

He kissed her again, one of the short, sweet varieties, before saying, "That's my girl."

He tightened his grip on her legs, leaned forward, and then he showed her just how much of a quitter she was *not* as he powered into her.

His fingers found her clit after a few moments, and now—like always—it triggered the bomb. This time, mercifully, Gage exploded as well.

Her gaze remained on his face as he came. She loved to watch it, loved to see how much being with her impacted him. It was the biggest ego boost in the world—the thought that she could put that pleasure/pain look on Gage Russo's face.

He hovered above her for just a moment or two before dropping to the mattress next to her.

She typically lay there beside him for a few minutes, but now that the fireworks had passed, she was ready to put the toy back in the box under her bed. She started to sit up, intent on going to the bathroom, but Gage stopped her with a hand on her upper arm.

"Lay back down. I'll do it."

"That's okay," she said.

Gage—the strong bastard—pushed her to her back, holding her down with his hand around the base of her neck. The touch sparked fresh arousal despite the fact she was more than sated, but she pushed it away.

"I put the plug in. I take it out."

"Is that some sort of moral code you live by?" she joked.

"Always. Now be still."

Gage tugged the toy free slowly, watching her face as he did so, obviously catching every slight wince or expression of "God, that feels good."

"This should be embarrassing," she mused quietly.

Gage shook his head as he pulled the toy completely free, dropping it to the floor by the bed. "Nothing we do is embarrassing, Penny. It's natural, easy, fun. We fit...in bed."

She wasn't sure if she heard or imagined the pause after fit.

She was her own worst enemy, and this was going to end badly for her. If only she had more experience with casual affairs. Or you know, *any* experience.

But she didn't. So Gage wasn't only going to be her tutor in the ways of sex and seduction, he was also going to teach her what a broken heart felt like.

A fact that was driven home when he pushed himself off the bed and reached for his clothes.

It was on the tip of her tongue to ask him to stay.

But the words didn't come. She couldn't let them. She might not be able to stop the inevitable fallout, but she had to at least try to mitigate the disaster.

He bent over the bed to give her a quick goodbye kiss, just as he'd done the past few nights.

"I'll see myself out. You stay there. You look cozy...and well fucked." He tucked her in, brushed a strand of hair off her face, and then he was gone.

Again.

Chapter Fourteen

Gage stood in front of the island in his kitchen, chopping onions and garlic for his tikka masala. It wasn't until he'd finished the task that he realized he was humming and smiling like some unhinged idiot.

All because he'd had the less-than-brilliant idea to invite Penny Beaumont to his apartment for a home-cooked meal.

Who the fuck was he?

He'd never—and Gage meant *never*—invited a woman back to his place, let alone cooked for her. This penthouse apartment was his inner sanctum, his Batcave, his Fortress of Solitude.

The sun had set just a few minutes ago, which meant Philadelphia was beginning to light up below.

He heard her knock and looked at the clock. She was fifteen minutes late, which meant she was arriving exactly when he'd expected her to. He chuckled, washed his hands, then went to open the door.

Penny, who was never without an excuse, immediately launched into hers, by way of greeting him as she walked in.

"Oh my God, Gage. I'm so sorry I'm late. I couldn't find my damn keys and then Luna yakked all over the—Jesus Christ."

Penny stopped just over the threshold and fell silent. He knew his apartment was impressive, with floor-to-ceiling windows that ensured his view was spectacular. He owned the top two floors of a building that overlooked Penn Square.

"This is where you live?"

He took her jacket and felt the irresistible desire to kiss her. But there was a little voice in the back of his head telling him he needed to stop doing that so much. He was pretty much obsessed with her kisses. Time to start dieting—restricting the kisses the same way he would calories.

He would try to reserve the kisses for those times when he was leaving. Always as she lay boneless, replete, sleepy in her double bed while he made a hasty escape.

He tried not to acknowledge the fact that it was getting harder and harder to return to his own bed—alone—each night.

"This is where I live."

She held up two bottles of wine, one white, one red. "Wasn't sure what we were having for dinner, so I just brought both."

Gage took one of the bottles from her. "Come on. I'll give you a tour and we can drop these off in the kitchen." He led her through the bottom floor, which consisted of his living room, eat-in kitchen with a balcony, dining room, home office, and gym. He gestured toward a closed door. "That's the family room, which in my case means gaming room. I'll show you that after dinner, otherwise we'll never eat."

Penny laughed. "Wise decision. Ordinarily, I'd argue, but I can smell whatever it is you're making and my mouth is already watering."

"Chicken tikka masala."

"I've never had that."

"Really?"

"My mom and dad's cooking was pretty basic and unadventurous, the menu the same thing every week."

"The same?"

Penny nodded. "Hamburgers on Friday night, alternating lasagna and spaghetti weeks on Saturdays, big pot of soup on

Sundays. The weekdays were usually easy stuff since both my parents worked. Dad taught late at the community college on Tuesdays, so Mom dubbed that can night. I always had SpaghettiOs with hot dogs."

"Of course you did," Gage said sardonically. "Well, then, I hope you'll like the masala."

"Judging by the smell alone, I'd say it's a safe bet that I will."

"Maybe you should hold off on that proclamation. I have to confess I haven't made this particular recipe in...a very long time."

Since his mother's death.

The recipe was her favorite, one that the two of them had made together time and time again. Gage couldn't begin to understand why he'd decided to make it now, or why he wanted to make it for Penny.

Actually, he knew exactly why. But he was playing a game with himself this week called Denial. And while he'd lost to Penny twice in recent weeks, this was a game he couldn't lose. No matter what. The stakes were too high. Even for him.

He led her upstairs, pointing out his two guest rooms before guiding her into his bedroom. "And this is the master suite."

Her eyes widened as she took in the large space in silence. "That's the biggest bed I've ever seen in my life. Do you know how many cats you could fit on there?"

Gage laughed loudly. He'd suggested once that she would probably sleep more comfortably if she kicked the cats out of the bed. Penny had looked at him like he'd suggested she put them all out on the street to fend for themselves.

He reached out, his resistance in tatters—she was just too fucking adorable—and pulled her into his arms. His original intent had been a hug, but then he decided he wanted a quick kiss. In the end, he grabbed her and held on, wrapping his arms around her waist as he kissed her senseless.

Penny had taken some special pains with her appearance tonight, managing to pull off a perfect blend of new and old versions of herself. She was wearing a muted pale-green blouse, one of too many he'd bought for her at the boutique before realizing he hated her in plain, boring clothing. She'd paired it with a black pencil skirt he'd bought as well, but because it was short and showcased her ass and legs, he didn't mind it at all.

Old Penny shone through in her shoe choice, which was a pair of black high-top Chucks. She'd failed to master the art of walking in heels, though to be honest, he wasn't certain she'd tried again after the night at Enigma.

"I like your shoes," he murmured, his lips still touching hers.

Penny grinned. "I took the El."

"You and your public transportation."

She rolled her eyes. "Forgot I was talking to Richie Rich."

Gage didn't feign offense. He had a lot of money and it showed. In his apartment and in his chosen way of traveling around the city—typically with a driver. He got a lot of work done in the backseat of his SUV.

He kissed her again, and once more, it lingered as his hands found their way to her face. He cupped her cheeks, angling her face just right to deepen the kiss even more.

"Maybe you should have saved *this* room for after dinner too," she whispered after several minutes of playing tongue tag. Penny's enthusiasm for kissing was contagious.

He placed his forehead against hers and forced himself to take several slow breaths. She wasn't wrong. He'd been a minute away from saying to hell with dinner and tossing her onto his bed so they could continue with their... He forced himself to use the word *lessons* in his mind. Maybe if he practiced calling it that enough, he'd start to believe that's what all of this was.

But that wasn't the plan. And he really wanted to stick to his plans for her tonight. He glanced at his bed, aware that Penny hadn't spotted the straps attached to his headboard. He'd tucked them out of sight, under the pillows. He wanted to explore bondage with her, suspecting she'd enjoy the sensation of being held captive, helpless, at his mercy.

But first...sustenance.

"Come on. You can help me finish making dinner." He took her hand, grinning when she groaned and murmured, "Great. More cooking," in a disdainful tone.

When they reached the kitchen, he tossed an apron over her head, reaching around her to tie the strings at the back. Penny leaned in, her hands resting on his chest, letting him know that—like him—she preferred a lot less personal space when they were together.

She looked down and laughed when she read the apron, which said, "I like my butt rubbed and my pork pulled."

"Christmas gift?" she asked.

Gage nodded. "From my brother Conor."

"Well, that's good to know."

He gave her a curious look. "What is?"

"That Conor has a sense of humor. I haven't been around him enough to get a feel for his personality. Matt, on the other hand…"

"Is the poster child for serious workaholic and miserable bastards everywhere," Gage finished.

"Yeah."

Gage turned toward the stove and started making the sauce, while Penny leaned against the counter and watched.

"Matt wasn't always that way, you know. When we were younger, the three of us boys were close, tight knit. Matt was the ringleader, the one who always had a plan. We built tree forts in the backyard, waged hellacious Nerf gun battles that lasted days, built cathedrals out of Legos. He was legit the best big brother ever. Always had ideas for how to fill our days, and they were always epic. He laughed the loudest, ran the fastest, and made every single second fun."

Jesus, Gage thought. Where the hell had that come from?

"Wow. I'd love to meet that guy. What happened to him?"

"Dad was old-school wealth. Thought himself above pretty much everyone in the world, king of all he surveyed, so he was all about grooming the heir to his throne."

"Just the one?"

"Yep. I was the spare, and Conor was in no man's land. Not that either one of us would have traded places with Matt. Dad was a humorless prick and a strict taskmaster. When Matt reached the ripe old age of thirteen, Dad decided it was time for him to stop doing 'kid shit' and grow up. After that, Matt didn't play with us much, and over time...he sort of morphed into my dad's mini-me. Personally, I miss the old Matt."

"I'm sure you do. That couldn't have been easy on you and Conor."

Gage shrugged. "Like I said, things changed after that. I was eleven and Conor was nine. Conor was a bookworm, so he just sort of disappeared into his bedroom, always had his nose in a book."

"And you..." she prompted.

He'd been looking at her, but the conversation had drifted too close to places he didn't travel. Not even in his own thoughts. So he turned back to focus on the food. "I found video games, D&D."

"You played alone? Or...let me guess...you had your own nerd circle back in school, didn't you?"

He shook his head. "No. Not really. I played with my mom." Before Penny could ask any more questions, he reached into a drawer and pulled out a corkscrew, handing it to her with the bottle of red. "Why don't you pour us some wine? I've reached the critical point in the recipe."

He hadn't. He could make this meal with his eyes closed, but he wanted Penny to think he needed to concentrate.

"Wine glasses?" she asked.

He used the wooden spoon he was stirring with to point to a shelf to the left.

She drifted over to grab two glasses, instead running her finger over the spines of the cookbooks on the shelf above. "Is this your mom?"

Gage had been watching her peripherally, and he internally

cursed. He had one picture of his mom displayed in his apartment. Just one...and it wasn't even a big one. Just a snapshot that Conor had taken after Christmas one year with the Polaroid camera he'd had to have, proclaiming it the coolest thing ever. He and his mom had been baking cookies when Conor walked in and yelled, "Say cheese!"

The two of them had looked up, both with big goofy grins on their faces, him with flour in his hair. The picture was starting to fade, which killed Gage. It wasn't like he didn't have a bunch of others, tucked away in an album. It was just...he loved that one.

He'd put the photo in a small frame and tucked it there, overshadowed and practically hidden by his mother's cookbooks. He'd inherited some of Mom's jewelry and artwork, but it was the cookbooks he treasured the most.

Not that he ever used them. Hell, he hadn't opened a single one of them since her death. When he moved in, he'd set them up on that shelf, along with the picture. A pathetic shrine if there ever was one.

"Yeah," he said, turning his attention back to the sauce.

"She's gorgeous," Penny said, picking up the small frame.

Gage felt a ridiculous amount of pride in her comment.

"You look just like her," Penny continued. "Same hair color, same eyes, same smile."

It was true. While his brothers both inherited more physical attributes from their dad, he was the outlier, the one who'd looked just like their mom.

Penny put the frame back down and reached for the Indian cookbook.

Gage felt a weird sense of panic, like he didn't want her to touch it.

"The glasses are right there, next shelf down," he said, too loudly, pointing out the obvious. Penny's hand hovered in midair, her fingers a mere inch from the cookbook. She changed direction and grabbed the glasses.

Gage could practically read the questions lined up in her

mind, but she didn't ask them, which was unlike her. And he wondered why.

What had she seen in his face? Heard in his voice? He was usually better at shielding his emotions.

He dipped out their plates, adding a piece of naan bread to each, then carried them to the kitchen table. The floor-to-ceiling windows by the table afforded them an amazing view of the city at night. Penny sat down, admiring it for a moment before picking up her wineglass. "I can see why you eat here. Though the view from the living room is pretty spectacular too. Should we toast to your mom? For teaching you how to cook?"

He nodded, a lump forming in this throat. "To my mom."

They tapped glasses and took a sip.

"My mom was an artist before she married my dad. She illustrated a couple children's books and was forever working on her own comic book."

Gage had no idea where those words came from. He hadn't talked about Mom in years. Maybe it was because he was eating her favorite dish, the smells in the kitchen right now evoking so many memories.

Or maybe it was because he wanted to talk to Penny about her. She was a good listener, and...he wanted her to know him better. As more than her boss or her gamer friend or her damn sex tutor.

"That's so cool. I can't draw stick figures," she joked.

"She was the one who taught me how to play D&D. She had an incredible imagination, and she was never too busy to play with me and my brothers. Of course, Matt was never around much after Dad got his hooks into him. And Conor always preferred his books to games. Big weirdo. So she and I would play video games together."

Gage was glossing over the details, lying by omission, telling Penny only the parts that he could repeat without pain. Because talking about his mom's darker days would tread too close to a place he couldn't go. Not with her. Not even with himself.

Penny smiled. "You were lucky. My mom is shit at games. I swear to God she drives PacMan into the ghosts within the first thirty seconds every damn time."

"That couldn't have been easy for you," he joked, before continuing his own story. "A lot of times, it was just me and Mom, hunkered down in the family room, fighting asteroids, racing *Mario Karts*, rocking out to *Guitar Hero*. You should have seen her playing 'Devil Went Down to Georgia.' Never missed a note on the expert level."

Penny's eyes widened appropriately. "Shut up. That song was hard as fuck!"

"Tell me about it. I never managed to master it, but my mom was a natural."

"So you don't just look like your mom, you act like her too."

"In some ways," he said hesitantly.

He was saved from having to think too deeply about that when Penny took a bite of the masala, closed her eyes, and groaned. "Holy shit. This is so good."

Gage smiled, pleased she liked it. "Right?"

"If I knew how to make this, I'd cook it every damn day."

Gage dipped his naan in the sauce. "I'll make it for you again sometime." He wanted to kick himself the second the words were out. Or at least until Penny gave him a bright, delighted smile.

She had a great smile.

"Okay. I'm going to hold you to that."

They ate in silence for a moment more, both enjoying the meal.

"So it sort of sounds like your parents were one of those opposites attract kind of couples."

Leave it to Penny to put a romantic spin on it.

He shook his head. "No. They were a mismatch. My mom was very beautiful, and my dad liked beautiful things. He came from money, while Mom's family was dirt poor. He saw her and decided he had to have her. So he wooed her. And my mom, who'd never had anything, had her head turned by the handsome rich boy who lavished her with gifts. Once they got married, the thrill of the chase was gone, and Dad moved on to the next challenge—which in his case was attaining more wealth, acquiring more companies, more real estate, more prestige in the community. At one point, he talked about running for political office. My dad was the type of person who only wanted something until he had it. Then he'd get bored and find something else to chase."

"Couldn't have been a very happy marriage for your mom."

Penny was astute and empathetic. But she was also walking too close to a line he couldn't cross, a conversation he couldn't have, words he'd never say.

"She had me and my brothers," he said dismissively. They continued to eat, the conversation moving on to safer topics. When they were finished, Gage said, "How about we fill these wine glasses and finish the tour? I'll show you the gaming room."

"Sure. That sounds great. But I'd prefer to pick up the tour where we left off."

He frowned, confused. "Where we left off?"

"In your bedroom."

Chapter Fifteen

Penny had wanted to continue the conversation about his parents. There were a million more questions she had about his mom, his dad, about how they died. They'd both clearly passed away young, but the details surrounding their deaths weren't something anyone at work discussed.

It was obvious Gage had adored his mother, loved her deeply, so it stood to reason he would have been devastated by her passing. Could she blame him for not wanting to talk about it? She'd be gutted when her parents died, absolutely gutted, so she'd let the subject drop.

And ordinarily, she'd be all in on gaming, but she wasn't interested in playing tonight.

Tomorrow officially marked the end of the lessons.

The self-flagellation part of her was hoping Gage would want to drop the tutor title and pick up the boyfriend one. It was a dream, and an unlikely one at that, but Penny was nothing if not a wishful thinker.

She'd never been in love before, but there was no denying that was what this was. Gage had warned her not to fall in love with him, and she'd lied, promised she wouldn't. Even though that wasn't something a person could control.

Heartbreak was inevitable at this point, so she might as well ride this train all the way into the station. Gage had taught her about flirting and seduction and sex—and while he didn't realize it, he was also teaching her about the pain associated with unrequited love.

"Bedroom, huh?" he said, reaching his hand out to hers. She took it, rising from the kitchen table. Gage started to lead her out of the kitchen, but she resisted.

"Shouldn't we clean up the dishes?"

Gage shook his head. "No. I want you naked. In my bed. Right now."

"Oh."

"And, Penny?"

"Yeah?"

"I have serious plans for you tonight."

She'd never heard anything more sensually threatening in her life.

Gage led her back upstairs to his bedroom, neither of them saying a word. Their hasty pace basically said it all. They were anxious for the rest of the night—the best of the night—to begin.

As they entered his room, Gage stopped just over the threshold, gently pushing her forward. She turned to face him.

"Strip."

One word. In *that* voice.

Penny instantly bent down to untie the laces before she toed off her Chucks. She'd toyed with the idea of trying the heels again—God knew they went with the outfit better—but the idea of wobbling on those torture devices on the El felt beyond her abilities. Besides, the only part of her outfit Gage had complimented tonight had been the shoes, so she was glad she'd chosen comfort over fashion.

She reached down, hopping on one foot—an awkward process, given her tight skirt—to draw off her socks. She caught a lightning-flash grin on Gage's face when he saw her brightly colored socks covered with frolicking kittens. She hadn't been too discerning about sock choice since they were completely hidden in the high-top sneakers.

Gage reached out to stop her after she'd pulled off the socks. He gripped her upper arms, drawing her attention.

"Sexy, Penny."

She recalled him saying those same words on the dance floor. Sexy, not silly. Now, like then, it was easier said than done. Because attempting to be sexy felt silly to her, like she was a little girl trying on her mom's bra and filling it with tissues.

Her expression must have given away her feelings, because Gage didn't release her.

"There's something you need to figure out, Penny. Something you need to understand and feel all the way down to the depths of your soul."

"What's that?" she whispered.

"You are beautiful...so *incredibly* beautiful."

"Gage," she started, blinking a couple times to bat back some pesky tears.

"As soon as you accept that, you'll know your worth, and you'll project it to the world. Nothing will stop you then. Not even yourself."

Now, as always, Gage gave her a few moments to let his lesson sink in. And sink in it did.

Confidence had never been an issue for her at work. She knew her shit when it came to computers, cybersecurity, programming. So much so, she could almost be described as cocky at times. She had no trouble fighting for higher pay or going for promotions because she knew she could do the job and do it well.

The same didn't hold true when it came to her personal life. Penny had filled out at least a million of those online dating profiles over the years, but she'd never—not once—managed to click the button to upload the thing. The same confidence she had when it came to her career didn't exist when it came to herself.

But in that moment, with Gage's words...she realized she'd never needed an external makeover.

Well, okay, her hairstyles had sucked, and the glasses *were* kind of big and ugly. And some—just some—of her clothes had bordered on too tatty to wear in public.

But she understood now that all the surface changes in the world weren't going to help her achieve her goal if she didn't see herself as beautiful, as worthy of attention and love.

"You're a really good teacher," she said after several minutes, aware her tone was thick with unshed tears.

And because he was Gage, the very definition of confidence, he gave her a cocky grin and said, "I know."

Then he released her, took a couple steps back, lifted his hand, and repeated his original request. "Strip."

This time, Penny didn't attempt to rush, didn't seek to shed her clothes in a mad dash. Instead, she reached to the side of her skirt and pulled the zipper tab down slowly, her gaze locked with Gage's.

The expression "fake it 'til you make it" drifted through her mind. Because while Gage had said he saw her as beautiful, it was going to take her some time to truly believe that all the way to the depths of her soul, as he requested. So she let the admiration, the naked desire in his eyes, guide her through her sexy striptease. She pulled her confidence from *him*. Something he was making easy because, damn...no one had ever looked at her the way Gage was right now.

Once she'd lowered the zip, she shimmied the tight skirt over her hips, leaving her boy-cut panties on. They weren't as sexy as a thong, but Penny had spent a lifetime pulling wedgies out because they were freaking uncomfortable. She would never understand women who willingly embraced the concept of flossing their ass all day long.

Gage's gaze lowered, and she realized she'd probably done this striptease in the wrong order. Her blouse hung low enough that

—apart from her upper thighs and brief glimpses of her panties— she'd revealed nothing yet.

She lifted her fingers to the first button on her blouse. She'd left one more unbuttoned than she normally would, something she could tell Gage had appreciated. She'd caught his gaze drifting to her cleavage over dinner more than a few times.

Once her blouse was open, she slipped it over her shoulders. She was wearing the balconette bra he'd bought her from the salon because she loved the way it pushed her breasts up, made them look sexy.

She dropped her blouse to the floor then hesitated. Much of her shyness with Gage had faded, but there was something about the way he was looking at her right now that was too...intense. Too much.

While she dithered, wondering what to do next, Gage took the decision out of her hands. He closed the distance between them, running his fingers along the top of her breasts.

"I love your tits," he murmured. "I dream of putting my cock right here," he pushed one finger into her cleavage, "and fucking until I'm coming all over them."

Gage had revealed himself to be quite the king of dirty talk. And Penny was here for it.

She reached out, anxious to get him to the same state of naked as well. Not because she was uncomfortable but because she loved looking at him, touching him. The man was chiseled, hard in all the right places.

Gage brushed her hand away. "Keep your hands by your sides."

She did as he asked. "Fine. Now give me my show," she demanded.

Gage tsked at her command, something she should have anticipated. He didn't take orders in the bedroom. Not that that fact stopped her from trying nightly.

He slipped one strap of her bra over her shoulder then the other.

Without their support holding the delicate lace up, the bra slipped lower, revealing the tops of her areolas. Gage used his pointer finger to draw the bra completely down, the tip of it tickling through the valley between her breasts. The second they were fully revealed, he was there. His head lowered so that he could take the right nipple into his mouth, sucking it hard enough that she saw stars.

She'd teased him last night about his tendency to go left, jokingly accusing him of "playing favorites" when it came to her breasts. He'd promised to correct that oversight in the future.

Well, the future had arrived, and Rightie was mighty happy right now. Gage was a master of foreplay, never in a hurry to move on to the next part. The man could spend hours just playing with her breasts. Penny, on the other hand, was too new to all of it. As such, she found herself constantly pushing for more, desperate for the orgasms she knew were right there within her grasp.

"Gage," she gasped. "Please." She kept trying to rip his shirt off, but he kept catching her hands, pulling them away. After the fifth time, he straightened up and looked at her, his expression sterner than she'd ever seen.

"I can see I'm going to have to save you from yourself before you cross the line and I'm forced to punish you."

Penny's eyes widened. "Whoa. I realize those are all pretty basic words, but when you put them in order like that, they suddenly become seriously hot."

She expected Gage to give her one of his signature grins that always made her feel like a million bucks. She loved being able to make him smile, laugh. Not that he was a miserable guy, but it was just another way he made her feel special...cool, even.

But nope. Not this time.

If anything, Gage's expression grew darker, even more forbidding. He reached around her and unhooked her bra, dropping it to the floor. She expected him to go back in for round two of "booby time," but he didn't even look down, his gaze locked on hers.

Then he reached lower, pushing her panties over her hips.

"Take them off," he demanded.

She did as he asked, curiosity winning out over the sudden flutter of nerves this new, super-alpha Gage had ignited.

Penny stood in front of him, completely naked, in direct contrast to his fully dressed figure. She waited to see what he would do next, demand next.

She didn't have to wait long.

"Go lay down on the bed. In the middle. On your back."

She turned, doing exactly as he asked. His huge bed was so unbelievably comfortable, she groaned. Her mattress was ancient, a hand-me-down from her parents when she got her apartment. Maybe it was time to stop buying a bunch of silly crap on Amazon whenever she got bored or wanted mail—there was nothing like getting a package in the mail—and invest in a new mattress.

She considered that for a moment, wondering if now was a bad time to ask Gage where he'd bought his.

Yeah. Probably a bad time.

Penny felt the bed shift as Gage knelt next to her. Still wearing way too many clothes. Dammit.

He ran his knuckles along her cheek. "You disappeared for a second."

She bit her lower lip, silently cursing herself. "It's hard for me to shut down my brain sometimes," she admitted.

"I've noticed. What were you thinking?"

Shit. She didn't want to tell him. "I was wondering where you got your mattress."

This time, Gage did break character, the stern alpha going soft as he flashed her one of his far-too-sexy grins. It was brief, but beautiful. And then, the Dominator—yeah, that worked—was back. She liked her new nickname for this version of Gage. Reminded her of the Terminator.

"Clearly, I'm going to have to work harder to shut down that active brain of yours."

The devil in her wanted to tell him he was welcome to try, but she held her tongue. Primarily because—before she could lay down the challenge—Gage lifted one of her arms above her head, binding it to his headboard with some strap she hadn't noticed before.

"Oh," she breathed, tugging to test the tightness. It didn't give. Not even a little.

Gage cupped her jaw. "Do you know what a safe word is?"

She nodded.

"Yours is stop, Penny. If I do something you don't like or if you get scared, just tell me to stop and I will."

She crinkled her nose.

"What's wrong?" he asked.

"That a pretty boring safe word. What about ukulele instead?"

Gage shook his head, though there was definitely amusement lingering behind his brown eyes. "Fine. Ukulele *or* stop will work."

She considered that as he bound her other hand. They were tied directly above her head, side by side, rather than spread-eagle style.

She watched as he reached under one of the pillows and pulled out a blindfold. "What other magic tricks do you have hidden in this bed?"

"A magician never reveals his secrets," he said as he placed the blindfold over her eyes, casting her in instant and complete darkness. "Okay?"

"So okay," she whispered.

Without her sense of sight, the others kicked in and she became more aware of every slight shift on the bed as Gage moved. She could tell when he stood up, could hear the soft swooshing sounds of him undressing, each article of clothing hitting the floor.

Then she heard a drawer open and close. She was curious about that. They hadn't used condoms, hadn't even discussed them again since the night he helped her get rid of her pesky virginity.

She jumped slightly when the mattress sank again under his weight.

"Shhh," he soothed.

Penny felt his thigh pressing against her side. He was sitting on the bed, facing her. Without the blindfold, she would have been studying his face, scrutinizing it to gauge his reaction to her appearance, to her body. She would have—most likely—felt slightly self-conscious, even though he'd seen her naked plenty by now.

However, none of that was present at the moment. By taking away her sight, Gage had found a way to lessen her insecurities simply by ramping up her...God...her *everything*. Her arousal. Her anticipation. Even the tiniest inkling of fear. Because she was bound, helpless, at his mercy.

All of her focus was on him, wondering what he was going to do next.

His hand touched her throat, his thumb stroking the side of her neck. Had he noticed her reaction to that grip the other night?

His fingers tightened incrementally, until it became more difficult to draw in air.

He was making her breathless again, but in a much different way this time. Her mouth fell open, but she didn't speak, uncertain if she wanted to ask him to release her or press harder. She wasn't sure she had enough air to make either request.

Gage loosened the hold then drew his fingers along the skin at the base of her neck, still tingling from his rough grip. He was a master at tapping into turn-ons she didn't even know she possessed.

Then, she gasped when she felt the brief burst of heat from his breath on her nipple, just before he sucked it into his mouth. She didn't try to hide her grin, her breathy giggle, and she imagined she could feel his lips tipping up in amusement as well.

"Yes. I'm starting with the left," he said, proving he knew

exactly what she'd found funny. "But don't worry about the right." To punctuate that promise, he pinched the right nipple firmly, squeezing it just to the point of pain, and a little beyond. "This beauty is going to be well taken care of as well."

After that, Penny forgot to think, forgot she was naked, forgot her own damn name, as Gage alternated between sucking, pinching, licking, and biting her nipples. She was fluent at masturbation, but her breasts hadn't ever been part of that. She hadn't thought, hadn't realized, exactly how sensitive, how much of an erogenous zone they were.

She was breathless, her heart thudding so hard, she was certain Gage must have been able to hear it. Worst of all, her pussy was clenching, seeking something—anything—to appease her burning need.

Gage didn't touch her there, his attention wholly focused on her breasts.

"Please. God, Gage, please," she pleaded, not for the first time. Hell, not even for the thousandth time. He didn't acknowledge her cries, didn't pay heed to her begging for more, for relief.

"What—!" Penny's entire body jolted upwards when she felt something much sharper than Gage's teeth squeezing her nipple.

"Clamp," he said. One word, but it packed a punch. "Breathe deeply. You'll get used to it."

She continued to thrash, thinking perhaps she could dislodge the vicious beast. Her nipple was inflamed, burning, and it was on the tip of her tongue to say stop or…Jesus, what the fuck was the other word?

Gage cupped her face, his lips tickling her ear as he whispered, "Breathe."

She stilled. Then did as he said.

And it worked. The flames she'd feared would turn her to ash shifted downwards, burning a no-longer-painful path from her breasts to her pussy.

"I need you," she whispered.

"I know. But I promised to treat both your gorgeous tits the same."

She didn't have time to react to that before he put the second clamp on. She expected to have to ride out more pain, more agony, but her body was over that.

"God!" she cried out. Her voice was hoarse. She no longer sounded like herself.

And still Gage refused to give way.

She felt his tongue, sliding its way through the valley between her breasts. Her D-cup tits had never felt so freaking huge, so swollen and sensitive. Just the slow, delicate touch of his tongue had her hips lifting from the bed, searching, demanding.

Gage continued his leisurely trip down her body, teasing her belly button for just a second before gliding lower.

He was finally—FINALLY—going to pay attention to her most needy part, and suddenly she didn't want it.

Gage was a sadistic bastard. While him going down on her when she was in a normal state of mind would have been incredible, right now, it felt more like torture.

"Please! I can't take anymore. Just fuck me. Just. Fuck. Me!"

Gage, damn him, continued along his merry way, as if she hadn't spoken at all.

"I'm going to kill you the second you untie my hands."

He chuckled but didn't change course.

The tip of his tongue wiggled against her clit. It wasn't enough. It was nowhere near enough.

He teased her that way for a few minutes, while she called him every nasty name in the dictionary, starting with the A's—asshole —and working down to the T's—twat.

She was trying to come up with U through Z when Gage took mercy on her and slammed two fingers inside her pussy.

She was wet enough to float a boat, but his fingers were thick and rough and fucking perfect.

Her back arched, and she screamed as she came so hard, she feared she'd broken a few bones.

Gage's fingers never stopped moving, slamming in and out,

drawing the orgasm out for hours, days.

Penny moaned when it finally started to wane, but Gage wasn't finished.

Shit. He hadn't even started.

She wanted to tell him she couldn't take any more. Her body was on system overload.

Stop.

The word was right there, on the tip of her tongue, but he spoke first.

"Take a deep breath and hold it."

She frowned, but did as he said, the air she'd just sucked in exploding out of her as he removed both clamps at the same time.

"Motherfucker!" she cried out. "That *hurts.*"

But it only lasted for a split second. Because Gage was there, his mouth shifting back and forth from one nipple to the other, softly stroking away the pain with his tongue, with his gentle kisses.

She wasn't sure how something could feel brutal and blissful at practically the same time, but those were the only words she could find to describe the powerful feelings thudding through her body like a stampede of horses.

She blinked a few times when Gage pulled the blindfold off. The room wasn't particularly bright, the only light provided by the city nightscape outside, but it still took her a second to adjust.

When she did, she saw Gage's gorgeous face as he reached higher, releasing one arm and then the other.

"I'd intended to keep you bound, but I want your hands on me," he murmured.

She wanted the same. She lifted them to his shoulders, using her grip to pull him down on top of her.

He kissed her, even as he moved into position, his knees pressing her legs apart, his cock brushing against her stomach before she reached between them to guide him to the place she'd sworn was too sensitive for more.

Gage broke the kiss, his gaze intent, serious.

"What are you thinking about?" he asked.

"You," she answered. "Just you."

He gave her a quick kiss. "Good answer."

Gage pushed inside in one continuous thrust. There was no seesawing in and out, no giving her time to adjust. He was thick and hard, and every time with him felt like the first time as her body struggled to take him in.

Once he was buried to the hilt, he captured her gaze once more. "Hold on," was all he said, before he began fucking her in earnest.

She met him blow for blow, lifting her ass, wrapping her legs around his waist, tilting her hips until he found that place inside that felt like her own personal internal roller coaster—thrilling, intense, exciting, even scary.

He hit her G-spot over and over and she came again, loudly.

Gage went over the cliff with her—thank God, because she really couldn't take another orgasm without splintering into a million tiny pieces.

As their climaxes eased, he settled over her, caging her beneath him, his forearms resting next to her head on the pillow. He kissed her softly this time, his lips worshipping hers in a way that was so sweet, almost innocent, it was in direct opposition to the way he'd just ravaged her body.

She wasn't sure how long he kissed her before he pushed away, lying down next to her on the bed.

Penny lay there, trying to will some strength back into her body. Gage had a way of fucking her until she felt like she was made of nothing more than Jell-O every single time they were together.

It took several minutes, but eventually she managed to push herself to a seated position on the side of the mattress.

"What are you doing?"

"Getting dressed," she said.

"Why?"

Penny glanced over her shoulder at him. Gage was a gorgeous

man, whether in a suit or jeans and a sweatshirt. But when he was naked like this, his hair messed up from her hands gripping it, he was absolutely breathtaking.

"If I stay here much longer, I'll fall asleep," she said as a way of trying to explain. Gage had never spent the entire night at her place, so she assumed he wouldn't want her staying at his.

"Do you need to go home? To the cats or something?"

She shook her head. "No. I fed them before I came. They're fine until tomorrow."

"Then come here."

Penny hesitated, but Gage wasn't having it. He reached out, gripping her around the waist to pull her back down on the bed. He was a strong man, so it was fairly easy for him to put her in the exact position he wanted, which in this case was her back to his chest as he spooned her.

"Stay with me tonight."

"I have work tomorrow." Penny literally wanted to smack herself in the head. Why was she arguing? This was exactly where she wanted to be.

"And I'm your boss. We'll shower together here, then I'll drive you by your place to put on some clean clothes for work. I'll take you to the office tomorrow."

"If you're sure." She wasn't certain how she knew, but there was a part of her that understood the invitation to sleep over was a big deal.

Which meant Big Dreamer Penny kicked Realist Penny to the curb, spinning cartwheels inside her head as she settled back in the bed next to him.

Then she landed the mother of all round-offs when Gage twisted her until she faced him, pulling her closer and wrapping his arm around her shoulders, so that she could use his chest as a pillow.

The last leg of the journey was complete.

Penny had fallen completely and totally head over heels in love for the very first time.

Chapter Sixteen

"We've got a problem."

Gage looked up as Matt walked—stomped, was probably more accurate—into his office.

"We really need to work on your greetings. Because that one's not only old and tired, but it's also inaccurate. Every time you say *we* have a problem, what you really mean is *I* have a problem."

"Or you *are* my problem," Matt corrected.

"What did I do this time?" Gage asked, hoping his brother, who seemed too damned omniscient, hadn't found out about his...affair with Penny. Gage hated the word *affair* the second he thought it, but he was incapable of giving it any other name.

"I told you to take care of the Penny Beaumont issue weeks ago."

It took him a second to realize his brother was talking about the headhunters, and he hadn't come here to bitch about the sex lessons. Gage scowled. "And I did."

"Is that so? I just got back from a late lunch with John Kelly."

John was as close to a friend as Matt came, the two men rooming together in college. In anyone else's world, John would be the equivalent to the buddy a guy met up with every six months or so for a golf outing, even though any common bond between the two had long since died and all they had now was a brief shared history. In John's case, Matt wouldn't spare the four hours for a golf match, so he had to settle for the occasional lunch.

Gage figured the only reason John was even still a blip on his brother's radar was because the two men were both successful businessmen with common interests—and for some strange reason, John refused to give up on the friendship.

"I fail to see a connection between John Kelly and Penny Beaumont." Gage feigned disinterest, not willing to let his mask slip even a millimeter lest Matt sniff out something he shouldn't.

Matt was clearly pissed, because rather than sit in the chair across from Gage's desk, he placed his hands flat on the surface and leaned forward. "John's expanding his IT department. He was thrilled to get Penny's resume a couple weeks ago. He asked me for a damn reference!"

"A couple weeks ago?" Gage repeated. "That's not possible." Two weeks ago, he'd agreed to fulfill the wager. Hell, he'd taken her virginity.

"Did you or did you not convince Penny to remain with Russo Enterprises?"

"I did. She agreed to wait until her upcoming annual review, at which point we planned to discuss her salary, the benefits package, and the possibility for advancement within the company."

Matt scowled. "Well, clearly you weren't convincing enough if she's sending out her resume. It's one thing for headhunters to be gunning for her. Another for her to put out her own feelers."

There was no way Penny would do that.

Was there?

"Are you sure John had the right name?"

Matt crossed his arms. "Oh yeah, I'm sure he just pulled the name 'Penny Beaumont' out of his ass. Her reputation precedes her. He knows she'd be the feather in any company's IT cap. I think he was trying to subtly brag that she was interested in *his* company over mine."

"Ours," Gage corrected. "And I can't believe she'd send her resume out after agreeing to wait."

Matt loomed even closer. "Fix this. *Now*. Before John Kelly or Frost Incorporated or some other fucking company swoops in and steals her."

Gage reached for his phone, the idea that Penny would betray him—no, the company—finally sinking in. His temper piqued.

"Penny Beaumont," she said when she answered, in that tone that was equal parts sweet and seductress.

"I need to see you in my office. Now," Gage stressed.

He could hear the eye-roll in her voice. "Printer again?"

"Dammit, Penny. Hurry up," he said, slamming the phone down.

Matt had been the picture of fury when he'd stormed into Gage's office...but his expression was different now.

"What?" Gage asked hotly, furious that Penny would do this, especially after everything they'd done together.

"When did you start calling her Penny?"

Gage frowned. "What?"

"She's worked here for six years and never—not once—have you ever called her anything other than Beaumont."

Fucking astute bastard. If Gage's blood wasn't boiling over Penny's duplicitousness, perhaps he would have found a way to answer. As it was...he couldn't think of a goddamn thing to say.

"You danced with her at Enigma," Matt mused, speaking to himself more than Gage. It felt like his brother was starting to put together pieces better left far, far apart.

"So what?"

"Why *were* you at Enigma? Alone? What did you mean when you said you lost a bet?"

Gage didn't respond, so Matt forged on.

"She's been dressing differently...wearing contacts, makeup, leaving her hair down."

"Is there a point to this?" Gage asked, aware he was perilously close to losing his shit. With Matt. With Penny. With the whole fucking world.

"Just an observation. Would her change in appearance have anything to do with the two of you spending time in your new gaming room together after hours?"

"Of course not. Penny is helping me start an e-sports team. I told you that. Besides, who..."

Gage didn't even have to finish asking the question. Connie had obviously reported back to Matt about him and Penny.

"You said no more office hookups." Matt's comment didn't sound as angry or annoyed as Gage would have expected.

Before Gage could respond, there was a knock at the door. Matt gestured for Gage to remain seated as he walked over to open it.

Matt's gaze missed nothing as Penny stood at the threshold. "Ah, Ms. Beaumont. So... *You're* back," he observed, taking in Penny's outfit.

True to his word, Gage had pulled Penny into the shower with him this morning, the two engaging in a very steamy, very wet quickie before they drove by her place for work clothes. Penny had pulled one of the boring ensembles he'd bought for her out of the closet, and Gage had finally had enough. He'd rummaged through her clothing until he came up with what she was currently wearing, one of her faded T-shirts from Goodwill—that said Run, Forrest, Run, in honor of her cat—and an extremely distressed, oversized pair of bib overalls.

For the first time in weeks, she looked like his Penny, and he'd fucking loved it when they'd arrived at the office.

Right now, he was struggling to find any of those fond feelings.

She was trying to leave him...er, Russo Enterprises.

"Back?" Penny asked, flummoxed by Matt's comment.

"Never mind. Just an observation. I was on my way out."

"Oh. Okay, well, have a great day, Mr. Russo."

Matt looked at her for a long moment, his brow creased. Then his gaze slid to Gage—and he realized his brother had completed the puzzle, snapped the last piece into place, seeing the big picture that Gage refused to acknowledge.

"I think perhaps you should call me Matt from now on."

Penny, clearly taken aback, stumbled for a moment. "Um, uh, yeah. You can call me Penny," she hastily added.

Matt nodded just once, the humorless bastard sending him a knowing smirk before turning to leave.

Penny walked in and shut the door, leaning against it. "Even when he's saying nice things, he's pretty fucking terrifying."

"You should have met my father," Gage muttered.

"Given the things you've said about him, I'm not sure I would have wanted to."

"Do you know how my father died?" Gage didn't have a clue where that question had come from.

Penny shook her head.

"He had a heart attack. While fucking one in a long line of mistresses he'd acquired after my mother passed away."

Penny didn't reply as she digested that information. Then, all she said was, "Oh."

Gage gave her a humorless grin that probably came off as vicious, given the way her eyes widened. "Don't you want to make some comment about the fruit not falling far from the tree? Call me a chip off the old block? It's nothing I haven't heard before."

Penny frowned. "I don't think you're *anything* like your dad."

Gage couldn't explain why those words felt like balm on a sunburn. He'd heard the dad comparison too many times from too many of his father's colleagues and cronies. It was typically accompanied by a slap on the back and nudge-nudge-wink-wink kind of smile that said they admired his love 'em and leave 'em playboy lifestyle.

The first time he'd heard the comparison, he'd had to excuse himself to the restroom, so much bile clogging his throat, he'd thought he was going to be sick.

Gage's feelings for his father growing up had been a blend of fear and grudging respect. After his mother's death, those two things morphed into a deep-seated hatred that had only continued to grow and fester, regardless of the years that had passed.

Not because he blamed his father for her death. Gage knew where that blame lie.

No. It was because his father hadn't mourned.

Two nights after her funeral, Dad had come home with another woman, introduced her to him and his brothers like it was just any other Tuesday night, then proceeded to take her upstairs to the bed he'd shared with Mom.

"Gage," Penny said, and he was aware he'd let too many of his emotions show on his face. Then he recalled why he'd asked her to come up here. She was trying to leave...and it didn't matter if it was the company or him, it was a betrayal that went bone deep.

"How did your mom—"

"Lock the door," he demanded, refusing to let her ask that question. She didn't have a right to that story. She'd gone behind his back, sent out her resume. Every syllable he spoke simmered with the rage he felt.

Penny stared at him for a full minute, like she was trying to decide if she'd be smarter to do as he said or run like the hounds of hell were nipping at her heels. If he weren't in the middle of a Mt. Vesuvius-style eruption, he might have admired her sense of self-preservation.

As it was...

"Do as I say."

Penny snicked the lock in place on the door, but she didn't venture any farther into the room.

"Come here."

"I'm not sure that's a wise move. You're in a weird mood."

"You're right. I am. That's why it would be smart of you to do. As. I. Say."

She walked to him slowly—too slowly. When she was within arm's reach, he grabbed her, pulling her against him, kissing her hard…so hard, her lips were smashed against her teeth. He didn't relent, didn't stop his rough assault, aware his actions were likely to leave a bruise.

He half expected her to try to shove him away, but when had Penny ever done anything normal?

Nope. She gripped his hair and returned the kiss tenfold.

Gage was the one to break the union after a couple of minutes, taking one small step away, the two of them breathing rapidly.

He unfastened one side of the overalls, flipping the strap over her shoulder. Then he did the same with the other. The pants were baggy enough that without the support of the straps, they slid to the floor in a heap.

"Step out of them."

She did as he asked, toeing off her Chucks as she did so. "Gage —" she started, but he shook his head.

"No more talking. There's only one word you're allowed to use and it's your safe word. If you don't want to say it, then you don't speak."

"I…" She paused when he raised one eyebrow, daring her to go against what he'd just said.

She fell silent, biting her lower lip, though he didn't think that action was based on nerves so much as a way to keep quiet. Silence didn't come naturally to Penny, now that they'd broken through her shyness around him. And especially not in the past couple weeks, as they'd grown closer. If the woman had a thought, she usually found a way to say it.

He pulled her T-shirt over her head.

Her eyes never left his face, and he could almost imagine her trying to look deeper, as if she could see through his skin and straight to his soul. He had to admit that if anyone could pull off that magic trick, it would be her.

But she was trying to leave him.

His jaw tightened, his teeth clenched.

"Bend over the desk."

She hesitated again.

Gage gripped her upper arm and moved her into the position he wanted. If he'd had to use serious force to do so, he would have pulled back, would have let her go, but Penny didn't fight him.

Once she was facedown, she lifted her head, started to look over her shoulder.

"Eyes forward."

She obeyed. And remained quiet.

Gage slid his fingers beneath the elastic of her practical boy-cut panties, sliding them over her ass and halfway down her thighs. He didn't push them off completely, leaving them where they were so Penny would feel the constriction around her legs, feel trapped.

He took several deep breaths, trying to cool off. He'd never touched a woman in anger, and he'd be damned if he'd start with Penny.

But she had to learn, had to understand that he wasn't going to just let her walk away without a word. The fact she'd sent that resume out, after reassuring him she didn't want to leave the company, hurt more than he cared to admit.

He lightly stroked her bare ass. He loved her ass.

He indulged in just one glancing touch, took another steadying breath, then he lifted his hand and slammed it down hard. Penny's pale cheek pinkened instantly.

She jerked, but her lack of cry or attempt to rise told him she'd been expecting the spanking.

His hand rose and fell at least ten times, until her ass was dark red, hot to the touch.

Penny didn't seek to escape him, and more importantly, she didn't say her safe word.

What she did was so much more detrimental to his state of mind.

She moaned in pleasure then lifted on her toes in order to meet each downswing.

He'd forbidden her to speak, something he was regretting

now. Penny never held back when they were together, never failed to tell him with actions—and words—how much she loved what they were doing. He missed that now.

"More?" he asked.

She nodded.

Gage bent over her body, caging her beneath him on the hard, flat surface. "Tell me what you want. In words."

"You. Hard and fast. And, Gage..." she added.

"Hmmm?" He placed a kiss on her shoulder, unable to help himself despite the fact he'd meant this to be a punishment for her deceit.

"Make it hurt," she finished in a whisper.

He closed his eyes briefly, praying for strength, for control, for some answer from the gods about what the hell he was supposed to do now. Because he was fucked. Royally.

He'd done the one thing he'd sworn never to do.

He'd fallen in love.

And she was trying to leave him.

Gage pushed himself upright, unzipped his pants, and withdrew his cock. It was thick and throbbing.

Fuck control.

And fuck *her*.

How could she do this to him?

He lined up the head of his dick and slammed in.

Penny grunted, the sound driving him on rather than giving him pause.

He thrust in with more force, more speed than he'd ever dared. Penny's groans turned to cries, louder—too loud. He covered her mouth with his hand as he continued to fuck her.

He sensed her trying to move, trying to find purchase, but he refused to relinquish a bit of the power. With his hand still over her mouth, he lifted her up until her back was pressed to his chest, holding her in place there as he pounded even harder. He didn't offer her the choice to do anything more than take everything he was giving.

Reaching around with his free hand, he pinched her clit, and Penny jerked roughly, coming hard, her pussy clenching him so tightly, he saw stars.

He didn't stop. He couldn't.

He fucked her through that orgasm, and then the next—a quicker burst, but given the way her body trembled, he'd venture it was just as potent.

And still he moved, slammed, beat a rough rhythm inside her pussy until she came again, her third orgasm defeating him, dragging him down into the deep abyss as well. She milked every drop of come from his body as she fell forward onto the desk, unable to hold herself up.

He'd followed her down, his dick going soft, still buried inside her, as he pulled in gasping breaths of air like a thoroughbred who'd just run the Kentucky Derby.

Gage didn't realize he was still covering her mouth until he felt her hand on his wrist, pulling it away.

Shit. He'd taken away her ability to say her safe word.

But even that knowledge, and the guilt that accompanied it, didn't overshadow what had driven him to this place.

"You're not leaving," he said huskily, his throat constricted, tight.

Penny lay still, fighting to find her own breath. "Okay," she said. "But Rich and Toby are going to wonder where I went."

"I mean Russo Enterprises."

Her response this time came slower, and while he could only see the side of her face, he didn't miss her confusion.

"What?"

Gage used the last dregs of strength remaining to push himself upright.

Penny, now freed from the confines of his body, did the same, rising on unsteady legs.

He sat in his office chair then pulled her down on his lap.

"I know I lost the bet, but you agreed to wait until your annual review so we could renegotiate your contract."

"Right," Penny said, as if he were a few eggs short of a dozen.

Her continued denial had his temper sparking once more. "Goddammit, Penny! I know about Kelly Corporation."

"I don't know what you mean."

"You're trying to tell me you didn't send your resume to Kelly Corporation two weeks ago? After the makeover, after everything we've done?"

"No. I told you, Gage. I love working here. You said I could be co-captain of the e-sports team. I'm not even sure what Kelly Corporation *does*. I mean...I've heard of them, but..." She shrugged.

One look at Penny's face, and he knew...whatever was going on with the resume and Kelly Corporation, she didn't have a damn thing to do with it. She didn't lie. It simply wasn't in her.

"Then how..." Gage mused aloud. "How the hell did they get your resume?"

And then, a light went on.

"*Shit.*"

"What?" Penny asked.

Gage didn't reply as he started to put one plus one together.

Connie had been at Enigma, had seen him on the dance floor with Penny. She'd acted as if she hadn't recognized her, but what if she had? Had she seen Gage intercept Penny at the door, seen the two of them leaving together? If Matt had been aware of the headhunters, of the Frost offer, then chances were good, Connie had caught wind as well. Had she decided to keep the offers coming in until Penny got one she couldn't refuse?

"I'm firing Connie," he muttered darkly.

Penny frowned. "From HR? You think she..." Penny shook her head. "Why the hell would she send my resume to another company?"

"She seems to have set her sights on me."

"Oh," Penny said. "I still don't get it."

"She saw us together at Enigma. And again last week in the elevator."

"Yeah, but I'm...not...I..." Penny stopped talking, a sudden sadness flooding her face—and that was when Gage discovered another truth.

A worse truth.

However, before the weight of that realization crashed in, Penny threw him off-kilter.

"Wait. Was that a punishment fuck? You thought I was sneaking around behind your back looking for a job, so you brought me up here to punish me?"

Gage rubbed the back of his neck. That was exactly what he'd done. What the fuck was wrong with him? He'd thought she was trying to leave him, and he'd totally lost his shit. He owed her one hell of an apology. And even that might not be enough. He'd fucked her in anger, covered her mouth, taken away her ability to say her safe word.

"Listen, Penny—"

She interrupted him. "Don't get me wrong. It was hot as fuck. The kind of sex that makes a girl want to be really, really naughty. You know what I mean?"

He groaned. She was literally going to be the death of him. She never responded the way he expected. Any other woman would be pissed as shit at him. But not Penny.

Instead, he could almost see the wheels in her brain turning as she tried to figure out how she could make him angry enough again to score an encore.

He chuckled, though the pressure on his chest was still there. "You don't have to be bad. If you want me to spank your ass again, just ask."

"Tonight?"

"You want me to spank you again tonight? Isn't your ass already sore?"

She shrugged. "It's tonight or never. Today's the last day."

Gage fought hard to school his expression. If he was a smart man, he'd tell her what they'd just done was the last lesson. He needed to walk away from this—from her—sooner rather than later.

Because it wasn't just his heart that was engaged.

That was the harder truth to swallow.

If it was just him getting hurt at the end of this, he'd take it, accept it as his punishment, his fault. But it was abundantly clear he wasn't the only one who'd fallen.

He'd told her—warned her—not to fall in love with him.

"Penny," he said softly.

She cupped his cheek, forcing him to look at her. To look at her and truly see what he'd been avoiding.

Love.

Penny was the braver soul, he admitted to himself. Not only had she recognized her feelings for him, but now he could see she'd already accepted the unavoidable fallout.

This beautiful, courageous, foolish woman.

"Please, Gage," she whispered. "Just one more night. That's all I'm asking for."

He swallowed hard then said, "One more night."

Chapter Seventeen

Penny took a moment to compose herself when she heard the knock on her door. After that interlude in Gage's office this afternoon, she'd returned to her desk, where she'd spent the last two hours of work staring at her computer screen and accomplishing nothing.

Fortunately, neither Toby nor Rich seemed to have noticed her distraction, her complete lack of productivity. Thank God it was the weekend.

She'd steal this night with Gage, and then...Optimistic Penny hoped he'd ask for more time with her. But Realistic Penny could be proven correct once again when Gage walked away from her without a backward glance.

Come tomorrow, she would either be the happiest girl on the planet or halfway through a gallon of chocolate chip ice cream, crying her heart out.

The worst part was...she didn't have a clue which outcome was looming. There were times when she thought Gage had feelings for her, when it seemed like perhaps the two of them were on the same page.

But there were just as many times when he'd refer to their

time together as just payoff on their bet, or furthering her education, or he'd quite simply close down completely.

She'd started to ask him how his mother died, and he'd completely cut her off. He only gave her glimpses of his past, of his relationship with his parents and brothers, which warned her that she'd built this thing between them into something it wasn't. He didn't want to confide his deepest secrets in her because they weren't a couple. Hell, up until a few months ago, they hadn't even been friends.

Tonight was it. If she could just keep saying that to herself, maybe she could make herself believe it.

Taking a deep breath, she shook off her fears and opened the door.

"Hey," she said, forcing a cheerful, not-worried, nothing-to-see-here smile. Then she added, "Oh, thank God. You just got a pizza. I was afraid you were going to make me cook again."

Gage breezed by her, heading straight to the kitchen and shaking his head. "You know, you're going to have to add 'can cook' to the list of attributes you have in mind for this future boyfriend of yours."

Future boyfriend.

Yep. She made a mental note to add chocolate chip ice cream to her very short grocery list for the week. It would come right after wine, cat food, and Lucky Charms.

"Oh, believe me. It's on there." She followed him to the kitchen, her ovaries joining the "fluttery" party when Gage bent down to pick up Hermione, cradling her in his arms like a baby, rubbing her stomach while she purred loud enough to beat the band.

"How are you, sweet thing?" he murmured as he petted her.

Great, Penny thought. *I'm now jealous of my cat.*

Forrest meowed loudly while weaving his way around Gage's ankles.

"I'm starting to think my cats like you more than me."

Gage gave her a wink. "I've got a way with pussies."

She groaned. "Set you up for that one, didn't I?"

"Yep." He put Hermione back down on the floor and flipped the lid on the pizza. "Got a large supreme, but remembered you picked the black olives off last time, so..." He did a voila gesture, and she realized he'd ordered the pizza without the olives.

For her.

And she hadn't even mentioned them last time, just quietly picked them off.

And he'd noticed.

Unable to stop herself, she closed the distance between them, lifting up on tiptoe to give him a kiss on the cheek for being so thoughtful.

Gage accepted her quick kiss, but when she started to retreat, he wrapped his arms around her waist and gave her a kiss that was a lot less sweet. Hell, it was practically pornographic. He pushed her against the counter more firmly, pressing their bodies together so that she could feel his erection against her stomach. Had he shown up in that state? Because damn, she loved the idea of that.

As they kissed, her fingers worked free the knot in his tie. He must have left his jacket in the car because he'd arrived without it. She slipped the tie free with one long, slow slide as Gage's lips left hers, burning a path along the side of her face to her neck.

"You smell so good," he murmured.

"Pina colada body wash," she replied. She'd taken a shower when she'd first gotten home from work because she and Gage had worked up a bit of a sweat in his office this afternoon. After her "punishment sex," they'd cuddled on his chair, making out until she'd found the strength to dress and return to her desk. Toby had given her a brief, curious look when she'd returned, thanks, no doubt, to the fact she was still flushed and sweaty.

So far, neither Toby nor Rich seemed to suspect anything between her and Gage, but she wasn't sure if that was because they were completely unobservant when it came to physical attraction, or if the idea of her with Gage was so out of the realm of reality, it never even occurred to them.

Penny started to work her way down the buttons of Gage's shirt, hating the way it hid his super-sexy chest. She could spend hours looking at him, if it wouldn't make her seem like a total freak. Once she hit the last button, she tugged the shirttails free of his dress pants, loving how hot he looked with his shirt hanging open.

Gage broke the kiss, grinning when her gaze drifted lower. She ran her hands over his hard pecs and abs. He let her look for just a moment or two before mumbling, "Tit for tat."

He pulled her T-shirt over her head in one quick swish, taking his own visual tour. She was more curvy than built, but her "extra fluff" didn't seem to bother him at all. More than that, he looked at her as if she was some priceless work of art.

They kissed again. It was leisurely, familiar. Because Penny knew this was most likely her last night with Gage, she refused to rush to the next part. She was going to steal every single second with him that she could.

"What about the pizza?" she whispered against his lips when the kisses lingered for several more minutes.

"I like cold pizza.

She smiled. "So do I."

Gage turned and closed the lid then reached for her hand.

They'd only just left the kitchen when there was a knock on the door.

"Are you expecting someone?"

She shook her head. "No." Walking to the door, she peered through the peephole. "It's Tony."

"Moretti?" Gage said darkly.

She nodded then quickly walked to the kitchen to grab her shirt and put it back on. "Wait in here?" she asked Gage, who had followed her. "I'll see what he needs. Won't take a minute."

Gage crossed his arms but didn't say anything. She couldn't tell if his sudden anger was based on the lifelong feud between the Morettis and the Russos or if—please—he was jealous.

She left him in the kitchen then went to open the door.

"Tony. Hi. I wasn't expecting you."

Tony smiled and lifted the dish in his hand. "Aunt Berta made lasagna today. She made too much, of course, so she put together an extra one for you. I had to drop some stuff off at a worksite on this side of town, so I offered to bring it by."

Penny took the dish with a smile. "That's so sweet of her...and you. How's her wrist?"

"Much better. It was just a sprain." He grinned. "She knows lasagna is your fav—"

Tony abruptly stopped talking, his gaze darting over her shoulder.

She didn't have to turn to know that Gage hadn't stayed in the kitchen.

Shit.

She glanced over her shoulder and realized it was even worse than that. Gage hadn't bothered to button his shirt either. Instead, he leaned casually against the doorjamb to the kitchen, as if the fact he was half dressed in her house was the most natural thing in the world.

How the hell was she supposed to explain this? He wasn't her boyfriend. What they were doing wasn't even technically dating.

"Tony," Gage said, his genial tone in complete contrast to his previous one.

"Russo," Tony said coldly, his gaze drifting from Gage back to her. She didn't need a mirror to know she was blushing like a fool. "Penny," he said, softer.

"We were just having some pizza," she said stupidly. She was pretty sure she couldn't pretend shirtless pizza with your boss was a thing.

"Pizza," Tony repeated, studying her face way too closely. She silently besieged him not to question this, not here, not now. He sighed. "I see."

Unfortunately, she could tell he *did*. She wore her feelings on her face. She'd been told that countless times, by her parents, by Rhys, even by Gage.

Tony wasn't her brother, though in the past year or so, he'd begun to treat her as a cherished little sister. He'd even come out and admitted he thought of her that way. Told her that she was important to him, and not just because of the bond he shared with her brother. He'd promised he would always be there if she ever needed help.

It was a sweet conversation at the time, but now she was starting to understand that her "adopted Moretti" status didn't just include support. It also came with that overprotectiveness Liza and Keeley had complained about at happy hour.

Regardless, Penny wasn't about to get into a conversation about this right now. She'd take a few days and figure out an explanation. Hopefully.

"Please tell Aunt Berta thank you for the lasagna. I'll return her dish in a few days."

Tony looked like he wanted to say more. A lot more. But instead, he just nodded. "Give Jess a call tomorrow. I know she'd like to hear from you."

Penny nodded, grateful that it sounded like Tony was going to hand the job of fifth degree over to Jess. Not that it would be any easier to explain this to her friend/future sister-in-law. She and Jess had gotten close, but they hadn't shared all their secrets yet... like Penny's virgin status, or the fact it had recently changed.

"Bye," she said, relieved when Tony left without another word. She closed the door, locked it, then turned and leaned against the surface. "You couldn't stay in the kitchen?"

"No. I couldn't." Gage didn't look the least bit guilty, which piqued her temper. He should feel sorry. He'd just put her in an awkward position with her family.

"You couldn't button up at least?" She pushed off the door and walked back to the kitchen, stomping by him to put the lasagna in the refrigerator.

"No. I couldn't." This time, his tone sounded less cocky, though still not contrite. For some reason, she thought he sounded confused. "What is Tony Moretti to you?"

"You know the answer to that. He's my brother's roommate, and they're...well...they're in a committed ménage. I guess that sort of makes me a sister-in-law-to-be."

"And the other Morettis? Do *they* think of you as a sister?"

Penny tilted her head, uncertain what to make of his questions. "Why are you asking? Why does it matter?"

Gage ran a frustrated hand through his hair. "Fuck, I don't know. I just don't like..." He let his words fall away but not before she saw it.

Jealousy.

It was another one of those blink-and-you'd-miss-it looks. She could sure as hell learn a thing or two from Gage about shielding her emotions. Whatever he'd been feeling passed as his expression cleared.

Or so she'd thought.

Gage didn't continue with his questions. Instead, he ripped her shirt off once more, as if the soft cotton was a personal affront, put there just to piss him off. This time, her bra, yoga pants, and panties joined it on the floor.

Once he had her naked, he took her hand, hastily leading her to the bedroom. He kicked the door shut then took her in his arms again, resuming the kisses they'd begun in the kitchen. His hands stroked up and down her back, the gentle caress in direct contrast to his rough claiming of her mouth.

"Penny," he whispered as his fingers tangled in her hair. "Penny..."

Her name sounded like a prayer, and for a split second, the words "I love you" tried to escape. Mercifully, she managed to swallow them down.

Feeling it was bad enough, but admitting it to him would be much, much worse.

She unfastened his belt, slipping it free from the loops. Gage took it from her before she could drop it. He doubled the belt, slapping the leather against his thigh a few times, all while watching her reaction.

Penny had loved his spanking, loved the pain, the heat of the burn, the way it had made her feel reckless, wild.

A slight smile tugged at Gage's lips, and he wrapped one firm arm around her waist, holding her against him as he lifted the belt and brought it down on her ass.

It stung for only a second. He hadn't put any real strength behind the swing. If anything, it had been a test wrapped up in a question.

"You said you wanted me to spank you again," he said.

"I did."

He lifted the belt again, striking her harder. The sting lasted longer, burned hotter. Penny moaned.

"I can't get enough of you," he admitted.

It was the most intimate thing he'd ever said to her, the closest he'd ever come to sharing his feelings.

And she wasn't the only one to realize that.

Gage dropped the belt to the floor. "Get on the bed, Penny."

She did as he said, sitting on the edge as Gage shed the rest of his clothing. When he walked over to her, the tenderness she'd longed to see on his face had been set free. Her heart did a flip-flop in her chest.

He moved her to the middle of the bed, caging her beneath him. He reclaimed her lips, kissing her as he worshipped every inch of her body with his soft touches.

After the most erotic, tantalizing foreplay of her life, she finally felt the head of his cock. Gage continued the kiss as he slid inside her. He lifted his head, looking deeply into her eyes as he reached for her hands, placing them to either side of her head, on the pillows, their fingers linked. He never broke the connection of their gazes as he slowly thrust in and out. In and out.

Neither of them spoke a word, yet Penny felt as if they were talking nonstop. She let him see, let him read everything written on her heart, holding back nothing, and Gage...

Gage did the same.

When they came together, it wasn't a tsunami, it was quieter, a gentle glide along a placid lake. But the impact was no less intense. Because of their shared intimacy, this felt like the most powerful orgasm she'd ever had.

Gage slowly withdrew, lying down next to her, still looking at her, still talking without speaking.

She was overwhelmed by the emotions he'd provoked. Gage had spent weeks teaching her about seduction and sex, but this had been her favorite lesson by far.

Because he'd taught her how it felt to make love.

If she hadn't been drowning in bliss, in happiness, in love, perhaps she would have been wiser. Perhaps she wouldn't have whispered, "Don't leave."

The transformation in Gage was instantaneous. His entire body stilled, stiffened, and the unspoken words of love that had been flowing between them evaporated as if they'd never existed at all.

Gage slowly sat up, turning his back to her as he threw his legs over the edge of the mattress. "I can't stay. I have..." He paused— then lied to her. "I have an early meeting tomorrow. I need to go home and grab a few hours' sleep, some clean clothes."

She was on the list now. One of the countless women offered a Gage excuse guaranteed to get him out of the bed and out of the apartment after he'd gotten what he wanted.

Penny sat up, pulling the sheet over her, suddenly feeling her nakedness. And not just in the physical sense.

Then she firmed her resolve. She refused to be one of those women who let the man have the last word.

"My birthday is next Saturday."

"I know," Gage said, without turning around. She was trying to take comfort in the fact he hadn't risen, hadn't started dressing.

"Jess and my family are throwing a party for me. At Divine. I don't want to go alone."

She didn't realize just how tightly Gage had been holding himself until she saw the dramatic drop in his shoulders. "And you shouldn't."

"Gage—" she started.

He turned to look at her, and she saw a resolve in him that she instantly hated. "The lessons are over, Penny. You're ready to put yourself out there. I promise...no man can resist you. You should ask that neighbor of yours to go to the party."

She nodded slowly.

Lessons. He was calling what they'd just done another lesson. Nothing more.

"Why are you so afraid of relationships?" she asked, painfully aware the old Penny never would have had the courage to ask that question.

"What?"

"Relationships. You've never been in one, right?"

"I've had girlfriends," he said, somewhat woodenly, rising from the bed. Gage was a master when it came to building walls, pushing people out. He started dressing, but she wasn't finished yet.

She picked up an imaginary sledgehammer and took a swing at his fortress. "When?"

His gaze narrowed. "Penny," he started, zipping his pants.

"When? Your last girlfriend. When did you break up?"

"Junior year in college."

"How old were you?" she pressed.

"Twenty-one."

Twenty-one.

"Gage. How did your mother die?"

He'd been in the middle of buttoning up his shirt, but he stopped, his eyes locking with hers. His shield had fallen away completely, and she had to swallow down the lump in her throat when faced with the raw, unbearable pain she saw there.

Gage didn't respond for a long time, so long that she thought he wouldn't.

Especially when he bent over to grab his socks and shoes, not bothering to put them on. He turned toward the door, and she knew this was it. Knew by the way he held himself that he was never coming back here.

He paused just on the threshold, but he didn't turn to look at her.

Instead, he simply said, "She killed herself," before leaving for good.

* * *

Penny sat on the couch, absentmindedly petting Harry while trying to summon the energy to get up and make something for dinner. Aunt Berta's lasagna had gotten her through the weekend, allowing her to wallow in self-pity and cry her eyes out without having to leave the sanctuary of her apartment.

On Monday, she somehow managed to pull herself together enough to go to work. Mercifully, her job was challenging, so she could throw herself into it without having to think about anything else. For ten blessed hours—she'd put in overtime—she figured out a way to shut the real world out and lose herself amongst the code, the data.

Her trouble began when she left work and went home. It was the hours between dinner and breakfast that left her with too much time to reflect, to feel. For the past three days, she'd been riding on Fruity Pebbles, sugar-free Red Bull, and precious little sleep. She felt like a zombie.

No, she decided, a zombie would probably feel better than this.

Today had been her annual review, and she'd expected it to be the first time she would have to face Gage since his departure last Friday night. As such, she'd been a bundle of nerves by the time she'd approached his office, her hands visibly shaking.

She could have saved herself the anxiety. Because Gage hadn't been there. Instead, Matt had done the review and given her a raise so big, she'd thought he'd screwed up his accounting—and pointed it out to him. Part of her worried the huge compensation was Gage's attempt at making up for hurting her. But Matt had assured her the math was correct. Then he'd gone on to praise her work, discussing how he'd like to see her position grow within the company. She'd tried very hard to be professional throughout the review, but she was afraid the best she'd managed was subdued. It didn't help that she kept trying to get a read on Matt, trying to determine if he knew about her and Gage. Sadly, the man's poker face was rock solid.

If the meeting had happened a month ago, or even a week ago, her feet wouldn't have touched the ground, and she would have called every single person she knew to tell them all the complimentary things he'd said. As it was, she hadn't even bothered to text her parents with the good news.

She sighed when someone knocked on her door. Company was the last thing she was up for, so she ignored it.

Whoever it was knocked again.

"Penny," she heard her brother call from the hallway. "I know you're home. I saw your car parked outside."

She pushed herself up, fully aware she'd have to have this conversation at some point. She hadn't called Jess this weekend, and she hadn't answered the phone when her friend called.

Penny opened the door and offered Rhys what she hoped wasn't too weak of a smile.

"Aw, kiddo," he said, stepping inside, shutting the door behind him, then instantly wrapping her up in one of his amazing, comforting hugs.

She thought she'd cried herself out this weekend, certain there couldn't be a single tear left that she hadn't shed. Rhys managed to find a few more. He didn't say anything for a long time, just let her hang on to him until she was able to pull herself together.

When she lifted her head from his chest, he wiped her cheeks with his thumbs. "Better?"

She shrugged.

Rhys put his arm around her shoulders and led her to the living room. They sank down on the couch side by side.

"Tell me about Gage Russo."

Her brother was never one to mince words or beat around the bush. He was also the best listener on the planet, so she told him.

Everything.

Every. Single. Thing.

About the bet, the makeover, the lessons.

He sat quietly as she unloaded every heavy feeling, only asking the occasional question here and there for clarification, but otherwise allowing her to tell it all without interruption.

"And then he left. I haven't seen him at work. Haven't spoken to him since Friday night."

Rhys sighed. "I didn't know you'd been so lonely, Penny. I'm sorry for that. I've been so wrapped up in my own life that—"

"Stop. Don't go that direction. You *should* be wrapped up in your life because you finally have one," she teased. She'd spent most of their adult years giving her big brother, the doctor, shit for his workaholic ways.

"Very funny. And I know you feel bad, and you might not get this right now, but I have to say...I'm proud of you."

"Proud of me?" she asked, bemused. "For sleeping with my playboy boss and catching feelings I knew wouldn't be returned?"

Rhys shook his head. "For acknowledging that something was missing in your life and for being brave enough to seek it out. I wasn't smart enough to know how pathetic my life was until Jess and Jasper crash-landed into it and knocked some sense into me."

"I'm sure you would have figured it out."

"I'm sure I wouldn't have. Sex lessons notwithstanding—and please don't feel like I need any details about those because I *really* don't—I think Gage taught you other, more valuable lessons."

"Like?"

"Like loving yourself. Knowing your worth. How to fall in love, and even what a broken heart feels like—nobody in the world escapes that one, and I don't think they should. It makes them appreciate the next person who comes along even more. He didn't leave because of *you*, Penny. You know that, right?"

She nodded. That was the one truth that had made her pain more bearable. "I know."

"He left because of *him*. And given the things you've told me, I suspect he's suffering as much as, if not worse than, you are."

She hoped not. She'd witnessed too much of the pain he still carried over his mother's suicide. She would hate to think she was causing him even more.

Rhys put a finger under her chin, forcing her to look at him as he said, "Now promise me you won't be one of those people who believes they can change someone. Gage walked away because he hasn't dealt with his past, and therefore, he can't give you what you want. You have to accept that."

"I do," Penny insisted. "I'm perfectly aware that the only person I can change is me. I've started the transformation, but I need to keep going."

"Going how?"

"I'm going full-on T. Swift. Gonna shake this off. Move on. I'm even going to find a date for my birthday party."

Rhys smiled. "That's my girl."

"My game isn't over yet. I still have a few more lives to play with."

He rose from the couch. "You and those damn video games. Put some shoes on."

"Why?"

"Because you're coming to dinner at my place. Knowing you, there's nothing in that refrigerator of yours but days-old takeout and frozen pizza."

"Actually, there's not even that much. I was about to have cereal for dinner," she confessed.

"Don't tell Aunt Berta that unless you're prepared for a very long lecture on the importance of good food."

Penny pretended to lock her lips, tossing away the imaginary key. While her chest was still tight, she felt infinitely lighter than she had an hour ago.

Thank God for big brothers.

Chapter Eighteen

It was nearly six on Thursday when Penny returned home from work with dinner in hand. Chinese takeout. Joining Rhys for dinner had been just the push she needed to get up and get on with her life. Being in a house filled with so much life, so much love, would have depressed the old Penny. Last night, it had done the opposite. It had renewed her purpose for seeking to reinvent herself.

She headed toward the door to her apartment then paused.

Taking a deep breath, she walked to David's door instead and knocked.

He answered it, clearly surprised to see her there.

"Well, hello there, neighbor," he said with a friendly smile.

"Hiya."

"Just getting home from work?"

She nodded. "Yeah. Me and my shrimp fried rice."

He laughed. "I just finished pork lo mien. Looks like we let the same Chinese restaurant feed us."

"Cooking for one sucks."

David agreed. "It really does. Never seems worth the bother. A lot of nights, I just heat up a can of soup."

"Sounds a lot fancier than my bowl of cereal. Listen, my

friends and family are throwing a birthday party for me on Saturday. I know you're still pretty new to the city and don't know a lot of people. I was wondering if you'd like to go with me. Great opportunity to get out and meet some really nice folks. There's going to be lots of food and booze and dancing."

David smiled. "You had me at food. I'd love to go with you."

"Great." Penny gave him the rest of the details, and they decided to meet right there in the hallway between their apartments at seven on Saturday. "See you then."

"Enjoy your fried rice," David added as he closed the door.

Penny crossed the hall to her apartment and walked in.

"Well, I did it," she announced to the cats, who meowed loudly. She pretended they were responding to her, offering their congratulations, even though she knew they were begging to be fed. Harry nearly tripped her in his race to the food bowl.

She fed them then popped open the take-out carton and began eating her own dinner while standing next to the counter.

She sighed after a few bites, trying to work up some enthusiasm over the coming party and her date with David. She knew she was taking a step in the right direction...but rather than excitement, she just sort of wished the whole thing was already over.

The silence that had been lingering between her and Gage felt like a dark cloud hovering over her head. She hated walking around the office like she was working her way through a minefield. She also hated constantly fearing *and* hoping she'd run into him, wondering what he'd say to her.

The longer they went without speaking, the more it bothered her.

She'd replayed Friday night over in her mind a million times, and she'd decided nothing had been said by either of them that should have ruined the friendship.

So he'd lied and made up an excuse to leave.

So she'd pushed him a little about his past relationships. And his mother.

They hadn't said hurtful things, hadn't yelled or screamed or insulted one another.

They'd put a time limit on the lessons, and it expired. That was it. Nothing more and nothing less.

Most of that was a lie, but she clung to it all like it was the God's honest truth. She had to...so that what she did next wouldn't feel like such a monumental mistake.

Picking up her phone, she typed out a text message, re-reading it three times.

I wanted to say thanks to you for the past few weeks, for the makeover, the clothes, the lessons. I'm sorry for the way things ended on Friday, and I hope that someday we can find our way back to being friends. Toby sucks at Dead by Daylight *and you're the only person who can give me a run for my money in GTA. I asked my neighbor to the birthday party. He said yes. I never could have done that without your help. See you at work.*

It was standard Penny. Easy, breezy, revealing nothing of her true feelings.

She hated it and considered deleting the whole thing.

One step forward, twelve back.

She swallowed her pride, drop-kicked the part of her that knew this was wrong, and hit send.

Because she missed him so bad it hurt.

That pain only continued to grow when she saw her message had not only been delivered but read.

No reply came that night, and there still wasn't one the next morning.

"Okay," she said to herself. "So...no more of that." She stared at her reflection in the mirror, looked long and hard. She pointed a very stern finger at herself. "You're allowed one backslide and that was it."

Glancing down, she spotted Forrest at his usual spot, his head cocked to the right, staring at the side of the bathtub as if it was the most fascinating thing he'd ever seen. She laughed despite the heaviness that hadn't left her since Gage left the apartment.

"Well, at least I still have you," she said to the silly cat.

Then she turned back to the mirror, Gage's words from their first night together coming back to her.

And she saw it.

No, she didn't just see it. She *felt* it.

She liked the person who was looking back at her. Yeah, she was a bit quirky, and damned if she couldn't see yet another fricking zit fighting its way to the surface on her forehead, and it probably wasn't normal to talk to cats as much as she did.

But who cared? All of that was part of who she was.

She smiled, determined to shrug off the last of her melancholy.

Today was the day she introduced the world to the real Penny Beaumont.

* * *

Gage pushed his keyboard away with a little more force than was necessary. Then he picked up his cellphone and re-read the text Penny had sent. He'd spent the better part of last night tossing and turning in his bed, telling himself to leave it alone, not to respond. What the fuck could he say to her anyway?

He'd consistently made a complete mess of things ever since making that second wager.

No. He'd been screwing up since the night he took her virginity.

Because sleeping with her had never been about lessons. He'd had sex with her because he wanted her so badly. Because he...

"Fuck," he spat out, slamming his fist on his desk.

"I see your mood is improving."

Gage glanced up, scowling. "Why don't you ever fucking knock?"

Matt shrugged as he and Conor walked in. "It's my company. I don't have to."

"It's *our* company," Gage said, playing his brother's stupid game.

Matt had accused him once, many years earlier, of not caring about Russo Enterprises. Of course, at the time, his brother had been right. Gage had been in a spiral for a couple of years after their parents' deaths, drinking, sleeping with countless women, always late to work, and when he was there, doing little of value.

He and Matt had gotten into the mother of all arguments one afternoon when Matt told him it was time for him to grow up and assume responsibility for their legacy, for *their* company. Gage, hungover and contrary as hell, had told Matt he could take *his* fucking company and shove it up *his* ass.

Time heals all wounds, and eventually Gage found his way out of the bottle. He'd started to apply himself to his job, tapping into his love for computers and technology, acquiring smaller companies and tech upstarts, adding those profitable ventures to Russo's already expansive enterprises.

Since then, Matt like to call Russo *his* company, forcing Gage to stake his claim, to admit that he cared about it as much as his older brother did.

His brothers helped themselves to the chairs across from his desk. It wasn't uncommon for Matt to stop by a couple times a day to discuss business matters. After all, they both had large offices on the same floor. However, Conor's appearance wasn't the norm. His brother preferred his privacy, so he'd set up his office at Enigma, working from the nightclub instead, claiming there were far fewer interruptions there.

"Let's make whatever this is quick. I'm busy," Gage barked, in no mood for whatever it was that had driven both his brothers to his office.

"Very well. I asked Conor to join me here for an intervention," Matt explained.

"What he failed to include was what the hell we're intervening in," Conor added, clearly annoyed at having his well-organized routine disrupted.

Matt must have been very persuasive—or demanding—if he'd gotten Conor away from his desk.

Gage was afraid he knew the reason behind this visit. After all, he'd bailed on doing Penny's annual review, which was his responsibility as her direct supervisor. He'd dropped her file on Matt's desk Wednesday morning, complete with all his notes about, and evaluation of, her current work, his suggestion for her salary increase, including stock options, perks he knew she'd love, and avenues for her possible advancement in the company.

He'd lied and told his brother he'd double-booked himself, that he needed Matt to handle Penny's review. Matt had, of course, seen right through the lie, but to Gage's surprise, he'd agreed to do it without further questions.

Gage should have known he'd have to pay the piper later.

Later had arrived.

"Cut to the chase," he said like a man facing the firing squad.

"What's the deal with you and Penny?" Matt asked.

"Penny who?" Conor chimed in.

Matt replied without looking away from Gage. "Beaumont."

Conor's confusion seemed to grow. "The IT girl?"

"Yeah," Gage responded miserably. "The IT girl."

"What about her?" Conor asked before the light came on. "Wait. You've got something for the *IT girl*?" he asked, absolutely aghast.

"What's so strange about that?" Gage asked hotly, his brother's tone pissing him off even more.

"Are we talking about the same woman? Isn't she the one with the crazy hair? The big glasses? The mom jeans?"

Conor obviously hadn't seen Penny lately. Not that it

mattered to Gage. New version or old, his feelings for her were completely the same.

"I'm in love with her."

It was the first time he'd said the words aloud.

Conor whistled. "Damn. Never thought I'd see the day," he said, while Matt remained silent.

Gage felt like he should say more, try to explain, but saying those five words had been hard enough. And after that, what more *was* there to say, really? He'd done the one thing he'd sworn never to do.

Given his heart to a woman.

Left himself open for a whole shit-ton of hurt.

Conor was the first to recover. "Okay. Well, then, what's the problem?"

Gage thought that should be obvious. After all, that *was* the problem, wasn't it?

"I'm...I can't...I'm not doing that." Wow, captain of the debate team, he would never be.

"Doing what?" Conor asked.

Gage couldn't find a way to put it into words. And even if he could, he wasn't sure he would say it anyway. It had been too many years since he and his brothers had been close, since they'd shared any real confidences.

While Conor was confused, Matt was the picture of understanding.

"We don't talk about her," his older brother said after a moment or two. "We've never talked about her."

Gage swallowed hard to dislodge the tennis ball currently clogging his throat.

"Who?" Conor asked.

Matt glanced at their kid brother. Just one look, and Conor got it. Gage knew the second he did, because his little brother's expression closed down.

He recognized the look because it was as if he was staring at his own reflection in a mirror.

"Shit," Conor muttered, looking away from them, out the window.

The three of them sat there in silence, and Gage doubted they'd manage to break through these invisible walls they each threw up whenever they were together. Too many years had passed.

After Mom's death, something that had already been cracked, thanks to their father, shattered completely between them. Matt, who'd been Dad's shadow until then, pulled away from the family, walking around like a man with a score to settle. His anger grew more muted with time, fading to coldness after Dad's death. Gage never understood why it was their father's death that vanquished the fury that never seemed to leave Matt after Mom's suicide. But vanquish it, it did.

Gage had assuaged his pain with booze and women, using both to keep him so numb, he never felt anything.

As for Conor, who'd only been nineteen when Mom died, he just...disappeared. Into his books. Into his work. Into himself.

"You loved Mom," Matt said. "You were the closest to her. I knew her death was hard on you, but..."

"I can't understand why she did it," Gage confessed. "I've *never* understood it."

Conor lifted one shoulder, though he still refused to look their direction, avoiding eye contact. "I think we have to accept we'll never know. She didn't leave a note, didn't talk to anyone. All we can do is make assumptions. And what good would that do any of us?"

"Knowing the reason why won't bring her back," Matt said with that same finality he used when he didn't want to discuss something.

Gage's temper spiked. "It won't bring her back, but it would help *me*. I want—I *need* to know."

"No, you don't," Matt asserted.

"Fuck you, Matt!" Gage yelled, tired of his condescending

prick of a brother. "You don't get to dictate how I feel about this! What if...what if it was my fault?"

Matt reared back in his seat, his face pale. "Why in the hell would you think that?"

"You said it yourself. Mom and I were close. Tight. Right up until I left for college. After that, I didn't come home very often, didn't call her as much as I should have. I got too wrapped up in girls, and drinking with my frat brothers, and being an immature jerk. She was estranged from her family after she married Dad. She never felt comfortable around the other women in our social circle. She suffered from depression. We all knew that!"

"She took medication," Matt said quietly.

"The doctor said she'd stopped taking it before..." Conor's words fell away.

Matt gave their younger brother a sharp look. "You talked to her doctor?"

Conor nodded. "Yeah, I did." It was a simple answer, but Gage would guarantee there was a hell of a lot more hiding beneath the surface, and his curiosity was piqued.

So Conor had been seeking an answer too.

"She went off her meds?" Gage asked.

"A few weeks before. Against the doctor's advice. Told him she didn't like feeling fuzzy all the time."

Matt crossed his arms, and Gage could see him shutting it all down. Going rigid with the attempt.

Gage was sick of his stoic, emotionless brother always pretending nothing touched him. "She was isolated, Matt, alone, with just Dad, who was an unfeeling dick on a good day."

He paused. One of them had to throw out the first olive branch...so he tossed it, opened up about the cancerous feelings that had consumed him since the day Matt called him at college to tell him that Mom was dead. "I should have remembered all of that, I should have been there for her more, should have—"

"Stop," Matt said, putting his hand up. "Stop right now."

Gage thought for a moment that Matt was going to stand up,

storm out. His older brother held his gaze, cold, distant, and he clearly did not want to have this conversation.

It took ice time to melt. Gage saw the moment it began to.

Matt took a ragged breath, and for just a moment, he laid the pain he was feeling bare for Gage to see. "Mom's death was not your fault. I didn't know that you've been thinking that all this time. If I'd known, I would have..."

Old habits died hard. Matt had been a controlling bastard for years, and his words touched that sore spot. Gage struck out, hating himself for it even as he did it.

"What, Matt? You would have told me to stop feeling that way? I know you're a control freak and you like to think you rule the world, but you can't tell me how to feel or what to think."

"I know that." Matt studied his face, and now—like so many times before—Gage got the feeling his brother wanted to say something.

Gage wanted to push, wanted to scream at Matt to just spit it out, but how far could he take this discussion before he took it *too* far? This was the closest the three of them had come to a real, honest talk in over a decade, and even as much as it hurt, Gage didn't want them to leave.

Don't leave.

He really was a fucking head case.

"What does Mom have to do with your feelings for Penny, Gage?" Conor asked quietly.

Gage shook his head. He knew, but he couldn't say it.

"You loved Mom," Matt answered for him. "She was your whole world when we were kids. The video games, D&D, comic books...the two of you loved the same things, spent hours together."

"That's true," Conor chimed in. "I loved Mom, more than I can say, but she wasn't just Mom to you. She was your best friend."

Matt agreed. "And in the way of young sons, I'd venture to guess she was your first love. I can remember when you were in first grade. You insisted you were going to marry Mom when you were a big boy."

Conor grinned. "Yeah, that tracks. Sometimes I was jealous of your relationship with her. Not enough to put a bookmark in *The Lord of the Rings* and play *Guitar Hero* all the damn time, but still..."

"Mom was beautiful. Inside and out," Gage said.

"She was. But none of that answers my question," Conor pointed out, looking from Gage to Matt.

"Did I ever tell you the last thing Mom said to me?" Gage asked, perfectly aware he hadn't. He hadn't told this story to another living soul.

Both his brothers shook their heads.

"It was Christmas break, right after New Year's. I wasn't supposed to go back to school for another week, but one of my buddies had gone back early and was throwing some big-ass party. I decided to cut my trip home short so I could go, the idea of getting wasted with my friends and fucking some blonde sorority girl taking precedence over family time."

Gage closed his eyes and rubbed his brow, the next part hard to remember. "I'd packed up my shit and was standing by the front door. Mom had made all these plans for us for that last week, an *Indiana Jones* movie marathon, a video game night, a couple new recipes she wanted us to make together. You know how she was when we came home from college."

"She always had big plans, a way to make every single day special, different, fun. I think she needed those plans to..." Conor paused.

None of them finished that statement. They all knew. Mom struggled to keep her dark feelings at bay. It helped her to plan fun things. It was like she had to schedule her happiness in order to find it, because feeling joy didn't come naturally to her.

Conor continued talking. "That same holiday, she'd planned a *Lord of the Rings* movie marathon with me, found out my favorite author was doing a book signing a couple hours away. She had a whole list of ideas for us. But I was invited to go to California with my best friend's family right after Christmas, so I asked for a rain check."

Matt sighed. "We can all play the blame game if that's what you think will help. I was no better. I was already working here by that time. Dad was putting me through my paces, piling more and more onto my plate. I can remember putting Christmas dinner in my planner and only allowing two hours for it. Scheduling it like it was just another meeting. I was worried about that too because Dad had only scheduled *one* hour for dinner."

"I didn't know that," Gage admitted, wondering how the three of them could have let so many years go by without talking about this. About her.

"What did Mom say to you?" Conor asked, leading Gage back to his story.

"I was saying my goodbyes, in a hurry to get on the road. Like missing five minutes of some stupid party would be the end of the world. Mom hugged me, and she had tears in her eyes. She said, 'Don't leave.'"

"Jesus," Conor whispered.

"I left. And then...*she* left." Gage swallowed heavily.

"Gage—" Matt started.

"The thing with Penny started as a bet over a stupid video game. She wanted to reinvent herself with a makeover. And with lessons."

"Lessons?" Conor asked.

"In seduction...sex. She asked *me* because she knew I didn't tie any feelings to the act. She just wanted a tutor in how to flirt and fuck, and as king of the heartless playboys, I fit the bill. Last Friday was supposed to be the final lesson."

Conor leaned forward, resting his elbows on his knees. "What happened?"

"I took her to bed, but it wasn't her lesson. It was mine. Because...Penny taught me how to make love that night. You see, while she hasn't said it, I know she's in love with me too. So when it was over and we were lying there, side by side, she put herself out there. She's a hell of a lot braver than I am."

"What did she say?" Conor asked.

"She said, 'Don't leave.'" He closed his eyes briefly. "Guess you don't have to be a genius to figure out what I did."

"You left," Matt said. "Those words...they triggered you, and you left."

"Yeah. And even knowing that, I can't make myself go back to her because..."

Matt wouldn't let him stop there, finishing for him, making him face all the hard truths. "You're afraid of loving her."

"I..." Gage blew out a long, slow breath.

"Because you're afraid you'll lose her."

Matt didn't ask a question, so Gage didn't respond.

"Do you trust Penny, Gage?" Conor asked.

He leaned back and thought about that. Because it wasn't just the love he'd been afraid of. In a lot of ways, that was the simpler of the two things to give Penny.

God knew she was easy to love...with her kick-ass gaming skills and dance moves, the adorable way she talked to her cats like they were human, her easy smile, quick wit and sarcasm, and her unique sense of style—that he'd stupidly, foolishly fucked up.

It was just as he told his brothers. He was in love with Penny.

Trusting her though...that was going to be a hell of a lot harder. And not because of a goddamn thing she'd done but because he was apparently fucked up, and he hadn't realized just how much.

He could feel the weight of Conor's and Matt's gazes on him, waiting for an answer. He wished he had one to give.

When the silence drifted too long, he declared defeat by simply shrugging in response.

"I'm sorry, brother," Conor said. And for the first time, Gage felt that connection that had been lost for so many years ago, reforming.

He gave his younger brother a ghost of a smile. "Thanks."

Of course, bridging the gap with Matt was going to be much harder, if his scowl was anything to go by. Not that Matt made it easy, falling silent, as was his way when he was finished with a conversation.

"I fired Connie today," Matt said at last. "I was able to confirm that she was the one who'd sent Penny's resume to John Kelly. Apparently she's friends with someone in his HR department, who didn't realize Connie's intentions were malicious. She had access to Penny's personal identifiable information, and she used it. Definitely grounds for termination. When faced with the proof, she was forced to confess. She didn't take your rejection well. Security escorted her out a few hours ago."

"Is she going to be a problem?"

Matt shook his head. "No. I took care of it. She won't bother you again."

There was a lot left unsaid in that sentence.

Gage had seen his brother in action when someone was perceived to be a threat to Russo Enterprises. Matt was ruthless, brutal, and he took no prisoners.

But it wasn't the company he'd been protecting this time. It was Gage—and somehow, he sensed Connie had gotten a thousand times the usual level of ruthless and brutal.

God help the woman.

He wasn't sure if he was grateful or sorry he hadn't gotten to see it. The word *bloodbath* drifted through his mind.

"Thanks," Gage said.

Matt nodded once then rose. "Very well. We'll leave you to your work."

It was on the tip of Gage's tongue to retort with "that's it?" Because as far as interventions went, this one sucked. Matt hadn't offered him one ounce of advice or given him a clue where he was supposed to go from here.

Conor gave him a crooked grin. "Come by Chives tomorrow around one. I've got a new chef, want to see what you think of his food. We'll have a late lunch and a couple of drinks. I'll even pull out the good bourbon."

In addition to his nightclubs, Conor ran two high-end restaurants in the city, soon to be three apparently, if his deal with supermodel Harper Branson went through.

Gage nodded, touched by the invitation. "Thanks. I will." Then he recalled Penny's comment about Toby and Rich. He'd been a shitty friend the past couple of weeks. "Mind if I bring a couple of buddies along?"

Conor shook his head. "The more the merrier." Then he left, stepping around Matt, who'd paused at the threshold.

Matt stood there for a moment then turned to look at Gage. "You weren't to blame for what happened to Mom. And contrary to what you think of me, I know there's only one person I can control in life, and that's myself. The same goes for you. Figure out what you want then find a way to get there. No one is stopping you or holding you back—not me, not Mom, not Dad. The only person blocking your path right now, is you."

Gage leaned back in his chair, Matt's words resonating with him long after his brother had taken his leave, as he considered his next course of action.

He had a decision to make.

Was he going to get out of his own way?

Or not?

Chapter Nineteen

"**W**orking late again, I see."

Penny looked up from her computer, bleary-eyed, exhausted. She blinked a couple of times, her contacts drier than the Sahara. They must have affected her vision because there was no way Matt Russo was standing next to her desk. She'd worked at Russo Enterprises for six years and she'd never seen Matt in IT. Not once. He'd declared this department Gage's domain and steered clear.

"I, uh...yeah," she replied stupidly.

"It's Friday night. Most of the employees were sneaking out of here early, ready to get a jump on their weekend."

Penny could attest to that personally. Gage had called Toby a couple hours earlier, inviting him and Rich out for lunch at Chives tomorrow with him and his brother, Conor. From that point on, work ceased as her two sweet, clueless friends stressed out over what to wear.

No wonder the three IT gurus were so tight. They were birds of a feather, social misfits, all of them failing to learn simple things like how to fit in because they'd spent all their formative years studying how to level up instead.

She'd offered advice, revealing that she'd been to the Enigma before, another swanky Russo establishment, though she didn't admit it had been with Gage.

Once they'd gotten over their shock—assholes—that she'd been inside such a cool place, they'd grilled her relentlessly, seeking out every bit of information. Penny had answered all their questions patiently—and in great detail—because, while Gage had told her what to wear the night she'd gone to Enigma, she really hadn't been prepared for a lot of the rest. She'd ordered the same drink as Keeley, and followed Liza's lead on how to stand and flip her hair and survey the room casually.

And none of that had mattered, because she'd still fucked up with the dancing.

While she was sad that clearly she'd lost Gage as a friend, she was grateful that he'd listened to her in regard to Toby and Rich, not tossing them over with her. Of course, it sucked to be the one thrown out, because that meant Toby and Rich were going out tomorrow afternoon—with Gage—while, as was the norm, she'd be home. Alone. With her cats.

The fact that she had plans tomorrow *night*—the dreaded birthday party—offered zero consolation at all.

"Penny," Matt prompted.

Shit. She'd drifted into outer space again. In front of her boss.

"Sorry, I'm, uh...I've been reviewing code for vulnerabilities and remediating it. I was hoping to make some headway before calling it a night."

Matt nodded. And then, God help her, he pulled Toby's rolling office chair from his desk closer to hers and sat down.

Were they going to have a real chat? About what?

Oh my God.

He knew about her and Gage. He had to. It could be the only explanation for this unheard-of visit.

"I must admit, I'd admire your work ethic," he said.

He'd said as much at her annual review a couple of days earlier.

"Thank you." Penny searched for something to say. Maybe if

she could come up with some random yet fascinating conversational topic, she could distract him from...whatever the hell it was that had driven him down here.

She'd heard through the office grapevine that Connie in HR had been fired and escorted out of the building today. If the same was about to happen to her, at least it was after hours, so there would be fewer witnesses.

Small comfort, but still.

"So, um, are you going to Chives tomorrow with the other guys?" she asked, barely able to hide her slight wince.

Yeah. Great way to distract Matt on the subject of Gage.

Start a topic *about* Gage. Jesus Christ.

Matt shook his head. "No. I wasn't invited."

"Oh." Penny considered that. Apparently, Matt had been with Gage the one time she'd been at Enigma, according to Liza anyway, so it wasn't like they didn't get drinks together. "Why not?"

This time, she didn't manage to hide her wince at all.

Matt grinned, something she was fairly certain she'd never seen before in her life. It was the first time she'd ever considered him...handsome. He was usually too stern, too serious, his eyes dark, his expression uninviting. But relaxed and smiling? Wow.

Of course, Gage was still way hotter, but the Russos definitely had good genes.

"Because I'm a humorless bastard," Matt replied easily. "And my brothers don't usually consider hanging out with me a good time."

"Yeah. Humor is hard," Penny agreed. "Hey, you know, I gave my dad a joke-a-day calendar one year for Christmas. Maybe you should look for one of those. Then tell your brothers a joke whenever you see them. Break the pattern, you know?"

"That would certainly be one way to break it."

"If jokes aren't your thing, you could go the trivia route. The same year I gave my dad the joke calendar, I gave my mom a *Jeopardy* one. She texted me and my brother the day's question every night. Although maybe that isn't a good idea, because it usually ended in warfare. My brother and I are competitive as fuck, and we engaged in more than a few arguments when one of us forgot to phrase the answer as a question or we felt an unfair disadvantage because of bad cell service."

Aaaaand that was a lot of useless word vomit.

"Shit," she cursed. "Did I just say fuck? Um...God. Sorry about that."

This was why she should stay in her head.

"I'm familiar with the word fuck...as well as the word shit."

Wait. Was Matt Russo making a joke?

"I do like trivia," he admitted. "Though I'm not sure there would be much of a competition if I started something like that with Gage and Conor. Conor is a walking encyclopedia. I blame it on the fact he's read every book ever published."

"Seriously? Wow. What a nerd," she joked, delighted—and somewhat awed—by Matt's loud burst of laughter.

"Yes, he is. Gage is too, of course. Just in a different way."

Penny narrowed her eyes playfully. "If you're insinuating that playing video games and D&D twenty-four seven, or cosplaying at Comic-Con—I rocked it as Poison Ivy, by the way—makes you a nerd..."

Matt held up his hands in feigned surrender. "I'm not the one who dubbed this department the nerd circle. I believe that was your coworker Toby's doing?"

Penny sighed. "Yeah. It was. And yet he's going out tomorrow to some cool restaurant for fancy-ass lunch and drinks, while we're..."

"I'm probably going to be at work," Matt said.

"I was thinking of working out this weekend. And by workout, I mean *Beat Saber* 'til I drop."

"Both very good ways to avoid real life."

She couldn't tell if the last part of his statement was a confession or a condemnation. Either way, she couldn't argue with it. She'd been with Russo Enterprises long enough to know that

Matt didn't have any more of a social life than she did. At least she could say she'd had one briefly with Gage. But now that the lessons were over, she was struggling to follow through on them.

Not because her self-esteem had vanished but because her desire had.

She wanted to be with Gage, not with David, not with some as-of-yet unknown suitor, and all the pep talks in the mirror in the world weren't going to change that fact for a long time.

Regardless, she felt as if she should at least defend herself.

"I'm not completely avoiding it," she said. "I'm actually going to a party tomorrow night. My birthday party," she tacked on to the end, struggling to infuse her tone with any enthusiasm.

"Happy birthday," Matt said.

"I'd invite you but—" She shut up fast.

Matt chuckled. "I wouldn't ruin your party that way. I suspect the guest list is rather Moretti heavy?"

She nodded. "Yeah. It is. I wish I understood why... I mean... you're a nice guy. I just don't get..."

"Nice is a subjective term." Matt sighed. "One that I don't think too many people in the world would use to describe me. And they would be correct," he added, his expression hardening, halting her from arguing that point.

She recalled Rich sprinting into their office this morning after going downstairs to the snack bar for a soda. Matt's PA, Henri, had been there as well, and he'd filled Rich in on how Matt had fired Connie, how he'd heard her yelling, then crying, then outright begging. He said when Matt opened the door and told him to call for security, his face had been stone cold, completely unmoved by the emotional woman.

"You fired Connie," Penny pointed out.

"I did."

"Was it..." Penny mentally decided fuck it and took the bull by the horns. "Was it because of me?"

Matt studied her face for a moment. "Don't you think I should have?"

Penny lifted one shoulder. "I don't know. I guess." Maybe she should be pissed off at Connie for fucking around with her career, but she didn't have room for any more emotions right now. Her entire being was consumed with the broken heart. She'd have to revisit her Connie anger at a later date.

"I didn't just fire her because of you. I did it for Gage, as well."

"Gage?"

"I didn't like the way Connie was attempting to insinuate herself into his life by deceit and lies."

"You care about your brothers."

"Of course I do. There's nothing I wouldn't do for them."

"And yet you say you're not nice," she replied with a smile, proud to be able to prove him wrong on that point.

"You're a fascinating woman, Penny Beaumont."

Fascinating was one of those words that could go either way, as far as she was concerned. Because being interesting wasn't always a compliment.

She tried to figure out which way Matt was leaning. She hadn't landed on an answer when he rose and pushed Toby's chair back into place.

"Was there something you needed?" she asked when it became apparent he planned to leave.

Matt tilted his head as he held her gaze. "I was trying to understand something."

She paused, waiting for him to explain, but he didn't.

"And now you do?" she pressed.

He nodded and walked toward the door. "Yes. I believe I do. Go home, Penny. The work will wait until Monday. Enjoy your weekend and your party tomorrow."

"Goodbye, Mr. Russo."

"Matt," he corrected without looking back.

"Matt," she repeated quietly.

He left as Penny sat there, feeling like she'd passed a test she hadn't even realized she'd been taking.

* * *

Gage walked into his apartment just after dusk. He'd worked late, dreading the idea of coming home alone. The past few weeks, he'd left work right at quitting time, always in a hurry to get to Penny. Spending time in her small, brightly lit, cat-filled apartment had been the most fun he'd had in...well...forever.

His place seemed very cold, dark, and lonely in comparison. Maybe he should consider getting a cat. Or two. As Penny pointed out, he had a big enough bed.

Jesus. What was wrong with him? He put that thought away.

He'd skipped lunch, something his stomach was just now deciding to remind him of. Walking to the kitchen, he turned on the light, his gaze landing—as it always did—on the cookbook shelf, on the polaroid of him and his mom.

He walked over to the shelf and picked it up, carrying it over to the counter, replaying the conversation with his brothers. For too many years, he'd carried the emotions surrounding Mom's death on his own, slogging his way through grief, confusion, guilt, and anger, like a man treading in quicksand.

Hearing that his brothers had been doing the same thing all these years had offered a strange sort of comfort and made him feel a hell of a lot less alone. He was looking forward to lunch with Conor tomorrow. He'd missed his younger brother.

Actually, he missed both of his brothers.

While he was in a complete tailspin over Penny, he felt as if he'd turned a corner in regards to what was left of his family.

He was going to rebuild the bridges he, Matt, and Conor had let crumble. He wanted them back in his life. There wasn't much he was sure about at the moment, but that was one thing that was solid and true.

Gage ran his finger over the glass of the frame, spellbound by Mom's genuine smile. She had suffered depression for most of his life growing up, so whenever he could make her smile for real— not one of those pasted-on fakes she wore a lot of the time—he felt like a million bucks. Conor had captured one of those moments, which was why this photo meant so much to him.

He wasn't sure why he hadn't told Penny about Mom's depression, why he'd given her the impression that everything—with the exception of Dad—had been sunshine and roses, that they'd wiled away every day blissfully playing games and having fun.

Too many times, Mom had been holed up in her dark bedroom, sleeping or just...staring into space. On the bad days, Gage would sit next to her, trying to cajole her out of her heavy mood by playing video games next to her, giving her a blow-by-blow of the action, hoping to capture her interest enough that she'd join in.

His phone vibrated in his back pocket, so he pulled it out and quickly read the text from Conor, confirming lunch for tomorrow at one. Gage placed his phone on the counter, the cell's home screen shining up at him.

In a weaker moment, he'd made the selfie he'd taken of him and Penny cooking spaghetti together the background photo. He was wearing a horrified expression as Penny stirred the sauce behind him, laughing at his antics. His gaze traveled from Penny's smile to his mother's.

It was easy to make Penny smile, to make her laugh. It took no work at all. She was easygoing, with an incredible zest for life. The type of person who didn't have to plan fun like his mother, but who could find it into everyday ordinary things.

He turned his phone off.

Enough, he thought.

Then he ignored himself and walked back to the bookshelf, found himself reaching for the Indian cuisine cookbook that he hadn't opened since his mother's death. Apparently, the night was young and there were still plenty more hours to fill with self-flagellation and misery.

This cookbook had been the one he and his mother used the most on their Monday night kitchen dates.

He carried it to the counter and started to flip through, seeking out the masala recipe he'd made for Penny. He hadn't needed to consult the cookbook, as he had the recipe committed to memory.

When he found the page, he gasped...his eyes widening when he spotted the familiar stain.

One night, he'd dropped the spoon he'd been using to stir, right onto the book, red sauce spattering the top corner of the page. The stain had always been there.

That wasn't what had taken him aback.

The stain was now encompassed in one of his mother's doodles. She'd turned the fading red into a dragon's fiery breath. Also, there was an incredible caricature, a younger version of himself, battling the beast with a wooden spoon, the words "Gage the Brave" written beneath the drawing.

Gage the Brave.

He began flipping through the cookbook, shocked to discover five more drawings—all of *him*, though his ages varied throughout. There was even one of him in his Greek letters, his hair longer, like he'd worn it his junior year of college.

The drawings adorned their favorite recipes, and all included him battling some food-shaped beast with that sword-like spoon, and always at the bottom of the picture, the words "Gage the Brave."

He stared at the last caricature, wondering when she'd drawn it. It had to have been during the final months of her life. Maybe even the final weeks. In the picture, he had chopped off one head of the spaghetti-headed hydra, and his spoon was just about to lop off another. It was a wonderful drawing, full of detail, despite the fact it was crammed in amidst a recipe, most of the artwork adorning the edge of the page. His gaze kept returning to the expression on his face. Because he didn't look fierce or angry or scared, as one might expect when battling a hydra.

Instead, he was smiling. He looked...happy.

Mom had told him once that she admired his zeal, the way he

never took things too seriously, always saw the best in people and situations. She'd remarked that she was glad he hadn't taken after his father...or her. That he wouldn't go through life lonely or sad because he was capable of loving others without reservation or fear.

His mother seemed to live in constant fear. When Gage had suggested once—just once—that she divorce Dad, Mom had shaken her head, claiming she could never leave him because he wouldn't just ensure she was penniless, he would make sure she'd never see her sons again.

He considered her life, how difficult it must have been for her. She'd fallen in love with a man who didn't love her back. His mother was soft, sweet...and weak. Never strong enough to fight back, to fight for her own happiness.

By the time Gage was old enough to understand relationships between men and women, his parents' marriage had devolved into a loveless one, as the marriage he'd held up as the standard for what he *didn't* want.

Then he recalled a promise Mom had insisted he make. That he would always remain true to who he was. She'd assured him there wasn't anything he couldn't defeat in life as long as he approached every aspect of it with his open mind and open heart.

He hadn't thought about those conversations in years, but now...

An open heart.

An open mind.

Could it be that simple?

For weeks, he'd told Penny to take long, hard looks at herself, forcing her to see past the insecurities, to recognize the amazing woman she was. Now, he realized he was guilty of closing his eyes too. His mother had seen things inside of him that he'd never let himself acknowledge after her death.

Now...

The heaviness that had hovered over him like thick fog for days on end lifted, evaporating like it had never been there.

He missed his mom. He would always miss her.

But more than that...he realized that somewhere along the line, he'd forgiven her. He wasn't sure when that had happened, exactly, but it was certainly recently. And it wasn't something he'd reached alone. Talking to Penny about his mom hadn't buried him in a deluge of heavy feelings like he might have expected. Because the things he'd shared with her had been the good memories, the things that had made him love his mother more than words could express.

Gage returned to the picture of his mother. "I met a girl, Mom," he said quietly. "You would love her."

He looked at the drawing of himself once more, and he heard his mother's voice.

Gage the Brave.

Gage, be brave.

Then he turned his phone back on so he could see Penny's smiling face.

Yeah. Decision made.

He was getting the fuck out of his own way.

Chapter Twenty

"**I** need advice. Romantic advice."

Gage was amused by the reactions of the three men sitting with him at Chives. Toby and Rich looked flabbergasted by the request, while Conor grinned widely.

Toby practically vibrated with shock. "You want help? From *us*? About *dating*?"

"Made your decision, have you?" Conor asked, chuckling at Toby and Rich's identical open-mouthed expression.

Rich looked from Conor to Gage. "Decision? About what?"

"There's this woman," Gage started. "I'm in love with her."

"Really?" Toby squeaked. "You? In love? Wow! Never thought I'd see the day."

"Why not?" Gage asked.

"Because you've always said no woman was going to tie you down. That you liked variety. That marriage was the equivalent of eating the same thing for dinner every night for the rest of your life."

Gage vaguely recalled making that joke, but it had to have been two or three years ago. Penny had made the comment that Toby and Rich tended to hang on his every word. Damn if this didn't prove it.

"I changed my mind," Gage admitted.

"Does the woman love you too?" Rich asked.

"Of course she does," Toby replied, as if it would be impossible for any woman not to fall madly in love with Gage.

He chuckled. Penny had never said the words, but she'd shown him her feelings in so many other ways. "Yeah. I'm pretty sure she does—or did. I screwed things up."

Conor snorted. "Come on, bro. Stop stringing them on. Give them *all* the facts, or you're never going to get the right answers from them."

Rich frowned. "What facts?"

Gage sighed. "It's Penny."

"Penny?!" Toby exclaimed. "*Our* Penny?"

Gage nodded, then, because he'd made his damn mind up and he wasn't backing away from what he wanted, he said, "*My* Penny."

"I guess that explains why she's been dressing like a girl lately," Rich murmured, even as he shook his head in amazement. "Wow. Penny and Gage," he said, putting the two names together as if trying them out.

"When did this happen?" Toby asked.

"About a month ago."

"Gage got a little too close to the fire and backed away," Conor explained, mercifully keeping it simple.

Toby scowled. "Did you hurt her? Is that why she's been so quiet this week?"

Gage had expected Toby's outrage on Penny's behalf, and despite the fact it was directed at him, he was delighted to see it. Penny had called him out over hurting her two friends, and now Toby was ready to lay down the same gauntlet. Toby and Rich were solid, and he was glad Penny had guys like them in her court.

"I fucked up. That's why I asked you guys out today." That wasn't entirely true. When he'd asked his brother if he could invite Toby and Rich yesterday, his intent had been slightly different. He'd wanted to subtly find out how Penny was doing.

However, after last night's discovery in the cookbook, his need for his friends' help had changed. "You're close to her. How do I fix this?"

"How bad did you screw up?" Toby asked.

Gage wasn't sure how to answer that. He'd avoided Penny like the plague this week. "You said she's been quiet?"

Rich nodded. "Yeah. She bailed on D&D night, and she stopped playing *Destiny 2* with us. Keeps saying she's too tired or too busy."

He tried to figure out how to give them enough details without revealing things he was certain Penny wouldn't want them to know, like wanting to lose her virginity and how it had all started as a bet. "We've been together for a few weeks, but, because I'm a dumbass, I was determined to keep it casual. Penny went along with it...until last Friday. She asked me to stay, and I made one of my typical lame-ass excuses and left." Gage hated that he'd done exactly what she'd asked him not to. Lumping her in with the other lovers he'd left immediately after sex, offering a lie in his attempt to escape.

Rich whistled and looked at Toby. "We've been keeping a list of those excuses. She hates it."

"I know," Gage admitted.

"Did you get into a fight?" Toby asked.

Gage shook his head. "No."

It was one of the things he loved the most about Penny. She was even-keeled, a thinker, not a yeller.

"You know, Penny's not a grudge-holder. I've done some stupid shit to piss her off a few times over the years, and it was always a simple fix. I just admitted I was wrong and apologized. Of course," Toby glanced Rich's direction. "I have no idea how she'd react in a...uh...a..."

"Relationship," Conor helpfully supplied, clearly enjoying the conversation a little too much.

Rich just kept shaking his head. "Penny and Gage," he repeated, as if those two words didn't quite fit together.

"We could have run a million tests and never seen this anomaly coming," Toby said. "Jesus. This throws all the dating data in the world into question."

Rich agreed. "Total breakdown."

"Thanks, guys. Super helpful," Gage grumbled.

Toby laughed. "You didn't seriously expect us to have any insight on this, did you? I do most of my dating in RPG—been getting lucky in *World of Warcraft* lately. I like to go old school sometimes."

Conor snorted. "Jesus. I can see why you guys are friends. You speak the same language."

They all laughed, and Gage acknowledged it wasn't really advice he needed. In truth, he was hoping for their blessing. These guys were two of Penny's best friends and, well...his too. "You really think we're a mismatch?" he asked Toby and Rich.

Neither man responded for a moment, looking at each other as they thought about the question. Gage respected that they were taking his concern seriously.

Then Toby looked at Gage. "You know, when I think about it, you and Penny are probably the perfect couple. You have the same interests, the same competitive spirit, which will ensure a lifetime of awesome gaming."

"You've got the same great taste in friends," Rich added. "And you're not allergic to cats, so that's a bonus."

Toby grinned. "She'd probably kill me for saying this, but I'm pretty sure Penny's been crushing on you since her first day at Russo Enterprises. She may have hidden behind her computer whenever you stopped by the office, but I always caught her peeking at you."

"You want to know a secret?" Gage said, leaning closer. "I was checking her out every time too. I told myself it was just to see what kind of crazy outfit or hairdo she was sporting, but the truth is, she fascinated me. Caught my interest right from the beginning."

Rich started shaking his head again. "Even so...Penny and

Gage. This is going to take some time to sink in. Hey, you know what? This opens up the avenue for couples' costumes on Halloween and at Comic-Con."

"There's an unforeseen perk," Conor joked.

While his brother was kidding, Gage could see Toby and Rich seriously considered that the true silver lining.

"Today is her birthday," Toby said.

"I know."

"She's having a party at Divine tonight."

Gage sighed. "And she has a date for it. Because I stupidly suggested she invite her neighbor to go with her."

"Jesus," Conor muttered. "You *were* fighting this hard."

"That's not a problem. You're a rich, good-looking guy. Just go in there all Shrek-like and grab Princess Fiona away from Lord Farquaad," Rich suggested.

Gage looked at Conor, who shrugged one shoulder.

"It's not a terrible idea," his brother said. "Penny might go for the romantic gesture. Doesn't sound like she's had much dating experience, so you riding in on the white horse, declaring your love for her, would definitely make an impression and tell her just how serious you are. Especially considering the place is bound to be crawling with Morettis."

"Me crashing her birthday party and breaking up her date with the neighbor she referred to as 'hot,' in front of all her friends and family, is a romantic gesture?" Gage asked skeptically.

"It is if your gift is better than his," Conor replied with a chuckle.

Gage blew out a frustrated breath. "Remind me to never ask you three for help again."

"Probably a wise call," Conor said.

"So what are you going to do?" Toby asked.

Gage grinned. "I'm going to get her a birthday gift."

* * *

"And that was how I came to the decision to move to Philadelphia," David said at last.

Penny prayed that marked the end of the longest, most boring story she'd ever heard in her life. She decided right then and there that in the future, she was not asking out guys she'd only talked to in the elevator. Because three minutes wasn't long enough to make an informed decision about someone's personality, or lack thereof.

As it turned out, David was only interesting for about three sentences, after which, his voice became white noise as he droned on and on and on. To make matters worse, his favorite—and apparently only—topic was himself.

She'd been trapped in this booth with him for half an hour, and she was fairly certain she could write his biography for him, right down to when he spoke his first word and completed his potty training.

She glanced across the restaurant, trying desperately to catch someone's—anyone's—eye, so that she could send out some sort of signal for help.

Keeley was the first to glance her direction. And God bless her, the sharp woman honed in on Penny's dilemma fast. She watched as Keeley walked across the room and whispered something in Luca's ear. He shot a look Penny's way, and she sent the same telepathic plea for help to him as well.

He and Keeley walked over to the booth.

"There's the birthday girl," Luca said, giving her a brotherly kiss on the cheek. "Didn't have a chance to say hello yet. Just got here. Was tied up at the worksite."

"That's okay," Penny said. "I'm just glad you made it. Luca," she said, pointing to David, "this is my neighbor, David."

"Nice to meet you," Luca said, shaking hands with the man. "I was hoping I could steal Penny for a dance."

David frowned and hesitated just long enough that Penny could tell he was annoyed by the request. If his lack of conversational skills wasn't a big red flag, this sudden and misplaced jealousy certainly sealed the deal. "Actually, we were right in the middle of a—"

"I'd love to, Luca," Penny said, hopping out of the booth.

"If you want to dance, Penny—" David started.

"I'll be right back," she lied. She intended to take her sweet-ass time. With any luck, she'd manage to keep a buffer of family and friends between her and her boring date until it was time to leave.

Luca led her to the small dance floor Keeley and Liza had created by pushing back a few tables. Gianna had put together a great playlist on Spotify, and Rafe was playing it over the restaurant's sound system.

"Thanks," Penny said, remembering her dance lessons from Gage. She began the appropriate bobbing in place to the fast beat, and Luca did the same. This dance had a definite Disney G-rating compared to the bump and grind she and Gage had engaged in at Enigma, but that was to be expected. Luca was a Moretti, while she was a "sister" by association.

The music was just loud enough and just fast enough to prohibit any real conversation, which suited Penny just fine. David had talked so much, she needed a damn break.

She'd tried to disappear into her head while he prattled on, but he had an annoying habit of finishing every other statement with, "You know what I mean?" and then waiting for the appropriate nod. He'd probably picked up that habit because it was the only way he could ensure people kept listening to his nonstop diatribe of mind-numbing crap.

She really wished she'd just come to the party alone, because David's monopolizing need for attention was keeping her from hanging out with the people she really wanted to celebrate her birthday with.

Rafe stood to inherit this restaurant, Divine, and apparently some other club from his grandfather after his passing. Apparently there was an interesting story behind Rafe and his grandfather that Keeley had promised to tell Penny but hadn't had a chance to yet.

She'd been touched that Rafe had let them use the place for her party. Of course, Penny suspected it had been easier for him to just agree after Keeley decided this was where they should celebrate. Penny had discovered Keeley was a force to be reckoned with when she had a plan.

Looking around the room, she was moved by the turnout of friends and family. Her parents were sitting at a booth with Aunt Berta, the three of them laughing and having a wonderful time as they plowed through generous helpings of meatballs.

Tony and Jess were also on the dance floor, while Rhys and Jasper were hovering near the enormous birthday cake Tony's Nonna had baked. Jasper was clearly dying to dive in, and she suspected it was only Rhys's hovering presence that was managing to keep the adorable kid from running his finger through the thick icing to steal a taste.

The restaurant was overflowing with Morettis, who never passed up the opportunity to party. Penny had met everyone here many times over the years, as they'd always welcomed her and Rhys to their family celebrations.

When Keeley, Gianna, and Jess had asked Penny who she wanted to invite, her friends had been somewhat dismayed by how short Penny's list was. That was when they'd decided to scale it up by including the huge Moretti family. At the time, Penny had been distressed by the prospect of being the center of attention at such a large party, but she had to admit, if not for David, she would be having a blast.

Toby and Rich were hanging out with Keeley's brother, Kayden, and Aldo Moretti. She was happy her friends had come and pleased to see they genuinely seemed to be enjoying themselves. The reason the three of them had always been thick as thieves was because none of them were known for the social skills at parties. Of course, lately, all three of them seemed to be coming out of their shells, thanks to Gage.

The second she thought his name, she felt the same annoying, painful pressure on her chest return.

She pushed it away, determined to enjoy the party. Her friends had gone to a lot of trouble, and she wasn't going to ruin it by succumbing to her broken heart. She'd save that pain for later... when she was home. Alone.

When the song ended, Liza's brother, Bruno, was there to take Luca's place. Penny glanced over to where Liza and Keeley stood, and Liza gave her a wink, letting her know they were both onboard for Operation Avoid David.

Penny smiled then laughed as Bruno grabbed her hands and started spinning her around old-school style to Billy Joel's "It's Still Rock and Roll to Me." Gianna and her boyfriend, Sam, danced next to them, and all four got into a bit of an old-school dance-off.

An hour passed in a blur of music and laughter and dancing as Keeley ensured Penny's dance card was filled. She'd shared dances with her dad, Tony, Rhys, Aldo, Kayden, and Oliver Collins, a Moretti cousin by marriage. She glanced across the room a few times and discovered David still sitting at the booth, scowling, despite the fact she'd seen quite a few people approach him and try to draw him into conversation. Liza had even invited him to dance, but he'd turned her down.

Finally, Keeley declared it was time to cut the cake. Penny fanned herself as she walked over to the cake table. Aunt Berta had lit the candles and everyone was singing. Penny thought she would hate this part, but looking around at so many wonderful people, all there for her, she just felt...blessed.

She'd approached this birthday feeling very much adrift, alone in the middle of the ocean. Surrounded now by family and friends, she couldn't help but feel lucky and happy and hopeful.

"Blow out the candles," Jasper yelled excitedly. "Don't forget to make a wish!"

Penny closed her eyes for just a second and made her foolish wish before blowing out the candles. Aunt Berta and Nonna started cutting the cake, handing her the first piece. She turned and discovered David standing next to her.

"Hi," she said, suddenly feeling guilty for leaving him alone for so long. It belatedly occurred to her that her lessons from Gage had been based on the assumption all her future dates would go well and she would want to seduce the man. They'd never covered how she got rid of the fish she wanted to toss back.

"Thought you'd forgotten about me."

"I'm sorry, David. It's just...it's my birthday, and I have a lot of family and friends who want to celebrate with me."

"Yeah. I can see that. Didn't realize I would be sharing you with an entire roomful of people on this date."

She wasn't sure why he *wouldn't* think that.

"I told you it was my party. I thought it would be a great opportunity for you to meet people, since you're new in town." She'd said as much when she'd offered the damn invitation.

"You seem to be friends with a lot of men."

What. The. Fuck?

Penny didn't have a clue how to respond to that, and any guilt she'd felt over leaving him alone morphed into annoyance. After all, it wasn't like he'd been trying to make friends. Toby and Rich didn't know anyone here either, but they were at least putting themselves out there, meeting people and having fun. David had remained at their table as she danced, sulking about the fact she wasn't giving him her undivided attention, even though she'd seen several people trying to engage him in conversation.

David shrugged, though she could tell he was annoyed at her lack of response. "I don't think this is working out."

"I think you're right."

"I'm going to call it a night. Think you can get a ride home?" he asked.

Penny nodded, relieved beyond words, even though she couldn't help but think leaving her without a ride home from her own birthday party was a serious dick move. "Oh, yeah. I'm sure my brother or parents will drop me off."

"Happy birthday," he said stiffly. And that was when she realized the fucker hadn't even bought her a card.

"Thanks."

Mercifully, that was it. He didn't try for a hug or a kiss or anything. He just turned around and left.

Penny blew out a long breath.

"I take it the date didn't go well."

Penny glanced up at the sound of Gio's voice. She shook her head. "Not even a little bit. And the worst part, the guy is my neighbor. So now I have to start looking for somewhere else to live," she said, only half-joking.

"I haven't gotten my dance yet."

She smiled widely. She loved the Moretti brothers. They were all hot as sin, but down-to-earth and sweet. "Did Keeley tell you that you had to dance with me?"

Gio gave her a funny look that told her she may have been mistaken about who'd been filling her dance card all night. Maybe everyone who asked had genuinely wanted to dance with her.

"Nope. Come on. I like this song. Even though the movie was sad as shit."

He took her hand and pulled her into his arms, as Lady Gaga and Bradley Cooper sang "Shallow."

"Why would you think Keeley made me dance with you?" Gio asked as they started swaying to the music.

Penny lifted one shoulder. "She dragged Luca over to rescue me from David, so I just assumed she'd kept doing that."

"I suspect that once she got you away from the neighbor, it opened the door for the rest of us guys."

"Maybe so, but in case you haven't noticed, Keeley is a pretty powerful woman when she wants something, so it sort of made sense for me to think she'd been the one making sure I wasn't hurting for dance partners."

Gio chuckled. "Yeah, she's something else. Personally, I blame Kayden for that. He's spoiled the girl rotten."

"That's not the way she describes her relationship with her brother. I think the words she uses are 'overprotective and overbearing.'"

"Can't exactly fault him for that. On top of being drop-dead gorgeous, Keeley has a wild streak a mile wide. Kayden's had his work cut out for him since their parents passed."

"Drop-dead gorgeous, huh?" Penny teased.

Gio grimaced. "Yeah. Maybe you should forget I said that."

Penny had assumed there was a bro code in effect when it came to sisters, an invisible line that none of the Moretti brothers or their friends would ever cross.

But there was something in Gio's tone that left her wondering if he was chafing under the restraint of that bond. Not that she could blame him if she was. Keeley really was awesome...and like he said, drop dead gorgeous.

She was tempted to tug at the thread, but Gio was quicker, managing to change the subject with ease. "You look great tonight. You doing something different with your hair?"

She laughed and nodded. "Yup. I've learned how to use a hair dryer and curling iron."

"It's very pretty."

"Thanks." This was the longest one-on-one conversation she'd ever had with Gio, and she was pleased by how well she was holding her own. The old Penny—the one with the wavering confidence—would have stammered and blushed through this entire dance. Tonight, she felt pretty and poised, two things that had very little to do with her makeover and more to do with...

Dammit...she went ahead and let herself think his name.

Gage.

After all, he'd been her damned birthday wish.

Gage had held a metaphorical mirror up and forced her to look long and hard until she saw all the good things that *he* saw in her. Obviously, she'd been her own worst enemy the past twenty-nine years.

And then—it was as if by thinking his name, she'd summoned the man himself.

Not that she realized it...until she heard Gio growl, his gaze focused on something behind her.

"Don't remember seeing your name on the guest list, Russo," Gio said.

Penny stepped out of Gio's arms, turning, surprised to see Gage standing there. "I invited him," she said without hesitation.

Gage, who'd been scowling at Gio, looked at her, not bothering to hide his outright jealousy. She'd never stood between two gorgeous alpha males who seemed determined to fight over her.

As far as birthday gifts went, she was pretty sure this was the best one she'd ever received.

It took Gage a few seconds to compose himself, and when he did, he smiled at her.

"Happy birthday, Penny."

Chapter Twenty-One

"I didn't expect you to come," she said, aware that Gio wasn't the only Moretti primed and ready to pounce if Penny gave any indication of distress.

"I know. And if you'd prefer I leave..." Gage glanced at Gio, and it was obvious that while he'd abide by her wishes, he wouldn't find it an easy task.

She shook her head. "I don't want you to go."

He gave her another one of his sexy grins, and the fluttering she hadn't felt since he'd walked out of her bedroom last week returned with a vengeance. That was when she realized she'd danced with at least five super-hot guys tonight, and not one of them had affected her like Gage did.

"Then I won't go." While Gage had been looking at her, the strength in his tone made it clear he was talking to Gio. But then his gaze traveled around the room, drawing her attention to the fact that most of the conversation had died away and they had an audience.

"Penny," Gio started, not yet ready to accept their new guest. "Listen—"

"Thanks for the dance, Gio," she said quickly, before walking off the dance floor. For the first time tonight, she was uncomfortable being the center of attention. She glanced back at Gage and tilted her head toward a table tucked in the corner.

He followed her—mercifully—without comment or one of his signature smirks, certain to provoke every Moretti male within a twenty-mile radius.

He joined her at the table, moving his chair close to hers.

Conversation started again, and a few people resumed the dancing, her parents—God bless them—leading the charge with Aunt Berta when the song "Shout" came on.

"Gage—" she started.

He touched her lips with just one fingertip, but her entire body heated as if he'd struck a match to a bonfire.

"I have a lot to say to you, Penny. And I'm going to say it all. I also owe you an apology, a big fucking one, and you're going to get that too. But not here, not right now. Your family and friends went to a lot of trouble to put this party together, and the things I want—I *need*—to say to you should be said in private."

"Okay."

"Okay?" he asked, as if surprised.

She nodded. "Yeah. Okay."

He chuckled. "You're so easy to be with."

She wasn't sure what to make of that. Perhaps he'd expected a fight? Maybe that was what she was supposed to do, make him work for her forgiveness, make him sweat a little, give him the cold shoulder, rant and rave and yell.

Maybe.

But none of that felt right to her. Because she'd heard the brokenness in his voice when he'd told her his mom committed suicide. It didn't take a genius to figure out he had some issues with commitment and relationships because of that.

But he was here now. With her. And that gave her hope. So she would wait.

"Where's your date?" he asked, looking around as if prepared to wage a battle.

Penny sighed. "That fell through spectacularly. The guy was

dull as dirt and, despite this being my party, he felt as if all my attention should be focused solely on him. When I didn't give him that, he left early."

"Good for you. Life's too short to date assholes."

"Another lesson?"

He shook his head. "The lessons are over."

She considered that for a second then said, "Good."

"So after David split, Gio stepped in?" he asked darkly.

"Jealous?" she teased.

"Completely, undeniably, murderously so."

Penny put her hand on his. "It was one dance," she said. "As friends. I think...I think his interests lie elsewhere."

Gage flipped his hand to hold hers, squeezing it. "Good. Because you're spoken for."

"I am?"

"I want to be your date for the night. No—fuck that. I want to be your boyfriend."

She gasped. "Boyfriend?"

"Yeah," he said, nodding. "I'm going to be your boyfriend. And then, in a few months, I'm going to be your fiancé. And then in a year—if I can wait that long—I'm going to be your husband. And we're going to have kids. Like, immediately. Honeymoon baby."

"What the hell are you talking about?"

"Do you like the sound of all that?"

Penny didn't hesitate, didn't need a single second to think about her response. She nodded. "Yeah. I do."

"Then when we get home tonight, we're going to talk, I'm going to explain why I left, I'm going to apologize, and then we're going to start the rest of our lives. Okay?"

She gave him her second "okay," and when he laughed that wonderful, boisterous, joyful laugh of his, she couldn't help but laugh too.

"Oh, hey. I got you gifts," he said, reaching for his phone.

"You didn't have to buy me anything. You've given me enough. The hair, the nails, the makeup, the clothes."

Gage waved her list away as if it was inconsequential. "Rich guy, remember? Here." He pointed to a picture on his phone, and her eyes widened.

"Holy shit. That's the biggest cat tree I've ever seen in my life."

"I know," Gage said, beaming. "The cats will love it. Look at all the hiding places for Luna. And there are two top perches so Harry and Forrest can both be alpha male. No more fighting."

"Gage," she said, "there's no way in hell that will fit in my apartment."

He pointed to the photo again. "I know. That's why it's set up in my living room."

She looked more closely at the picture and realized he was telling the truth when she saw the floor-to-ceiling windows and the Philadelphia cityscape in the background. "But—"

"And I got you this." Gage swiped to the left and another picture came into view.

"Whoa!" This time, she saw two top-of-the-line, all-the-bells-and-whistles gaming chairs. "Two?"

"Yours and mine. They're already set up and ready for us in the gaming room at my place."

She was starting to sense a theme. "You know, I do have room in my place for the chair."

He shook his head. "They're a matched set. They need to stay together."

"Gage—" she started once more, but he wasn't finished.

"Here. Last one." He swiped left again, and this time, she saw a simple stool next to his kitchen counter.

"Um…"

Gage was quick to explain. "Now, when we're cooking together—something we're going to do a lot—you don't have to stand. That seems to be your major complaint about cooking, right?"

She laughed, deciding Gage had managed to buy the most perfect gifts ever. Every single one of them proved how well he'd come to know her.

"I love them all, but I can't help but notice how they're all at your place."

"Yeah. I think you and the cats should move in with me."

She shook her head, wondering if she was ever going to find a way to wipe this big-ass grin off her face. "You're insane."

"Maybe. But are you gonna do it?" he asked, leaning closer to kiss her on the cheek.

"I think we both know I will."

"Come dance with me." Gage stood and held his hand out to her, and Penny took it without thinking, rising as well.

She caught sight of Gianna, watching them with interest, before she turned to the computer, clicking a button to change the music.

The first notes of John Legend's "Conversations in the Dark" started playing.

"I made a request when I got here and saw you dancing with Gio, asked your friend to play our song."

"We have a song?"

"We do. This one."

Gage wrapped his arms around her, the two of them swaying together as if they'd shared this same dance a million times before.

She'd never felt like she fit anywhere until now, right here, with him.

Gage, who had a surprisingly good voice, started singing the chorus, and she suddenly understood why this was their song. "I won't ever try to change you, change you," he sang. "I will always want the same you, same you."

It was as if every single word was written just for her, for them.

Gage had helped her change herself, while making it perfectly clear he liked every single thing that embodied her. Even the things she'd seen as flaws.

The awkward, nerdy cat lady with zero fashion sense.

The gamer girl who cussed like a sailor and chugged Mt. Dew like a teenaged boy.

The *Fortnite* dancing queen.

Even this new, more sophisticated, more experienced and confident woman.

He accepted—wanted—all of her.

And then, God, then...

His lips brushed her ear as he sang the promise in the song. "And I won't break your heart."

And Penny, who'd already fallen in love, fell forever.

She lifted her face to his and everything else in the room faded away as they kissed. It was a soft, slow kiss, so different from the countless kisses they'd shared before. Those had often been harder, faster—almost desperate—as if they knew their time was limited and they had to grab everything they could before it went away.

With this kiss, a whole lifetime opened up in front of her.

When they parted, Gage placed his forehead against her, the two of them grinning like goofy fools at each other as they continued to dance.

The song ended, and Penny had to force herself to leave his arms. A faster song came on, and Gage winked. "Your dancing or mine?"

She laughed and broke into the Robot. Gage followed suit, even though his was nowhere near as good as hers—and she made sure to tell him so.

They worked their way through all her silly dances then when the heat between them became too much to ignore, he pulled her closer.

"Time for my dancing," he murmured, as they pushed the limits of propriety with their sexy bump and grind.

After just a few minutes, he pulled a miniscule inch away. "Still not a fan of the bouncing dance?"

"You've shown me the error of my ways," she said, as he

stroked his hands up her thighs to her waist then around her back to rest just above her ass.

"Damn right."

"I should warn you," she joked when his hands started to drift lower. "My big brother is here. And my dad."

He paused then cursed. "Shit."

For the first time since Gage had shown up, Penny looked around the room. Toby and Rich were standing at the edge of the dance floor, neither man appearing the least bit shocked to see her dirty dancing with Gage. When they caught her looking, Toby gave her an awkward wink.

"You told Toby and Rich about us?" she asked.

He nodded. "Today at lunch. They were the ones who told me to crash your party and steal you away from the neighbor."

She laughed. "Wow. That was actually great advice."

Then she spotted her brother and Tony, both watching from their table. Neither man looked particularly angry, rather they were pensive...concerned. They cared about her and would always worry. She gave them a smile and a thumbs-up.

Rhys rolled his eyes, grinning widely, and Tony—while not exactly pleased—wasn't wearing his usual Russo scowl. Instead, he looked begrudgingly resigned, which she was calling a win.

"Penny," Gage said, drawing her attention back to him.

"Yeah?"

"Introduce me to your parents. Then...I want to take you home. Okay?"

She kissed him, a quick hit-and-run buss, before she said, "Okay."

* * *

Gage followed Penny into her apartment. While he had the bigger bed, he'd insisted they spend the night here because he'd missed the cats. And now that she'd agreed to move in with him, he intended to start packing up her stuff immediately. Or...well...first thing tomorrow.

They had other things to do tonight.

She took his hand after he closed and locked the door, intent on dragging him back to her bedroom. He resisted, tugging and guiding her to the living room first.

"Gage." She pulled back, the two instigating a tug-of-war that he won.

"Talk first."

It was apparent she'd forgotten his request to explain his actions to her as well as the fact he owed her an apology.

If he'd been in doubt about her and this relationship—which he wasn't—her actions right then would have sealed the deal. She was forgiving and kind, and life with her would never be hard.

They sat down side by side on the couch.

"I'm sorry I left last week."

She turned to face him, tucking one foot under herself. "Why did you?"

He'd had a lot of time to reflect on his actions, to try to understand what had driven him out of her bed when all he'd truly wanted was to stay right there and never leave. "My mother suffered from depression. It was bad. She spent a lot of time in very dark places, even though she took medication for it."

"Oh," she said, and he could see her rearranging everything he'd told her about his mother, putting the pieces back together a different way. "That couldn't have been easy for you."

"I hated the times when she...went cold. I tried to cheer her up, tried to cajole her out of it, but I don't know if you've ever known someone with depression."

"I haven't."

"It's a brutal disease. And when it's someone you love..."

She reached out, and he took her proffered hand, clung to it like a lifeline as he let himself say all the things he'd bottled up for years.

"Ever since my mom died, it's been hard for me to open

myself up to others. I trusted her. I loved her. She was more than a mom. She was my best friend. And...she left me. She *chose* to leave me."

"Gage, I'm sorry. I really am, but—"

He cut her off. "For a long time, I felt guilty about her death."

"Guilty? Why?"

"Because I left her first. I went off to college, joined a frat, didn't come home often because I was too busy with friends and partying and bullshit like that."

"That wasn't you leaving her. That was you growing up."

Gage nodded. "I know that. But holding on to the guilt was easier than setting the other emotion loose."

"What emotion?"

"Anger. She didn't deserve for me to be angry at her. She was sick. I knew that."

Penny let that sink in, her expression changing from sadness to understanding. "Gage—"

He forged on. Now that he'd opened the floodgates, he couldn't stop. "I was so fucking furious with her, I couldn't see straight. The only way I could deal with all the anger was with booze and fucking. I'm not proud of that, but..."

"Grief is a bastard, Gage. You found a way to deal with your pain. Own it. Learn from it. Move on."

He snorted. "You make it sound so simple."

She shook her head. "I don't think any of this is simple."

"I've spent the last decade pushing everyone away because I lost the ability to trust people not to leave. So...I made sure I always left first."

"That makes sense, but I don't think your mother *chose* to leave you."

Gage knew that. Now. For so long, he'd viewed her suicide as her leaving him, but now, he understood it was the only way she knew to escape the unending pain and loneliness.

"You're right. She didn't." He leaned toward her, kissing her forehead.

"I wish you could find a way back to your brothers. Maybe you could help each other. Because I'm sure they're struggling as much as you are. Your loss was their loss as well."

"It was. We talked a bit this week. First time since Mom died. And it did help a lot."

"I'm glad. I don't know Conor well, but I know Matt cares about you. I think it's just hard for him to show you."

Gage wondered how she could be so certain of that, but he didn't question it because she was right.

"I walked away from you because, despite all my best efforts, you made me feel things I hadn't felt in a long time. And it brought back some memories I couldn't handle."

"And now?"

"I'm going to stop being a coward. I'm going to be brave, because running and hiding comes with too high a price."

She tilted her head, confused.

"Losing you. I can't find a way to live without you, Penny. I wouldn't even know where to begin. I'm sorry I left. Sorry I hurt you. More sorry than I can say."

"I know. But, Gage, I understand why you did it."

He reached for her, using his grip on the back of her neck to pull her forward, to kiss her. Penny moved without hesitation, returning his kiss, her tongue the first to seek more, her hands gripping his hair in that way that told him just how much she wanted him.

"I realized something else this past week," he said when they broke apart.

"What's that?"

"That you asked the wrong person for lessons on being good in bed."

Penny shook her head, giving him one of her adorable grins, her eyes twinkling with mischief. "I'm pretty sure I didn't. Because, despite the danger of inflating that oversized ego of yours even more, you rocked my world."

"That's not what I mean. The trick to being good in bed isn't so much a question of ability. It's in choosing the right lover."

Penny tilted her head, clearly confused. "But—"

"Hear me out. I've slept with too many women in my life. Beautiful women who satisfied me sexually, who were competent, skilled, experienced. I made them come and they made me come... but not a single one of them made me *feel*."

"Oh."

"Penny, I love you. But more than that, I trust you. Completely."

He didn't realize he was holding his breath until she cupped his cheek and said, "I love you too."

Gage pulled her to him, trying to show her with his kiss exactly how sincere he was about the words he just spoke.

Penny, true to character, returned the sentiment, climbing onto his lap, straddling his thighs, her hands gripping his hair with that tightness that he was starting to find a turn-on because it was so very, very her.

"We have all night," he murmured against her lips as she fought to pull his shirt over his head. Then he added, "The rest of our lives."

His shirt gone, Gage started seeking the zipper on her dress that would help him strip her out of her clothing as well.

"I love the sound of that," she whispered.

He slid the zipper down then tugged her dress over her head in one long sweep. She was wearing one of those sexy bras that pushed her breasts up, and given that she was straddling his lap, they were in the perfect position for him to enjoy.

He slipped the bra straps over her shoulders and tugged the lace down until it rested below her gorgeous tits. He started for the left then changed direction at the last minute, stroking his tongue over her right nipple before sucking it into his mouth.

Penny's brief breathy laugh quickly turned to a moan. He played with her breasts, and it started to occur to him that forever would never be enough with this woman. His intention to take it slow, to savor her tonight, flew out the window.

Penny made him want too much, and when it came to her, he was a greedy bastard.

He unhooked her bra and tossed it to the floor, then he helped her stand for the few seconds it took to rid her of her panties. Once she was naked, he pulled her down onto her back on the couch. He didn't have the patience to walk to the bedroom.

Gage stripped off the rest of his clothes and crawled over her, his knees on the cushion, between her thighs.

Lowering his head, Gage kissed her for several minutes more, driving the temperature between them up so high, he feared they'd both die of heat exhaustion.

"Please," she pleaded.

"I love when you beg me," Gage teased, making no move to give her what she wanted.

"Asshole," she muttered, though there was no heat behind the words, just that twinkle in her eyes that told him she would always keep him on his toes.

"Maybe you'd get what you want faster if you called me daddy," he joked.

Penny reached between them and took his cock in her hand. "Maybe you should be a little nicer to the IT woman in charge of your penetration testing."

Gage laughed. "I love when you talk tech dirty to me."

He took her hand away from his dick, winking when she narrowed her eyes, obviously expecting him to continue tormenting her with foreplay.

Sadly, his control was in tatters. He guided his cock to her and slid in until just the head was inside. "What do you say we start our probing now?"

Penny laughed. "Oooo...a stuffing attack. I like your style."

Oh man. It was on.

"Well, look at that," he said, once he was seated to the hilt. "The magic quadrant."

Both of them were laughing, even as Gage began to thrust, increasing his pace.

"Gage!" she gasped after several minutes.

He reached down to stroke her clit, perfectly aware of how to send her into orbit. He tapped and tickled and, just as he expected, she came loudly, her nails scratching his back as she cried out his name.

Gage considered holding back, toyed with the idea of fighting for control, then decided fuck it. She felt amazing, and he was too close as well.

He gave into his own climax, his body going stiff as pleasure shook him to the very core. Gage held himself above her for a few minutes, both of them gasping, fighting to catch their breath, their gazes locked on each other.

"So beautiful," he whispered.

She smiled and blushed.

Then Gage closed his eyes for a moment, shaking his head. "Jesus."

Penny frowned, confused. "What's wrong?"

"Lift your head and look at my back. It's Forrest, isn't it?"

Penny did as he instructed then burst into laughter when she spotted whatever cat had decided his bare back would be a good place to lie down and take a nap.

"Yup," she said between chortles. "Forrest."

Gage didn't bother to shake the purring cat off.

"You knew I came with cats," she said when she could finally stop laughing. "Guess this just proves you need to get better at video games if you're going to keep placing bets. 'Cause I kicked your ass twice."

Gage gave her a confused look. "You're kidding, right? I won both those contests."

Penny narrowed her eyes. "Rewriting history?"

He shook his head. "Nope. Both times, I asked for a long-term contract. And I'm pretty sure I'm on the verge of scoring the longest contract you can get. A lifetime."

Penny looked like she wanted to argue—he loved her competitiveness—but in the end, she merely sighed. "Would you agree to calling both contests a draw?"

Gage pretended to consider her request, then he shrugged, feigning reluctance. "I guess, co-captain."

She laughed. "Gage?"

"Yeah?"

"Shake Forrest off. I want to have sex again, preferably in my bed. How about a little role play? I'll be Lara Croft and you can be Geralt of Rivia from *The Witcher*. God, he's hot."

Jesus. He really had found the perfect woman.

"I'm in, but I'm going to be Kratos from *God of War*. That dude is legit. Plus, he's got a beard like me."

"You and that damn beard. Fine."

Gage gave her a quick, potent kiss, then rose, forcing himself to go slow, so Forrest simply slid off gently. He took her hand, dragging her quickly to her room. Once they were there, he led her to her bed and playfully pushed her onto the mattress, following her down.

"Game on, Willow99."

Ready for more Italian Stallions? Book three (Keeley, Rafe, and Gio's story) releases September 2022! You can preorder it now!

Rough and Ready

And be sure to be on the lookout for the rest of the Italian Stallions series.

Down and Dirty
Wild and Wicked
Hot and Heavy
Steady and Strong

Tempted and Taken
Kiss and Tell

Want to see how Oliver Collins scored an invite to Penny's birthday party? Want to see how the Moretti brothers got their Italian Stallions nickname? Check out these books, standalone within the Wilder Irish series!
Wild Side
Wild Dreams
Wild Chance

Calling all fans of Mari Carr AND Facebook! There's a group for you. Come join the Mari Carr's Facebook group for sneak peaks, cover reveals, contests and more! Join now.

And be sure to join Mari's mailing list to receive a **FREE** sexy novella, Midnight Wild.

About the Author

Virginia native Mari Carr is a New York Times and USA TODAY bestseller of contemporary romance novels. With over three million copies of her books sold, Mari was the winner of the Romance Writers of America's Passionate Plume award for her novella, Erotic Research. She has over a hundred published works, including her popular Wild Irish and Compass books, along with the Trinity Masters series she writes with Lila Dubois.

Follow Mari:

www.maricarr.com

mari@maricarr.com

Join her newsletter so you don't miss new releases and for exclusive subscriber-only content.